Prominent Characters

Michael Morales Lopez, Junior

        Michael's parents Maria and Michael Lopez, Sr.

        Michael's brother Eddie

        Michael's wife Roseanne

        Michael's daughter Rosie

        Michael's girlfriend Corrine Casey

Lily Ann Arnold

        Lily's parents Margaret and Lester Arnold

        Lily's brothers Robert, Thomas and Jack

        Lily's son Jim Austin

        Lily's boyfriend Ron Hollander

The characters are fictitious. Any similarity between the fictitious names and those of living persons is entirely coincidental.

Dancing in the Rain

Peggy W. Fellouris

authorHOUSE®

AuthorHouse™
1663 Liberty Drive
Bloomington, IN 47403
www.authorhouse.com
Phone: 1-800-839-8640

First published by AuthorHouse 4/28/2011

ISBN: 978-1-4567-3251-6 (e)
ISBN: 978-1-4567-3252-3 (dj)
ISBN: 978-1-4567-3253-0 (sc)

Library of Congress Control Number: 2011902842

Printed in the United States of America

Pat
A super friend
and great Bridge
Player! Love,
Peggy

Dedicated

to

Dana, Molly, Jared, and Adam

Acknowledgements

My grateful appreciation to those who encouraged me to write, Eddie and Pete and my many friends who urged me to consider writing a novel, including Rhonda, Amy, Ronald, Charlie, Bob, Cary and Cheryl, Sandie Byrne and Tim Pears. Thank you to my dear friends who read the various drafts, Mickey, Sarah and Julie and their words of wisdom during the writing process. Special thanks to my instructors at Exeter College, Oxford University, England.

A special thank you to Robert, who was editing when he had to be called away and no words can express my appreciation to Amy G. who stepped in and became the editor, the one who pulled my work to completion.

Richard Ward assisted me with the selection of a publishing house, for which I am grateful. Of course I thank my daughters, Deborah and Anabel for their patience with me and my many questions. And thank you my readers whom may enjoy the "let's pretend" story of *Dancing in the Rain*.

Forward

A card reader told Lily she would meet her love on a certain day and a priest sent Michael forth to find his love. Is it Providence, God's divine guidance that puts them together or fate?

The novel follows Lily, a beautiful woman raised in a loving upper class family of considerable wealth and affluence and Michael, a handsome gentleman raised in a loving family of low socioeconomic standing who yearned for success and wealth. Each of their many trials and tribulations could not stop their love for one another.

It is important that you as the reader know of their youth as it is given throughout the story in an effort to remind you of the variance of their lifestyles and the great journey they undertake to find each other.

Chapter 1

THE PINK POLISH ON her toes glistened as she stepped into soft silk panties with lace inserts. She slid into the lovely garment while standing on the fluffy white bath towel, balancing herself first with one foot and then the other. The soft manicured fingers pulled the expensive garment over her slender smooth skin. Yes, she was a real blonde. She quickly adjusted her size 32 C bra, placed her feet into the new black leather pumps, and reached for her Red Cross uniform. A recent card reader said she would meet the man of her dreams today.

A single stroke of the brush left her highlighted golden blonde hair in place. Her reflection in the mirror was true, clear skin, sky blue eyes, high cheek bones with just the right amount of coloring, a roman nose and a gentle smile showing perfectly set teeth. One could guess such perfect teeth may have held braces in the early years. A rounded jaw line and oval shaped face completed the picture. Lily Arnold was ready to perform her volunteer duties at the military airport in San Diego, California.

The two women arrived early in the day. Lily was hoping it would be the day that Tommy, her brother, came home. The Air Force wouldn't give the families the exact time or day for their son or daughter to arrive back in the states, however, Lily and Martha, her friend from work, weren't going to take any chances. They wanted to be there to greet Tommy as he stepped off the plane. The two women, both Red Cross volunteers, were most willing to serve the returning servicemen.

Lily's friend Martha was a tall generously built young lady, with long dark hair pulled back, square shaped face with interesting brown eyes and just a hint of the distinguished looking smile lines she would have as she matured. Martha was a very good natured friend and Lily loved volunteering with her.

"Martha, it's a good thing that we wore our Red Cross uniforms or we wouldn't get this close to the men as they disembark. I really don't mind waiting tables and serving the coffee, do you?"

"Lily, are you kidding? All of these men are special returnees. It is not only patriotic, but it's nice watching them meeting and greeting their families." "Here we get a "front row seat, so to speak, waiting for Tommy. Do you think he will be on one of these planes?"

"Oh, I hope so."

"Won't he be surprised to see you in uniform, well, a Red Cross uniform?"

"His eyes will pop out. It was good of my parents to let us do this alone.

They are at home waiting."

As the first plane arrived, the announcement came over the

air, "U.S. Air Transport Plane 4557 is arriving with the men from Unit Squadron 918 who served the U. S. Army in Saigon." Other voices announced flights from the Far East and Europe, some Air Force, some Navy and still others, Marines." The room full of waiting families became silent. You could only hear a few whimpers, probably from a mother or grandmother.

"Martha, we need to see the pots are full of steaming hot coffee and don't forget to have creamers there too. Oh, yes, some cold drinks, especially Coca Cola."

"Lily, I like doing this, so you keep at the station. I'll watch the tables." She deftly placed the steaming hot coffee and desserts in front of flower arrangements and welcome home signs. Groups of families stood around anxiously waiting for their brothers or fathers, some parents holding children dressed in fancy outfits, others in their pajamas, and a few with babies wrapped in blankets.

"Here they come!" shouted one mother. Both Lily and Martha turned to face the opening door of the room. "Yes, here they come! Our men, our family! What a great day!"

The tears started down Lily's cheek. Martha was smiling, almost a grin. The entire room felt so jubilant! First came some of the men from the Army, with crutches, casts, being helped, carried, some holding back tears as their families rushed to them. Each and every soldier saluted the Commanding Officers as they strode past to their loved ones.

The ladies poured coffee and served desserts to both the men and their families as they hugged each other. Little children clamored to be held by Daddy. Each group spent a few minutes in the area. Martha mingled among the families. Lily maintained the station.

As time passed, plane load after plane load of men disembarked in much the same fashion. Then the Marines entered. My, how tall they stood as they saluted. Neither crutches nor casts bothered them. They seemed to be men of great strength.

One young Marine, very handsome, seemed to catch Lily's eye. There was something about him, not just spit and polish. As he lifted his cap, the head of black wavy hair framed his face, giving him a noble look. Warm tan skin and nice white teeth shined through a soft smile. A glimmer of happiness appeared through the quiet brown eyes, a strange but interesting combination. So clean cut, he could have been a poster boy for the Marines.

For just a short moment, they saw each other and no one else, almost as if they knew each other, had a connection.

Lily was suddenly curious. "Martha, could you go over near that Marine and see who comes to meet him?"

"Sure Lily, why, do you know him?"

"There is just something about him." Martha moved over near the Marine, smiled and asked if he would like a cold drink.

"No thank you," he said politely as he looked up at Lily.

At that moment, two young women ran toward him. Lily quickly thought, "Perhaps his wife or maybe his sister."

He hugged them and called them Mary and Nancy, not sweetheart or darling, Martha noticed.

"Oh well, he too, must be equally happy to be home," thought Lily. Perhaps Martha should see that he gets a full cup of coffee."

As Martha walked closer to him, she noticed two little boys playing with his gear. He was hugging them and laughing. Lily could not help but overhear them call him "Uncle Michael". The name seemed to fit him.

Their dialogue sounded like they were concerned about something. One of the women, perhaps a sister, was telling him that his mother wasn't feeling well. Martha shared the conversation with Lily.

Just then another plane was announced.

Martha lifted her eyebrows and turned to Lily, "I know your brother is due home, but you are really, I mean *really* excited and happy. You've missed him more than you've let on."

"Martha, it's hard to explain why Tommy is so important to me….He's been there for me…all of my life. Our home, as you know, because you've been there, is huge, swimming pool, tennis court, flower gardens, well…you know. Well, Tommy and I shared everything, every day, chasing butterflies, swimming, and playing with our dog, Duke. Tom taught me to button my sweater, to tie my shoes, helped me with many decisions as I grew up…every part of every day he was my life and I was 'Tommy's sister'. I guess you could say we are closer than twins," Lily said with a smile.

"Once the news reporting on the Vietnam War became intense, it became the talk of all the young men," she began explaining how Tommy was no different. God and country influenced everyone. Tommy soon joined the Air Force and was in flight school almost immediately. Lily hugged Tommy goodbye at the train station, holding back her tears. Tommy wouldn't like to see her cry. It broke her heart. She spent that night crying into her pillow, but Lily was proud.

"Oh, look Lily, the men are starting to come in." Lily straightened up, as if she were standing at attention.

Again, each uniformed man, saluted their Commanding Officer as they entered the area, many with crutches or casts, some carried and some being helped.

"Lily, this is so sad. Oh, look, especially that one with the aide." Her eyes went toward a rather tall man, with soft brown hair cut short, wearing dark glasses. He held himself erect as best he could while using a white cane, with a red foot on it. The aide was a step ahead and the fine looking Marine held onto his arm. Lily's eyes froze on the scene as the tears ran down her cheeks.

She carefully stepped forward towards him, touched his shoulder, and softly said, "Tommy, it's me, Lily"

Chapter 2

IT WASN'T A SHORT drive from San Diego to Los Angeles; however, having the limousine gave greater comfort to both Lily, Martha, but especially Tommy and the accompanying aide. Tommy's dark glasses and white cane seemed to take as much space in the thoughts of those in attendance as if it were an elephant in the car with them. No one wanted to say anything that would upset Tom, especially Lily. Tom asked the usual questions.

"How is Mom? Dad? Does Jack like college? How is he doing? And Lily, how are you doing? How is your job?

Lily proceeded to carry on as much of a conversation as possible, as much as she could that is, without asking Tom what had happened. She spoke of her position at the law firm, and the fact that she had completed her doctorate and would be finishing her law degree soon. Tommy was pleased.

He reached for Lily's hand. She quickly placed it in his. The four people looked very crisp in their uniforms, but soon they would be relaxing in their civilian clothing.

They arrived home. The limousine drove up the drive and stopped at the front door. Kate had been watching for them.

"Oh, Mrs. Arnold, Tom is home," she called as she went out the door to greet him.

Kate seemed to take the white cane and dark glasses all in stride, but Margaret was quite surprised at Tom's appearance. She looked at Lily and Lily shrugged her shoulders as if to say, "I don't know what happened." Then the aide assisted Tom up the two stairs to his waiting mother. She hugged Tom and cried with happiness. He was home from the war at last.

Just then, Lester came to greet them. He too seemed surprised. The family hadn't been informed of Tom's blindness. Lester quickly shook his son's hand and then reached forward and pulled Tom close to him. "I'm so glad you're home, son."

They all entered the house and into the living room. Everyone found their seat and began to relax. Tom's aide sat right beside him and asked if he needed anything to make him more comfortable. Tom replied, "No thank you, Jake. Once I go to my room, I shall be just fine."

The conversation included the young women and their roles as Red Cross volunteers. Without too much direct questioning, the family noticed Tom to be a bit tired.

"Tom, your room is ready for you. Pretty much the way you left it."

"Thanks, Mom. I think I'll rest and change. It must be getting near the dinner hour."

"Yes, Tom, and when Jack arrives, he will be right up. So

if you're asleep, you can expect him anyway. He was so excited knowing his big brother was home."

"That's fine, Mom. I'm anxious to see him, too.

After the aide assisted Tom to his room, he said that he would be leaving. Margaret invited Jake to stay for dinner, but he, too, was anxious to see his family.

"I'll return in about a week to assist Tom in becoming acclimated to his surroundings."

Lester expressed his gratitude as Lily walked Jake to the door. Jake lingered a moment then said, "Lily, he talked a lot about you and the close bond between you two. He is strong, but encouragement and belief in him will do it."

"What do you mean, Jake, "Do it?"

"I can't say. Just love him, and believe in him and what he is capable of doing."

"Well, thank you, Jake, and we shall look forward to seeing you soon. If there is anything we can do for you, please don't hesitate in letting us know. You know your role with Tom is vital to us."

"Thank you."

Jake entered the limousine and soon the drive was off. As Lily reentered the living room, Lester asked, "What was that about, Lily? I could hear Jake's comment."

"I'm not certain, Dad. I'm just not certain."

Shortly there after, Jack raced in saying, "Where is he?" as he went up the stairs, some two at a time, directly to Tom's room. About thirty minutes later, Jack could be heard finishing his sentence as he closed Tom's door.

Tom rested, and later Mom came in placing her hand on his shoulder and gently waking him for dinner.

"Mom, sit a while. I'll need a bit of direction to wash up for dinner." As Tom stepped forward very slowly to his attached bathroom, he asked, "What does my room look like?"

"Well son, very much like the day you left for the military. Let's see, your old football photos are on the wall where you hung them. The bed is in the same place, even with Kate pulling it out every now and then to dust. Oh, yes, your catcher's mitt is on the stand near the window. I guess, Tom, the only differences are the color of the draperies and the bed spread. Kate saw this soft blue set and thought you would like the fresh look. Oh, yes, and the blue towels match as well. It is all quite nice, Tom. Tom, when you are ready, your father will want to know what happened to cause the blindness."

"Yes, I know."

Tom was always very neat. He went to the closet and touched the creases in the pants. Chose one and slipped into it. Then he felt the jackets. "Mom, will this one go with what I have on?"

"Yes Tom, very well."

"Here's a shirt, son, a pull over."

Shortly afterward, Tom was ready and took his mother's arm.

She quickly and quietly described where they were. When they got to the stairs, Tom began stepping down with ease.

"Mom, it is easy to get around. As a kid, I'd count the steps, twelve in all, and the banister was fun to slide on, that is, when no one was around."

Margaret smiled as they reminisced a bit. She told Tom when they entered the dining room and placed his hand on the back of his chair. Tom was able to maneuver and sit comfortably. From years at his mother's table, he instinctively knew where the napkin, silverware and glasses would be.

Lily sat on his left, feeling she could help best from there. When she saw that Tom handled his napkin and silver so well, she was not only surprised but relieved. Tom could feed himself. The military had trained him and reoriented him back to family life quite well. The conversation was comfortable and the food was "Tom's favorite", according to Kate. Margaret looked to Lester with happiness and he back to her with pride.

Their family was back together, well almost. If only Robert was home, but Tom seemed pleased that Robert had telephoned to speak to him earlier.

Robert's frequent phone calls kept the family apprised of his activities and he of theirs.

Tom did quite well with managing the dishes and the room. Lily was at his side constantly. As soon as dinner ended, Dad asked Tom to accompany him to the library where they could share some male conversation. Neither Lily nor Margaret cared. Jack joined the men.

Lester Arnold was a very gentle, but direct man, and treated his sons as men. The three men spoke together for some time and every so often a few bits and pieces of laughter came through the walls. When Tom began to talk, they listened as he shared his adventures. It was easy to tell that he took great pleasure in describing all he could not see anymore. *Tom began the conversation*

"Los Angeles, California, is a huge, sprawling city," he said. "filled with many cultures and languages, seemingly spoken all at once. They have the most beautiful beaches and simply glorious weather. What are exotic Christmas flowers in the East are simply every day poinsettias that grow in nearly every yard. Most urban areas have Spanish sounding names, not at all the typical New England names, but really culturally diverse and interesting.

After a while, the conversation turned to the "old days" and it was clear that Tom wanted to reminisce. "Dad, you gave us a wonderful life and great values. Remember what it was like when you came home from your government assignments? Mom couldn't wait for you to get home. Remember how she would buy a new dress and jump every time the phone would ring? What a great life we had." Tom took a sip of his cognac and sat back in the deep wing chair, sleepily thinking back on those days.

Margaret listened at the door, softly smiling as she heard Tom's recollections. Yes, it was a wonderful way to raise a family. Funny how even the children realized that although Lester was often gone on business, she had lived for his return...

"Ma'm, you know he said he would be home this afternoon. He is never late." Katie assured Margaret who was adjusting her summer dress for the third time. Margaret had been shopping the week prior. The clerk at Neiman Marcus had been saving the soft pink Ralph Lauren dress specially ordered from The Collection. Margaret enjoyed the complement of pink against her skin. She preferred to be in soft colors when she was with Lester. He had often commented about it when they first dated. As she flipped through the Vogue magazine for the third time, her anxiety began to show as she waited Lester's return.

His trip was to Sweden this time; he had been gone for nearly a year. Katie, the housekeeper, had been baking and preparing many favorites for the head of the household, including fresh asparagus, eggplant parmigiani, apple pie, and even chocolate chip cookies. She smiled as she thought about how as children they would promptly help themselves to the cookies as soon as they came from the oven. Katie always put an extra dozen on the shelf, especially for Mr. Arnold. However, with Lester gone so much of the time, it was almost as if Margaret might be considered the head of the household.

There is Robert, the tall quiet son, away at boarding school. A studious young man, Lester visited with him at the Abbey. Robert enjoyed his studies and particularly math like his father, the engineer. Lester was particularly proud of his son and enjoyed the fellow students he associated with. Margaret had always thought Robert might be interested in a religious order, and found out that Robert indeed had the quiet personality necessary to enjoy his life at the Abby. The frequent letters and phone calls kept everyone in close contact with him.

Tom stood on the terrace, shouting through his curled hand, "Lily, come on, come over here! Mom is cutting the flowers, come watch!" The young man motioned "hurry up" with his hand. Young Lily's blonde curls bounced on her shoulders. The sunlight created highlights as she ran toward Tommy.

"Momma, can we help you?"

"Darling, watch out, the scissors are sharp. Oh, look! There is a butterfly, see it?"

Tommy always delighted in carefully following the flight of the Monarch butterfly. Lily stood near her mother watching Tommy very carefully. Tommy jumped up, trying his best to capture the elusive creature.

The gardener, watching the children, called to them. "Tommy, the pool is warm this morning." Tommy stopped, turned, and noticed his mother watching. "Thank you, Mr. Brown" as he dashed directly to the pool. Lily ran lightly on the grass as if the grass was tickling her feet. Jumping into the water from the side and feeling the pool water in her hair, made her wrinkle her nose and rub her eyes. Duke, the pedigreed Golden Labrador, was close behind. Lily enjoyed hanging on Duke as he played in the water with them. Their Olympic size pool gave them plenty of room to swim and play. Tommy used the diving board, and Lily clapped her hands and squealed with delight as she watched Tommy dive in. She swam over to the board only to jump in.

The family was not concerned about the children playing in the pool, because they had become experienced swimmers after many private lessons. The instructor often complimented the six year old boy and his four year old sister for their quick ability to become skilled at swimming. Tommy enjoyed his role as the big brother.

Tommy is truly Lily's big brother. Wherever you see one, you see the other. Margaret never seemed to worry about her, because Tommy was such a great help. Besides, there were usually several adults working in the yard. Many mornings, the parents enjoyed their coffee pool side, and often spent early evenings with a glass of wine on the terrace. The Arnolds enjoyed the well-cared for property.

Peering out the front window, Margaret called to Katie to answer the phone, "Kate, that phone just won't stop ringing. Please answer it. I have flowers in my arms."

"Yes, Ma'm. Katie had been with the family for many years, and had become more of a family member than an employee. She scurried into the room, wiping her hands on her apron. Katie was light on her feet and many times Margaret would find her dancing around the room with the children as they were growing up. Even though she was a bit chubby, it was not even a consideration to her. She loved to dance and let it be known that early in life she was quite the dancer. She would eagerly tell the children tales of her early dancing years and no matter how busy, Katie always had time for them.

Whether it was watching the children hugging her or intently listening to her stories, it was easy for Margaret to see that the children loved Katie dearly. Phone in hand, she looked toward Margaret and shook her head, acknowledging the call was not from Lester.

Margaret smiled at Katie and gave an assuring nod. She thought to herself, "That phone never stops ringing, and each time I think it is Lester. I can hardly wait for him to arrive. He will love this new dress, and the arrangement of the flower garden." She looked up, recognizing his step and cried, "Oh, here he is!"

Tommy and Lily had been busy all day, playing first in the swimming pool, then with the dog, Duke, and how they loved to pay ball. They would throw the ball and Duke would fetch it. Tommy helped Lily with the game. "Look Lily, this is the way you throw the ball." Lily was quick to understand the game. They heard their Mother exclaim, "Daddy's home." They squealed with glee and ran to the door. Kate would quickly wipe them dry and wearing fluffy white robes, they would hurry into the living room to greet their father. Dad always arrived with gifts and many hugs as he greeted them, "Hello, my darlings." He would pull off his tie and place his jacket on a nearby chair.

They were always happy to see him and equally as happy to receive their gifts. He never forgot to bring Tommy, Lily, Mother and even Katie a present, and always knew just what each would enjoy.

This time, Tommy's gift was a catcher's mitt, which he immediately put on pretending to throw and catch an imaginary ball. So pleased and proud, Tommy hugged his father, kissed his cheek, and whispered, "Thank you, Dad." Lester hugged him and held his son for an extra moment.

Lily loved pretty clothes and especially those made from silk. She often played with her mother's silk scarves, especially the Hermes and Chanel ones, inventing new ways to wrap the expensive cloth like a dress or sometimes a cape. On this trip, Daddy had brought her a big box with a bright red ribbon on it. He asked her to guess. First, "Is it pajamas?" "No," he shook his head. Then, "Is it a sweater?" "No," he said again and shook his head, delighted at the game. "No more teasing, my little darling. You may open it," he said with a big smile, showing his perfect white teeth.

Lily first pulled on the bow and the tissue paper covered in red hearts slid off. The box opened and Lily took a deep breath,

"Oh, Daddy, it is beautiful, so beautiful! May I try it on now?"

"Yes, of course, sweetheart."

Lily carefully slipped into the red robe. She touched it so softly and turned to Tommy to tie it for her. Her father called to her saying, "Come here, my little girl, Daddy will tie it." Lily smiled and hugged him tightly with both arms.

"I love you, Daddy. It is so beautiful. Thank you," she said, as she swirled around the room.

Slowly, with a mischievous look, Lester handed Margaret her gift. Margaret smiled and set it aside, giving him a knowing smile,

"I can wait until later to open it…"

"No, Margaret, the kids would like to see it."

Margaret agreed and carefully opened the beautiful box with pink paper and a large pink and white bow, revealing floral scented stationary. "Now Margaret, you can write me more often," he said. Everyone laughed, knowing that there wasn't a day that went by that she didn't write to him when he was gone.

"Thank you, darling, I shall," she replied, most pleased both with the gift and his sentiment of wanting more of her. Katie went into the kitchen to check on the dinner and make sure Lester's favorite vegetable, asparagus, wasn't overcooked. Lester waited until she returned.

"Katie, our good friend, I didn't forget you either!" he said, as he handed her a gift. She admired the small box tied with a lavender ribbon. As she pulled on the bow and pulled back the flowered paper, she could see it was her favorite perfume.

"Oh, thank you, sir. I am so pleased." Katie was always careful with her expenditures and appreciated the gift of expensive perfume, like Chanel No. 5.

One might have seen a small tear glisten if you were looking closely. Katie left the room and returned soon, announcing dinner was served. Prayers first, immediately followed by the aroma of classic dishes graced by savory sauces. When the lively meal ended, the children went upstairs with Katie to bathe and retire. Before long, the children's, "Good night, Mom and Dad" could be heard coming from their rooms.

As if on cue, Margaret heard Tom explaining how moments like those held him together during some difficult times, "It was these memories and so many others that kept me going while serving in the military. I know it might sound odd, Dad, but I want to thank you and Mom for giving us our way of life."

Both Lily and Margaret were pleased and relieved to hear their muffled conversation and laughter. Margaret wanted her family back together. Lily wanted her big brother to be just that.

Jake, Tom's aide, appeared each morning with the driver to take Tom to his physical therapy sessions. Rehabilitation was just that. Lovely nurses and therapists roamed through the rooms and hallways. Before long, Tom could tell them apart by the sound of their voices. He participated in the various exercises and quickly returned to his original physical condition. At various times, a room would house several men, all with dark glasses and white canes. Some even had dogs to assist them. Tom had days that seemed as if he was just going along to get along. That is, until Lily noticed a certain young lady that seemed to keep Tom engaged in his exercise program.

Chapter 3

DALLAS, TEXAS WAS A long way from San Diego, California, half way across the country, but the flight seemed short to the two sisters who were so happy to share the time with their brother. Dad, Eddie, and Nancy's husband, Jacob, were waiting at the airport when the family arrived.

Michael had a quick glimpse of the waiting crowd from the window. First, his sister Nancy stepped through the gate, then Mary. Michael knew his father would be first in line, so he posed a military salute. His father gave a gentle laugh, saluted back, and then hugged his youngest son. Tears of happiness flowed easily. How proud father and son were.

Eddie also did a mock salute and knew he was next. No matter how different the brothers were, the love of family was strong. The family's strong sentiment was as clear as their "Welcome Home Michael" sign. Jacob reached out with his hand to shake Michael's, just as Michael pulled Jacob to him. They hugged and laughed. It was a great feeling of relief and happiness to have Michael back in the family. So striking, so proud.

Dad had brought the large station wagon, all six quickly found their seats. "Here Son," Dad said, patting the seat closest to him, in the same way he did when they were little children. Michael slid into the one up front. It felt so familiar, so good to Michael.

Nancy spoke first, "Michael, the children are so anxious to see you, they hear all about how great and wonderful you are. They think you are eight feet tall, and fought the war with your bare hands!" Everyone laughed, but then looked at each other and grew quiet. A sense of foreboding filled the car.

It was an awkward silence. It was Mary who spoke up, "Michael you need to know…..she hesitated. "You need to know Mother isn't doing so well."

Michael turned as best he could, "what do you mean, not so well?"

"Oh she is going to be just fine," his father interjected. "It's just that she is in the hospital for now. We didn't want to worry you unnecessarily."

"The hospital? What happened?"

"Michael, it's her heart, but we have been assured that if she follows the doctor's orders, she will be just fine. I had a good talk with Doctor Leonardo. He said it was a very mild attack. That means everyone will have to jump in and keep her from doing everything, the way she always does. The girls have been great, and we men cannot let her wait on us hand and foot. You know your Mother, she thinks that is her job and hers alone. So we have to watch it. But Michael you are the best medicine. She will get well so much faster, now that you are home."

Now the proud father had his family back, whole, and they would go directly to the hospital where Maria was anxiously waiting for her family. Today was a better day than most of her days. Just knowing her youngest son was back in the United States, not only in Dallas, but actually back in her home made everything alright.

As the group entered Maria's room, Michael was first. He went directly to her open arms. She cried a bit and they looked into each others eyes as only a mother and child can do. They had reconnected. Then Michael looked over at the lovely young lady sitting in the chair next to the bed. He was just thinking he should know her when Eddie spoke up, "Mickey you remember Roseanne."

Michael hesitated a moment, "Of course, Roseanne, how are you?"

She smiled, blushed and said very softly, "Hi, Michael."

Michael was trying to update his thinking. He remembered her as a young kid hanging out with Eddie, and now, here she was a lovely young woman sitting at his mother's side

Eddie reminded Michael, "You remember her as a kid, huh? Well she's a woman now."

"You mean a lady, Eddie."

"Yeah, that's right, a lady. She comes out every so often to help Mom. Mom has gotten very close to her. She treats her like a daughter,." Nancy nodded in agreement.

23

Although always a cute kid, Roseanne had become a lovely young woman. Michael was impressed. The conversation eventually turned to Michael and Eddie's adventures growing up.

Mary spoke up, "Remember how Eddie and Roseanne were always together? Where you saw Eddie, you would often find Roseanne not far away," she said, as she delved back into their childhood memories.

Roseanne Rodriquez was a quiet girl from a quality family similar to Eddie's. Before Roseanne became a teenager Eddie would chase her, pull her hair and tease her, He enjoyed her company. Eddie always stood up for her or took her side when she was challenged.

"Come on Eddie, why do you always want her with you?" asked Bobby on the way to the beach. It was Saturday morning, Bobby, a school friend, and Eddie and Rosanne were on their way to White Rock, just outside the city off East Mockingbird Lane where the East Park road runs near the lake. It was the nearest body of water for the young people to enjoy. For most families in the area, this was their summer spot. It had its deep spots, but most of it was safe to swim in even without life guards.

"Listen here Bobby, Roseanne comes with me and that is that! I don't want to hear about it. You don't like it? I won't go with you. "

As a teenager it was easy to see that Roseanne was Eddie's girl. Sometimes he would fool around with Esther Ravelinni, but not enough to upset Roseanne. When Eddie and Roseanne would go to the beach, the fellows knew enough not to whistle at Roseanne. Eddie had a hot temper and quick fists; he was not one to be challenged even as a teenager and would always get even with anyone who crossed him.

The conversation about Eddie and Roseanne turned Michael's thoughts to the girl who was sitting next to his Mom. Roseanne had grown up just a couple houses away from the Lopez family home. Her parents were very much like the Lopez parents. Manuel Rodriquez and Michael Lopez Sr. were close friends. Their close proximity and similar cultures made it easy for the children to become friends and spend time in both houses.

Michael turned again to look at their childhood friend. Roseanne had really grown into a beautiful woman, She was only three years younger than Michael and five years younger than Eddie. It seemed as though Eddie also spent a great deal of time with Roseanne's brother Steven. Michael smiled to himself remembering how Roseanne had become Eddie's girl, then eventually, his one and only girl.

Maria was pleased, but tired and quietly went to sleep with a smile on her face. Mr. Lopez quietly invited the family to the coffee shop. "Let your Mother sleep" he said as he waved them out the door. "Let's sit down together and have some coffee."

"I'll wait here," said Roseanne.

"No, you come along too, replied Mr. Lopez "They have tea there, too."

While Maria was resting, the family and Roseanne went down to the hospital. As they enjoyed the refreshments, Mr. Lopez sat back in his chair and placed his hands in his lap. He seemed eager to talk and soon began to captivate his audience with his lively memories.

"My children, have you ever heard the story of how I became the luckiest man alive? A hush came over them and all eyes were on their father. It was easy to see that Mr. Lopez enjoyed reminiscing. He began telling the story, " It is sort of like a "Once upon a time story" he began… and they first laughed and then became quiet as their father told the familiar family narrative.

Michael Morales Lopez's parents loved and enjoyed their children. His mother Maria was a lovely lady, small in stature with dark hair, creamy complexion, bright brown eyes, and a lovely soft voice. Her great grandparents had immigrated from the warm sunny climate of a small village of Sabinas, near Monterrey, Mexico. Third generation American, her parents insisted she was to be educated in both Spanish and English. Maria was a good student, eager to learn and quickly acquired knowledge. A modern American like many in her class she joined the student council, Spanish club, young Catholics, and with a natural talent in music she led the Glee Club.

Maria was blessed with many of the old traditions, being

strictly raised, quick to obey and understood her Father was the head of the family. Her parents accepted the American way and rather than select a husband for her, when Maria reached her eighteenth birthday, she was free to date the man of her choice.

Michael's father, also named Michael Lopez, was raised by his parents in the old traditions, total obedience to his father and great love and kindness to his mother, church and family. He was five foot eight with a slim build. Anyone coming in contact with him could feel his charisma and grace. He dressed in light colors, pants, and jacket, usually a soft colored shirt with a contrasting tie. He exercised and took pride in his appearance. One might think his fingernails were manicured. Looking directly at you the tan skin was without blemishes, a fine nose and curved chin. His physic could be easily described, a trim physic, small mustache, full head of black wavy hair and spoke with a slight accent.

Mr. Lopez had been groomed to be a business man, with an education from Bentley Business School. Michael would run his own business. His philosophy was simple. He wanted one woman to be his wife for the rest of his life and then together to raise his family in the Catholic tradition.

After the stress of a busy week, Michael liked to rest and relax in the cool theater on warm Sunday afternoons. He really enjoyed watching movies, but he particularly enjoyed the musicals.

One beautiful day, Michael Lopez leisurely parked his car and looked at his wrist watch. It was a gift, given when he completed his business courses. He checked the time, not wanting to be late for the featured movie. Michael quickly walked the short distance to the theater and saw a small line of patrons waiting to purchase their tickets.

Before long, he had moved to the front of the line, money in his hand. He looked directly at the ticket seller. She waited to hear the number of tickets he wanted, all the while taking the few minutes to notice him. For the first time, Michael saw Maria in the box office of the local theater. He was very impressed with her beauty. He knew almost immediately that he wanted to meet her, but also knew he would have to plan any meeting carefully. She appeared a lady in every sense of the word.

Soon he became a steady moviegoer. At first he only smiled at her, and then as time went on, he made small talk. Maria had also noticed Michael and the fact he did not wear a wedding ring. Sunday evenings she would tell her mother about the very handsome gentleman that frequented the movies. Her mother smiled, but warned her to always remain a lady.

It was a balmy evening and Michael waited until the line of patrons diminished making sure he was the last to purchase his ticket. By now, he had learned Maria's name from an usher and had made sure she knew his. That evening, Michael asked if he might see her after work.

Being very proper, Maria said it would be too late. Her parents would be waiting up for her. Then she mentioned that the following

Sunday was her day off. Michael quickly made a plan for the following Sunday.

By the time that Sunday was over, he knew that Maria would be the love of his life. His search for the right woman was over. They dated for six months, attending concerts, going to dances, and having intimate dinners. It wasn't long before they felt comfortable including friends in their activities. They felt their love was real.

When they were together, it was as if there was no one else in the room or on the street. They only had eyes for each other. Other people also noticed the deepening feeling between the two; it was wonderful to see. They knew it was time to talk to the families. Michael was nervous; he wanted Maria's father to approve of him and like him. They both knew that would be the test. With the father's approval, they could get married; without it, they could not. No matter how much they loved each other, Michael knew that Maria had to have that approval.

Her mother loved Michael almost at first sight, but would her father was a question in both their minds. Maria had met Michael's family at a family dinner. His parents were delighted with his choice for a wife.

Michael shifted from one foot onto the other and finally knocked on the front door. He heard her brother shout in the background. Then the brother came to the door with a smile and a twinkle in his eye. He winked at Michael. Michael nodded his head, knowing Marie had told her brothers about their plans.

Michael was invited into the neat living room. He sat on the worn brown sofa, glancing about the room. He stood up when Maria and her father entered the room. Maria quickly introduced them and then joined her mother in an adjourning room.

Soon one could hear the men laughing, signaling all was well.

Once all the formalities of introduction had taken place, Michael spoke to Maria's father requesting his blessing. After a short conversation about Michael's financial situation and an admonishment to care and love Maria, the blessing was given.

Both families wanted an American life for their children. A small wedding was held in the Catholic chapel where Maria was a beautiful and radiant bride. The family held a small reception at home with traditional foods. Michael and Maria rented an apartment until a down payment could be saved and their first home was purchased. Maria was a fine wife, loving and supportive and later a good, nurturing mother. Michael's small auto sales business slowly grew into a fine dealership.

Their first child arrived shortly after the first anniversary, a darling baby girl named Nancy, after a favorite a sister-in-law. A second daughter arrived a bit sooner than planned, which they named Mary, after Maria's mother. Then came a son whom they named Eddie after a grandfather. Both parents were surprised when two years later another boy was born. Michael Sr. was doubly pleased when Maria insisted he was to be named after her husband, Michael Jr.. He became a delight to all.

The girls were both lovely. Nancy was delicate in size and features and grew into a beautiful little girl. She loved playing with her dolls and following her mother around the kitchen while she cooked. Nancy never missed an opportunity to mimic her mother by climbing on a kitchen chair and pretending to wash dishes. She also loved to set the table and help around the house. As different as night and day, her sister Mary preferred to play outdoors with the boys. Mary's kept her chestnut brown in a ponytail,, off her face and out of the way, while Nancy loved to sit at her dressing table, brushing her dark curly hair and styling it one way and then another. Maria loved both daughters and enjoyed their unique differences.

Her sons looked very much alike, dark wavy hair, shining tan skin, and quick amiable smiles. However alike they appeared, they differed totally in dress and style. Eddie was unconcerned about the neatness of his jeans or shirt, while Michael kept keep his clothes clean all day. The parents enjoyed the differences among their children and treated them equally. Their love had continued to grow, and their young family was the joy of their lives.

"Well, children, enough of the Lopez family story for now. Let's finish our coffee and get back to Mother's room. Your mother will get well, we must see to that," said Michael's father, getting up from the table." Mercy Hospital is one of the best in the country and seems to have a recovery rate above most hospitals as well.

The younger Michael felt encouraged and thought his mother *would* recover from her heart attack. From all he had heard, she was in very good hands. He turned his thoughts to Patsy, his high school sweetheart. For some reason, he flashed back to the prom and how Patsy looked in her gown that night. He was anxious to see her. They seldom wrote to each other. But he felt their relationship would pick up where they left off. Things were going to be great between them.

The first item on his agenda for the next day was a phone call to the Wilhemsen home. He dialed the number as easily as if he had never left.

"Hello, Mrs. Wilhelmsen."

"Yes, it is Michael, yes, Michael Lopez."

"Thank you. Yes, Mother is recovering nicely."

"Yes, it is good to be home at last."

Michael became anxious to be finished with the niceties and get to the question at hand.

"Mrs. Wilhelmsen, is Patsy there?"

"Oh, when will she return?"

"Please tell her I called."

Michael was more than disappointed when Mrs. Wilhelmsen explained that Patsy was out with Billy Kesner and would be home later in the afternoon. My Patsy? I couldn't believe it. I knew I couldn't have expected her to stay home and wait forever, but he thought they had an understanding. Maybe it was just him that had an understanding after all...

Michael thought about calling back later in the day, but he stayed in his room that night, holding back the tears. He couldn't get to sleep; he kept thinking about her and remembering how they had loved each other in high school and the promises they made when he left...

In far west corner of the cafeteria, sat the most popular girls in school laughing and obviously enjoying each other's company. Michael noticed that Patsy Wilhelmson, the prettiest of them all, was looking straight toward him. He brushed the cookie crumbs off his shirt and slowly strolled over to the group of girls. Their boisterous chatter turned to whispering as he came closer.

Michael had spotted a group of friends near Patsy's table and nonchalantly walked past them pretending he didn't see Patsy staring at him. He stood near the table with his arms folded and flashed his signature grin, bantering with his friends, The group of girls looked first to see what he was doing, then at Patsy. Still laughing, he looked around and walked over to the girls' table. He leaned over and asked Patsy what she thought of the school play.

"Did you like it?"

She looked away, causing him to say her name. "Patsy, did you enjoy the play? I thought I saw you in the audience, sitting up in the balcony area?"

Turning her head, he noticed her smooth chin and sensuous mouth. She looked at him and said off-handedly, "It was alright." As everyone at the table giggled, Patsy leaned toward them saying, "Okay I'll see you later." In their teenage language that meant "leave now." Almost immediately after she spoke, they all rose and left for their classes.

Patsy's curly dark hair bounced as she leaned over the table, the light brown highlights catching the light. Her V neck yellow sweater contrasted nicely with her shirt and the classic style jeans, completing the typical teenage uniform. Now that they were alone at the table, she returned to his topic, this time sounding more positive, particularly about the part Michael had played in the production. Their conversation moved from one topic to another until the bell sounded for the next period's class. As he walked her to her class, he asked if she would go to next week's dance.

"You don't waste much time, do you?" she said, flashing him a smile and leaving him to wonder if that was a "Yes."

By the time the day of the dance arrived, Michael wondered why he had been so upset over Rachel, his last girlfriend. True, she was pretty and they had gone together for two years, but Patsy was exciting, funny, *and* beautiful. The dance was magical and she was magic.

Michael stepped forward and reached for her hand, "Let's walk over to the punch bowl.." They walked over to the records and began discussing various favorite songs and bands. Time evaporated as they danced every dance, talking, laughing, and ending the evening with an unspoken understanding that they were an item. Senior year was suddenly looking much better!

Patsy was most attentive to Michael from then on in class and outside of class. They spent all their time together, sharing activities, dances, movies, or just hanging out listening to music and doing homework. Eddie had Rosanne and now he had Patsy. "Wow this is nice," thought Michael.

By early spring, every student was talking about who their senior prom date would be, what they would wear, how they would get to the prom, and what after prom party they were going to. Mr. and Mrs. Lopez were to be chaperones which answered most of the questions Patsy's parent's had about the evening. Although the Lopez parents were very nice, they were also very strict. Michael and Patsy had been a couple for most of their senior year, so there was no surprise that they would be going together.

Mr. Lopez drove Michael to Patsy's home. Michael was standing in front of the door when Patsy's father opened the door. Patsy was still up stairs. The parents exchanged greetings. Soon Patsy's mother came to the top of the stairs. She looked pleased as she turned to see her daughter come out of her room. She spoke to Patsy and then from the top of the stairs she announced Patsy was ready. Michael could not believe how stunning she looked. To say she was exceptionally beautiful was no exaggeration Michael was more than pleased.

Photos were taken, first with parents and then just the couple as the flurry of directions was shouted out, "Stand here, put your hand over here, another photo at the stairs, now all the parents get in the picture." The picture taking continued until the couple pled to be let go. It was to be the night they would always remember. Michael knew from this day, he could easily view Patsy in his future, college and after. Patsy was *the* one.

Both Michael and Patsy, like most of the students, had been busy all year selecting and being selected by the college of their choice. Michael could hardly wait for his letters of acceptance. He had applied to several colleges and Universities, but had his heart set on Texas A & M. He felt confident that he would be accepted there, but another event changed everything for him.

It was a cold day in the middle of January when John F. Kennedy, the President of the United States addressed the nation's men. President Kennedy said, "Ask not what your country can do for you, rather ask what you can do for your country." His words rang in Michael's ears and he felt his heart well up and his tears flow. When he finally composed himself, he began to think over what he must do to answer the President's call.

Chapter 4

AFTER TEN DAYS, MOTHER had regained her health enough to be back in charge of her home. It was good to see her progress. Michael, being Michael, soon returned to the local Marine base. After thinking it through and reminiscing on his Civil Air Patrol days, he completed all the paperwork to be a drill instructor and awaited determination.

"This will be a good thing for me and something I know I can do well," Michael thought. The Marine Corps had other plans. An officer approached Michael with the devastating news," You're too young to receive that placement."

Again Michael's quiet anger came forth; too young to drink, to vote, to train men, but not to young to go to war. Then Michael remembered his youth and the problems that his anger had caused. If nothing else, he had learned the lessons of his youth and learned them well. He knew he had to come to terms with this disappointment as well. He shrugged it off. "It doesn't pay to be angry, it just gets you in trouble."

"It would be better to do something more pleasant than direct combat that's for sure, maybe a peaceful assignment in a foreign country," thought Michael as he sat down in a straight back chair and thought about his options. "There must be something better than a Drill Master." The hallway was stark with wall board full of notices. He thought hard about how to make sense of the rest of his enlistment. "What's next? How do I make a plan, when I don't have any idea about what step to take next?" A crooked sign up sheet on the wall board caught his attention. It was haphazardly hanging by one corner. He stood up and walked over to straighten it out and then noticed the word, "Overseas". Underneath it was an informational sheet for overseas Marine security guards.

"Security guard? Isn't that a job for old retired men? There certainly aren't any old men in the Marines...well maybe the officers. Maybe this is a possibility for me," thought Michael. "Yeah, a foreign country. That will teach Patsy... No," he considered. "Wait a minute. That's not fair. Patsy is entitled to her own life."

Michael looked over the sign up sheet and it directed him to the right office. Yes, there was a position opening. The officer in charge looked him over. Yes, he appeared the right height, weight and total all over appearance. Michael was pleased at such a nice reception and signed on the dotted line.

Camp La June, North Carolina was very pleasant. Not the extreme heat of Texas, just the even temperature of a spring day. The grounds were kept in great condition especially for having so many men pass through the camp.

The security guard unit was seen as the "cream of the corp." It was most difficult to obtain a status in the group with a drop out or dismissal rate of over fifty percent of the men.

Sixty days of intense training in Washington D. C. followed the days in Camp. Not only was there strict classroom training but constant vigilance whenever outside of class. These men were selected to represent not only the entire United States Marine Corp, but the United States of America. "Selected" was the word. Michael would now be placed in Saigon, Germany, Italy, or even Paris, France.

Written orders were the word of the day. The serviceman who represented the mailman in civilian life brought the envelope to Michael's quarters. Michael was sitting on the side of his bed, and looked up somewhat surprised when he was handed the envelope. He knew it was two days early. He had been accepted and placed in Paris, France.

As he held the letter, Michael remembered how he felt when he was a member of the drill team in the Civil Air Patrol (CAP). Those were the days.

Back then, Michael and Bill Richardson were paired on the school's tennis team. They were paired well, at the same playing level and evenly distributed coordination. The young men were extremely handsome in their white tennis clothes. Michael and Bill played tennis together most summer mornings, sometimes singles and some days they would find another couple and play doubles. The tennis courts at Grover Public High were in good condition, but it was important to arrive early or you would be playing in the hot sun. It was early August, in more than a warm summer, when Michael finishing a game of tennis with Bill, was walking across the park. He was almost to the drinking fountain when he spotted Russell Morell. Russ, as most called him, was recognized as an outstanding student and an even better leader.

Michael called to him, "Hey Russ, slow down." Russ stopped and turned around. Happy to see the tennis players; he extended his hand. After shaking hands and slapping backs, Bill asked, "How have you been Russ, haven't seen you around lately".

"Oh, I just came back from summer camp at the Air Force Academy."

"Air Force Academy? Where is that?"

"Oh, in Colorado."

"Yeah Mike, it was great," Bill continued, "You learn so much and have some real fun, not like summers here, just hanging out."

"Sounds good, Russ. How did you get to go there? Your Dad, huh?"

"No Mike, anyone can go, well, after you pass the requirements."

"What requirements Russ?" Mike cut in, his interest piqued now.

"Mike, we are going to have a Civil Air Patrol (CAP) meeting next Thursday. Why don't you come with me? It can't hurt, even if you don't like it. In fact, you're just the kind of guy they are looking for."

This not only appealed to Michael, it was straight in the direction he wanted to align himself. He would not, could not forget the upcoming CAP meeting. Thursday arrived. The meeting was in the library and Michael was eagerly awaiting Russ. They went directly to the community room, quietly walking through the reading room. Russ introduced Michael to several new members. Michael knew many of the members already. They soon quieted down and the speaker was introduced.

The Commanding Officer, Richard Wilkinson, was quite a presence. He was in uniform, average height, wavy hair with a very pleasant, inviting, expression. He spoke to the teenagers as if they were important young men. The group of some 30 young men in all, were all fashioned in the same way, neat hair cuts, strong bodies, similar dress, and they all seemed to have an air of pride. "Yes, that is what it is, pride. And I am going to have some of that myself." thought Michael.

Michael realized the impact the meeting was having and thought, "I meet the requirements, high scholastic grades, excellent health, good posture, and a strong desire to excel. The next day, he shared his decision with his parents at the dinner table saying, "I was more excited to become a member than I can ever remember, more excited than when I pulled the neighbor kid out of the lake, more excited than when Ellen hugged me at her birthday party, yep, way more excited."

Later in September, he was to be sworn in as a member of the Civil Air Patrol, He would be a CAP, and a real proud American. Wondering how the swearing in ceremony might go, Michael looked at the audience thinking about the evening. He noticed his mom and dad in the crowd, with Nancy and Mary. They kept giggling at the candidates; they liked the uniforms Michael guessed. But where was Eddie? Michael had counted on him being here. He had promised…

Mr. Martinelli was always testing Eddie's loyalty. Poor Eddie, he thinks he is the boss, but actually he has a big boss now. He wasn't interested in college or the professional careers, at least ones that most families are proud of. He has to do whatever Mr. Martinelli wants him to do. Strangely, Eddie likes it that way. Michael's thought came to an abrupt end when the music started.

The day had finally arrived and Michael was happy. Being at the American Embassy in Paris, France had seemed like a dream to Michael. He walked past a highly polished desk, on highly polished marble floors, thinking that "spit and polish" was made for this place, when he looked up and saw a beautiful young girl talking to a distinguished man. Just then, jarring him from his thoughts, another Marine spoke to him, "Hey Mick, the girls are waiting near the fountain." It was his room mate, Jared.

Bastille Day is celebrated in Paris, just like July 4th in United States. The fountains were flowing like French champagne. What a wonderful place! As Michael and Jared walked through the downtown area of Paris, the young ladies seemed more than delighted. They engaged the two young men for the entire day and much laughter and merriment took place, well into the wee morning hours. If Patsy could only see me now...

The detail of our assignment and orders were very clear. We had no problem completing each and every assignment. And early completion meant an early evening with the very fine ladies. Paris is *the* place, there's no place in the world like it. Tough duty they say. I guess they weren't in 'Nam, that's all I can say. 'Nam was tough; this place is like candy in comparison. Michael and Jared shared quarters. No one was concerned about the time of night they came in and being young in Paris, in uniform was like being number One!

One rainy dreary day, the Commanding Officer was meeting with the men regarding regulations. Who should enter the room, but one of his very attractive secretaries. Michael told Jared to go on ahead and he lingered long enough to be alone with the captivating lady, long enough to learn her name was Nicole Freeman and yes she would go out with him that evening. Michael enjoyed Nicole's company, especially since she was from the United States.

It was impossible to remember who, where and what happened during those two years in Paris. The sight seeing was most fulfilling, the language poetic, and the people warm and friendly. Most of all, he seemed to enjoy Nicole Freeman during those two years. Although there were many French women, Nicole was his frequent companion.

She was a sweet young lady and Michael was a man of the world at the age of twenty-two. Despite the entertainment, the two young Marines never relinquished their very serious assignment of taking complete charge of the security of Number 5 Embassy Building.

Chapter 5

Tom could now shower, prepare simple sandwiches and even pour tea for himself. Lily was so happy and proud of his progress. He practiced many of the daily living skills at the rehabilitation's facility. Lily often brought the daily paper and read it to Tom. She would joke and tease him about times in their youth, such as when he taught her to ride a bicycle and how he helped her learn her prayers. She so wanted Tom to know how important he was to her. Lily would hold his hand or touch his shoulder, place her cheek next to his just to let him know she cared.

"Tom, remember when you told me how important it was to pay close attention to whatever you do in life?" Lily encouraged, "You said you must first consider the results before you make a move. I've never forgotten that and you shouldn't, either."

As the days and weeks progressed, Lily seemed to think there was something special about Tom's relationship with a certain physical therapist. Her name was Colleen Riley and if Tom could only see her beautiful red hair and bright smile, he would have been even more impressed.

Lily happened to be reading the Sunday paper to Tom when Colleen walked in the lounge area complimenting Tom on his ability and the ease in which he performed the tasks he had been practicing.

"You must be Lily," the woman said. "Tom talks about you frequently."

"Then you know I'm his sister. And you must be the magician that has gotten Tom to be so handy, even with the teapot!" Lily responded. All three laughed, oddly comfortable with each other. "Whoa Lily," said Tom. "Don't give Colleen all the credit, my hard work counts, too!"

Colleen answered, "Yes, Tom really has been goal oriented. He will be quite self-sufficient; he puts his concentration and energy into each exercise. A great man, as well. What a great brother you have here Lily!"

"Thank you. Tom really looks forward to his sessions here."

"Lily," said Tom "I think Colleen wants me to get back to work."

"Okay Tom. Anyway, I've some shopping to do for Mother. I'll see you at home," she said as she bent down and kissed his cheek.

That evening, Lily questioned Tom about Colleen. Tom was pleased to talk about her. He certainly was impressed and pleased with Colleen, and even more than interested in her.

One day at the rehab, Lily pushed the issue "Tom would you like to invite Colleen over, perhaps for dinner with the family or coffee? Tom was delighted with the idea, "But it might be too soon for a family dinner, don't you think?" he asked. He very much wanted Lily to set the scene for him. "Lily will you help me out for the occasion?" Lily was delighted, sporting a wide smile at the suggestion.

"Can you ask her if she would like to come over for coffee next week?" she asked.

That was just the push the couple needed to get over their inhibitions and Tom's fears. Colleen soon became a frequent visitor of the Arnold home. When they were together, Colleen's training enabled her to make Tom seem like he had no disability at all. As time went on, Tom told his dad that he was going to ask Colleen to marry him. Dad urged Tom to do so, even asking Jack to go with Tom to purchase an engagement ring. Dad told him not to buy anything too fancy, but "one she'll be proud to wear," he instructed.

Later that day, Jack asked the question no one had yet asked, "What if Colleen doesn't want a blind man for a husband? What happens then?"

He continued with his hard comments. "Well, why are you looking at me like that?" he said. "I'm certain the thought has crossed your mind, too…"

"Son, it's not something we wanted to think about, but you are right," said Dad. We only assume the two are in love and want to marry. She may say no. When I asked your Mother to marry me, I was worried"

Tom came around the corner, and joined the conversation,

"She should have been worried!" They all laughed, breaking through the uncomfortable feeling of being caught talking about his blindness.

Just then, Lily poked her head in the room, saying, "What's so funny?"

"Come on in, Lily," said Tom. "I want you to hear this, too."

"Look," he said. "I am nervous, but I am not going to throw away my chance at happiness. If she says "no", well, at least I tried. Someone once told me that if you live too much in the past or the future, you will miss out on the enjoyment of the present. To me, that seems like a pretty good philosophy. One thing you may not know." Tom said, "At my last appointment with Dr. O'Brien, he assured me this blindness may not be a lifetime affliction. He told me that it was a psychological blindness."

"He said the trauma of being shot down and having to drag my co-pilot out of the way caused a physical manifestation, in my case - blindness. And, he said the day may come when my sight will return and then, my degree as an electrical engineer from Notre Dame will keep me busy again." By this time, his mother had walked in as well and they all looked at each other in disbelief. Lily grabbed her mother's hand and choked back the tears.

Tom came home several nights later alternately whistling and singing. Colleen had said, "Yes." Tom's seeing eye dog, Major, seemed equally as happy.

Finally, the day had come. Excitement was in the air. The

magnificent church was full of friends and relatives, and the aisles and altar were decorated with large bouquets of flowers. The bride and her many bridesmaids were in the bride's room of St Andrews Episcopal Church. What a large and beautiful structure. Jack was Tom's best man and stood close to him in case he needed anything. He kept telling him who was arriving and where they were seated. For today, Tom would not wear the dark glasses.

"Jack, put these in your pocket."

"Sure, but don't you want them?"

"With all the pictures, I'd rather not have dark glasses on. You know. I'll just put my hand on your shoulder. OK? Just go slow."

"What about your cane?"

"Just leave it, I don't need it right now." Tom chuckled, "You aren't going any where, right?"

"No," he laughed. "I guess not!"

The music started and all eyes were on the bridesmaids walking up the aisle accompanied by the groomsmen. Each of the six women looked extraordinary; their gowns flowed as if in a breeze, sky blue and the satin slippers matched the dress and they carried bouquets of pink baby roses.

Margaret and Lily both looked beautiful in their closely matching ivory suits and pink corsages. They stood in the front row watching the procession. The happiness they had for the soon-to-be-wed couple was evident to everyone there.

The change of music indicated the bride would come down

the aisle in her full glory to stand by the man she would soon call husband. Colleen was magnificent; the gown was outdone only by her beauty. White seed pearls throughout the bodice matched her pearl and diamond earrings. A small tiara crowned her abundant red hair and shoulder length veil. She held her father's arm lightly and seemed to glide down the aisle never taking her eyes away from Tom.

Jack beamed as Colleen's father kissed his daughter and let her go and joined her mother. They made a very handsome couple, her father in a traditional tuxedo and her mother in a satin pink dress with a matching corsage.

The priest, who was also a family friend, began the ceremony. As the vows began Tom reached for Colleen's hand before Jack could assist him. Their eyes seemed to meet and Tom's expression had changed. His eyes searched her face and rested on her eyes. Colleen slowly began to realize that Tom really was seeing her. When he said "I do" Tom choked back his emotions. He could see his beautiful bride. As she had walked down the aisle to meet him, he began to see her outline and then her image became clearer. All the pain was released and his heart was full. God had restored Tom's eye sight. As he said "I do" he also breathed a prayer of thanksgiving, "Thank you God. Colleen you are so beautiful." The priest heard Tom's words. He paused for a moment, then decided to continue without the interruption.

The priest ended the ceremony and the couple turned to be

introduced for the first time as "Mr. and Mrs. Thomas Arnold." Tom smiled at his wife and kissed her once more, then turned to the audience smiling brightly. "Today God gave me a beautiful wife, wonderful friends, and my eyesight, and I thank Him." The applause was immediate and resounding. As it quieted, he said, "Thank you each and every one for making this a day to remember." There was complete silence for a moment and then they all applauded again and cheered them as the couple and wedding party returned down the aisle and prepared for the celebration.

Chapter 6

Lily loved having Tommy to talk to, even if it had to be by phone. Every time she had a decision to make or a conflict to solve, he was there.

"Tommy, are you pleased with the Abbey?" "Well, I want to go to a school that I love, too. My friend, Jodie is at St. Catherine's and just loves it, but Mom told me I will be going to St. Mary's in Racine, Wisconsin, next year. No! I don't want to go there! What? Yes, the nuns wear those winged hats. No, I don't want one. Tommy you are so silly sometimes. Okay, Okay, I'll listen."

"Tommy, please do me a favor and tell Mom you think St. Catherine's is a great girls school. Yes, you know Dad thinks I must go to an all girls' school, but he never mentioned which one. No, no, Tommy, it is not St. Mary's I want... it is St. Catherine's. Don't forget."

Lily hung up the phone feeling quite confident that Tommy could persuade their mother to let her attend St. Catherine's School for girls. Lily knew Tommy would be on her side, but with Mom it wasn't always easy to get her to change her mind.

Lily arrived, bags and baggage at Saint Mary's, the school of her Mother's choice. "Hey! Lily Arnold!" A tall well proportioned brunette with a happy smile on her face came forward. She looked down at the luggage, recognizably impressed with the style and brand, put her clip board aside as she reached out to Lily. Lily grasped her hand. The breeze was blowing her long blonde hair across her face.

Lily, friendly and accustomed to meeting and greeting people, spoke first. "Hi, you must be Maryanne, Maryanne Cranston?" Lily eagerly questioned. Maryanne looked a bit older.

"Yes, as a member of the senior class, we are assigned to new students. And you are my assignment." Both girls laughed.

Relaxing, Lily replied "Thank goodness, how would we ever know the ropes?"

Pointing her finger at the cart, Maryanne reached for the small case. "Put your luggage on this red wagon and you can pull it to the building."

Laughingly Lily said "What a cute idea." School was a bit like camp, she thought, a "do it yourself package. Oh well, it works."

Quickly Maryanne replied "Well, no men to carry the stuff" then shrugged and continued on, "Being a small school, the dormitory is above the chapel."

Both laughed, and Lily commented, "I wonder why…"

"That should keep you being a good girl." Maryanne emphasized the "good girl."

After struggling to place the luggage carefully in the cart, they started towards their rooms. With great pride, Maryanne continued the tour, "The beautiful Gothic structure, ringing bells and beautiful statues all perfectly placed make for an amazing picture, don't you think? She paused to see if Lily was properly awed by the sight. "You must have noticed on the brochure. The facilities are well known and admired both far and near. The students come from all over. You are from California, right?"

"Yes, and Wisconsin is totally foreign to me. But you are right, the brochures show it all, but even they don't do them justice."

"The chapel is most splendid."

"Well, when you're not at your studies, or sports, you will find the chapel becomes your friend."

"St. Mary's has an adjacent convent, that way the student body and nuns stay all together."

Following room assignments, meeting new room mates, and touring the buildings for the second time, Lily and the student body were greeted by Sister Hildegarde.

"Good morning Ladies"

"Good morning Sister Hildegarde"

Sister Hildegarde, later known as Mother Superior, was warm and friendly. "Ladies, and I mean ladies, you are here not only to learn your lessons, and that is important, but you will be attending to your spiritual needs, that is attending the church services as are presented by our religious order. We are interested not only in your studies, but in the proper spiritual care of you, as a unique individual."

"Now regarding your school lessons," she continued, "you will become a well rounded student, learning through all the disciplines. Grades are a standard of where you are in the learning curve, but we feel it is more important for you know how and why to apply that knowledge. During your the three years here, you will become well prepared for which ever college you choose."

One young girl whispered to another "Good God we took enough of an entrance exam, if we passed it and we had to, to get here, we can go anywhere." Her friend giggled. "According to her we can only go up." More giggling.

Sister Hildegarde paused, looked at the two girls.

Her look was enough. Both girls sat straight up and gave her their full attention. She then continued. "And you probably will not need a prayer book by the time you graduate. You will know the services by heart." the student body laughed. "And now regarding your deportment at this school, you all come from families which have taught you manners and proper dress. You will be expected to maintain …her voice continued for another few minutes with the introduction to the school. Lily liked her immediately.

Even with the very strictly regulated schedule, the girls were full of laughter and easily assimilated into the routine. Days flowed into weeks and months. Lily was not disappointed by Sister Hildegarde's promises. She loved the school. It fit her just right.

During Lily's student years she took her studies very seriously and never faltered with her religious practices. In fact, Sister

Hildegarde called Lily aside many times to request her assistance in particular events or holidays, putting her in the lead student role. "Lily, August 16th is a special day for the Community of St. Mary's. There will be three rosaries said that day. Would you please make sure all the students bring their own rosaries? Thank you. That will be a big help."

"It will be my pleasure, Sister Hildegarde." Back in her room Lily was talking with another student, Joanie.

"Sister wants this to be a special holiday. I think she wants a buffet for the evening meal. What do you think?" asked Joanie.

"Joanie, I think the buffet is a great idea, and we can easily arrange it with the cooks and the wait staff, but first double check if it is a fasting day."

"Lily you are so right. No wonder you are always head of the class." They both laughed.

Another thing Lily really loved, particularly coming from California, were the seasons. During the months from November through March in Wisconsin, you could see always see snow flakes in the air floating downward to the snow covered ground. It pleased Lily to just watch out the window. Weekends of down hill skiing and cross country skiing become the regular off campus activity. The girls would gather around the trip notices, leaving in small groups planning their ski outfits and buses that will take them to the slopes.

Lily loved the snow and would frequently be the first on the bus. After returning from an exhausting day on skis, she would telephone Tommy and share the fun time. They reminisced about their many family trips in the mountain area of California.

During Lily's junior year, Lily was summoned to the Headmistress's office. "Lily, you have completed two and a half years of studies here at St. Mary's."

"We have watched you grow and mature each year."

"Sister Mello, I have truly enjoyed my stay here. As you know, the school really wasn't my choice, but it was my Mother's. Apparently mothers are very wise women. She certainly selected the right school for me."

"Well, Lily, we have been watching your actions and your devotion not only to your studies, but to your prayer life. Sister Hildegarde has been very impressed with you. As a matter of fact, all the Sisters of our community have noticed you. We are now wondering if the Lord is calling to you."

Lily was startled, "Oh Sister Mello, that has not entered my head – at all."

Well, perhaps you aren't aware that your actions are the actions of an Aspirant."

Lily placed her hand over her mouth, rather stunned and caught off guard. "An Aspirant, you mean, to become a nun? "Oh, Sister, I don't think so."

It had not ever occurred to her she might be singled out as an Aspirant.

"Sister Hildegarde has made a request. Instead of returning home for the Christmas break, would like you to spend time in the convent quarters and begin searching your soul for a commitment to the order."

"Thank you, Sister Mello. Please tell Sister Hildegarde I shall think about this conversation and pray about it very carefully. I will let you know when I decide."

The student halls were filled with happy voices as the Christmas season approached. Christmas music played throughout the school and decorations made the girls feel festive. Plates of cookies were piled near the punch bowl, calling to the girls as they moved in and out of each other's rooms, making preparations for the holiday.

On Friday, late afternoon, the snow was falling and Lily had been waving and shouting good bye until the last student had left for the train station and all the taxis and private cars had left their tracks in the snow. It was hard for Lily, watching her friends leave for Christmas break to enjoy their families and relax for the winter break. She suddenly wondered if she had made the right decision…

Every day, the bells rang out for services. Following service, Lily enjoyed a quiet light meal followed by silence until the morning bell rang. Lily felt cozy and warm in bed; she stretched and knew she had slept well. She eagerly prepared for the early morning service.

Silence is broken at the breakfast meal. The nuns discussed the hearty breakfast. "Good morning Sister." was repeated as each arrived in the dining hall. Finally the entire group had arrived and Sister Hildegarde shared the morning greetings. Lily was greeted as if she were already one of the community. Sister Hildegarde could see that Lily seemed to fit among the group. It pleased the Mother Superior to see that Lily had chosen to remain.

Following the meal she spoke directly to the possible Aspirant. "Lily, you will need to follow these instructions, and wear your veiled hat. The Community of St Mary's has residences in Racine, Wisconsin and Boston, Massachusetts, giving an Aspirant a small choice in placement." And with a smile, Sister Hildegarde said "One day, you too, could be wearing one of our winged hats." Lily nodded and smiled back.

While Lily was known among her classmates for having a sense of humor, she knew she had to leave the pranks and foolishness behind her now in order to seek the Lord and discipline herself in prayer. The schedule stated that an Aspirant was to discipline herself by waking up as the bells rang on the hour, dress, including the veiled habit and go to her private kneeler and read the prayers on the prayer card. The bell rang more than once during the night.

On the first night, Lily obeyed cheerfully, the second night Lily slipped on her robe and habit and read prayers at the kneeler. By the third night, Lily simply placed the habit next to her pillow.

When the bells rang she remained in bed in her night attire, placed the hat on and read the prayers.

After the first week, she had become disappointed in herself and her lack of discipline. "To discipline oneself isn't as easy as I thought," Lily mused, "or maybe it just isn't the kind of lifestyle I am fit for…" She knew she had to return to the office and admit her feelings to Mother Superior. Sister Mello was working at her desk and she stopped and put down her pencil and looked up.

"What an angelic face," thought Lily. "Sister Mello has a look, an expression I don't have and certainly don't feel. This I know for certain."

"Good morning Sister."

"Good morning Lily, did you sleep well?"

"Yes Sister, I was hoping to see Sister Hildegarde, is she available?"

"Of course, she makes herself available for all of us. Anything special?" she asked. At that moment the door was open and Sister Hildegarde entered the room.

"Did I hear my name?" she asked.

"Oh, yes Sister, I need to talk with you. Could we have some privacy?"

"Sister Mello, would you be kind enough to check on the prayer schedule for me? It is in the library."

"Of course Sister," she answered and left the room.

After a heart to heart talk, Sister Hildegarde emerged from her office with her arm around Lily's shoulder. Lily immediately ran to the telephone and called Tommy. "Tommy, I'm coming home for the rest of the vacation!"

Tommy was waiting at the airport when Lily stepped off the plane. She ran to him and they embraced for a few moments. He looked at his little sister, "Wow, you look great. You are really growing up. How was your Aspirant experience," he asked, searching her face for the answer.

"None the worse for the wear, as they say. Really wasn't what I expected, though." She laughed, took his hand and they headed for the baggage area chattering all the way.

Christmas at the Arnold's home was filled with traditional holiday food, beautifully wrapped gifts, bright decorations, and plenty of hugs. Visiting friends and relatives created lively scenes with the sounds of glasses clinking and the familiar scents of holiday food . Tommy had brought a friend home for the holidays, Johnny Hill, the very charming Johnny Hill. Instead of creating a wedge between Tommy and Lily, Johnny fit right in and the trio became a familiar sight throughout the town during winter break.

By the time the vacation was over, something unfamiliar had stirred within Lily. Something she struggled to name, but became swallowed up once she returned to school.

Lily graduated as valedictorian of her graduating class. A leader in every way, she had become a striking young lady, self assured, and full of grace. Beginning the class address, Lily spoke of the declining morals of the country and its involvement in the war. She contrasted her words with stories of hope. She spoke of success, "real success if you are willing to work for it." She ended with comments on the life of St. Francis.

Her parents Margaret, Lester, young Jack and of course Tommy all sat in the front row, watching her admiringly and nodding every so often at her remarks. Lily knew Tommy would move heaven and earth to be at her side for this important day. Lily's speech was received with a round of applause. Names of renowned families were called out as each girl reached for her diploma. Following a fancy brunch, students and their families prepared to leave the campus. Luggage was dragged to the waiting automobiles, good byes and promises to keep in contact were shouted back and forth.

Chapter 7

S UMMER HAD ARRIVED AND the Arnold family enjoyed the sunny days on breakfast, by the pool for a cool dip or at one of the private clubs with friends. As always, Tom and Lily were enjoying the day. Tommy was telling Lily about his college days and helping her weigh out her college choices.

"Dad, I have narrowed it down between two schools. I am stuck between Wellesley College for women and Princeton. What do you think?"

"Lily, Wellesley is certainly an excellent school, if you have your heart set on it. It's in New England and I think you might enjoy that area, but, perhaps it's time to go to a co-ed school. Princeton isn't terribly far from New York City. It is in New Jersey and is well known for its business courses. Besides, it is very historical and is in a small town. You might enjoy a few years there." Lily could tell her father was trying to guide her into her final decision. She was finding it difficult to make the choice. She had been accepted at all the colleges she had applied to, but still had not made a formal decision. It was a lot to think about...

The following day, Lily and her mother made their plans for a day of shopping. They thought they would start out at Bonwit Teller, a lovely up scale store, and then go to Bloomingdale's for lunch followed by more shopping, this time for shoes. Bloomingdale's had a fine restaurant, specializing in salads. The seating area was most pleasant, white table cloths and napkins to match, all with a small blue border. Each table had fresh flowers, and set at just the right height to not interfere with conversation. Waiters with freshly starched uniforms carried the trays and placed the dishes, asking if the ladies would like anything else.

During lunch, Lily returned to the conversation about colleges with her Mother. She wanted more details about Wellesley. Her mother agreed it was a fine school for women. Lily said its motto was most intriguing "Not to be ministered unto, but to minister."

"Oh, how nice, Lily. I didn't know that."

"Yes, and they are very dedicated to teaching students its philosophy of living for the sake of others." And as the conversation volleyed between the shopping and the colleges, Margaret asked Lily if she had already had this conversation with her Father. She questioned her about their ideas, "What did your father say? Did he have any suggestions? You need to make a decision."

"Well, Mother, Dad is pretty strong on Princeton in New Jersey."

"Well, that settles it, Princeton it will be or should I say "Princeton here we come?"

Lily rolled her eyes, turned her head and began laughing. "I should have known, Dad would have the last say."

"Your father is very wise. He would have had his reason for indicating Princeton. Did he mention a course of study?"

"Yes, he thought I should go toward my strengths, Business Administration, with a major in Management."

"Well, Lily now can we concentrate on other things since you have selected the school and the course of study?" They both laughed. "Now let's get a head start and find the right clothes for Princeton."

Lily did indeed enroll at Princeton for her under graduate work and study Business Administration, majoring in Management as her father advised. Four years at Princeton, gave Lily a nice taste of New York City, from theatre to nightlife. Lily didn't date anyone special at school and began to enjoy many phone calls back and forth to Johnny Hill, or should we say "Hi Johnnnneeey," as she answered the telephone when he called.

Holidays and summer vacations brought Lily right back to home base. Many conversations with her parents, especially her mother, influenced her into agreeing to continue her studies at the University of Southern California towards a Doctorate of Philosophy in Psychology upon graduating from Princeton. All this pleased her mother.

Her parents said little more regarding her education. "She is certainly old enough to decide on her own career" said her Father one evening.

They knew Lily would discuss any plans with Tommy. Tommy had completed his doctorial studies in Civil Engineering and had joined the military as an officer. He called regularly and they kept a flurry of letters back and forth.

Lily wrote to Tommy daily. Lily never wanted a mail call to go by without Tommy hearing his name called. Often the letters were full of everyday home like events.

"Dear Tommy,

This morning our cat had kittens, three no less, out in back by the Cabana. You know Mom, she was delighted and soon had a basket for them. By tomorrow morning they will be named!

"Dear Tommy,

Kate made Dad's favorite cookies. I guess she misses him, too. I wonder what he will bring Mom this time. She keeps talking about a trip to Niagara Falls. Maybe she'll receive the tickets. She loves those small trips, just the two of them."

Dear Tommy,

"Sandra, the girl in my office had a baby boy. She and her husband are sounding out names. I threw your name in the hat, so to speak. I wouldn't be surprised if they decide on it."

Dear Tommy,

"I had a newsletter from The Community of St. Mary's. They received a check for $50,000.00. It seems that one of the fathers of a former student left the endowment in his will. Nice, don't you think?" They have been having a fundraising drive for some time to have some repair work done on the school. Praying is good, but you need the money, too."

The whole family missed Tom, but for Lily it was painful to not be able to pick up the phone any time and just hear her brother's voice. Even from far away, he had great influence on her. "You know Lily, law is becoming the way to go for a lot of women. When the time comes, Lily, you might want to consider Yale for law school." Influenced Tommy. He knew Lily was a good student and she enjoyed all aspects of academia. Keeping up with her studies would be no problem, and her father would see that she was employed while continuing her degree. Lily had never considered law, but she found herself writing for catalogues and poring over them struggling to make the right decision. "Life seems like a constant crossroads of decisions..." Lily thought.

Johnny Hill had become a regular visitor to the Arnold household. He was handsome, charming, and was always ready to lend a helping hand to Lester Arnold, who considered his friend's son one of the family.

When Lily was home from school, Johnny began to come over

even though Tommy wasn't at home anymore.. He also seemed to be spending a great deal of time with Lily and they were becoming more than just friends.

Los Angeles was a big beautiful city and Lily was offered a wonderful summer position in a law office while continuing her studies. Johnny would call on her whenever he could for lunch, dinner, or even a walk in the park. Flowers arrived for Lily on special days and special occasions. It was apparent to everyone that Johnny was courting Lily.

The Western Union carrier rang the door bell. He had left his bicycle thrown off to one side in the driveway. Katie answered the door. "Mrs. Arnold it is a telegram. It's from the military, M'am."

"Oh, dear God, please don't let it be bad news. Please!" Margaret exclaimed. Margaret signed for the envelope asking Katie to give the young man a gratuity. She heard a "Thank You" and the door closing. Her hand trembled. Neither Lester nor Lily were home. "Well, I must open it whatever the news." She read it out loud, "We regret to inform you… what, We regret to inform you that your son Lieutenant Thomas Richard Arnold has been wounded and is …..Oh, thank you God, thank you." Tom had been wounded, but it was not life threatening and he was being cared for at a VA hospital and would be transferred closer to home soon.

That evening, the family were discussing Tom's situation when Lily spoke up, "Listen, at least he will be close enough that we can visit him often."

Jack turned to Johnny Hill "That's right, and we can take turns." Tommy's injury and sacrifice for his country struck a nerve in Johnny. Uncharacteristically, he disappeared with only a quick note to Lily that he would see her in a couple of months and that he had to take care of some business. Lily was unsure about his whereabouts, but knew he would be back. He always did what he promised. One late afternoon, Johnny opened the door to Lily's office. All heads turned and the room was quiet then Johnny spoke, "Is it convenient to see Lily?" There he was standing in uniform with a great smile.

Somehow she had known all along that he had joined the service. He was home from boot camp, looking even more handsome than ever. He had flowers in one hand and his hat in the other.

Not knowing what Johnny would say, Lily asked him to one of the other rooms. She took the flowers and laid them on a desk, then turned and hugged and kissed him. He had both arms around her, not just a light kiss this time. They had both grown up in his absence.

"Lily, I love you and want to share my life with you, but for now, all I can do now is ask you to wait for me."

"Oh, yes, Johnny I'll wait forever for you." She asked for an early lunch and they left the office arm in arm, and walked out and down the street in the warm beautiful sunshine.

Following a short leave, Tommy was back to light duty, but now it wasn't just a letter a day for Tommy, now it was two letters a day, one for Tommy and one for Johnny. The letter for Johnny was always signed, "I love you, come home safe to me."

News about Vietnam was not good, the television and radios gave daily commentaries on all the issues. Letters from the men were few and far between. One of Tom's letters indicated he would be back in active service soon. Lily learned Tommy was back in the air. Johnny too was a fighter pilot, following in Tommy's footsteps. Lily knew the prayers by heart and was a frequent visitor to the downtown chapel. "Dear Lord please keep our men near and dear to you…"

One Sunday, a black Cadillac with a driver was in the driveway. Lily looked out the window and saw Mr. and Mrs. Lawrence Hill, Johnny's parents.

As informal as Johnny's visits were, his parents were very formal people and had never come to the Arnold home unannounced. For a minute, she hoped it was a surprise visit from Johnny. When the doorbell rang, Lily had already flown halfway down the steps calling out to Kate, "I'll take care of it, Kate." As she opened the door to greet them, her delight turned to shock. The anguished faces of Johnny's parents said it all. Her tears came.

"Oh, Lily - it's Johnny…"

"Please come in," Lily struggled to mouth the words.

"Mother can you come here, the Hill's are here. Please Mother."

Mrs. Hill held Lily tightly, suddenly sobbing uncontrollably.

As Margaret Arnold came in to the room, Mr. Hill choked out his words, holding back the tears, "It is our son John."

Margaret gasped and began crying. She couldn't help but feel so much sorrow for Johnny and the Hills. It was a message no mother wanted to receive.

"Maybe it's not true, maybe he is just in a military hospital?" sobbed Margaret.

"No Mother." Lily cried out.

Mr. Hill suddenly lost his composure and answered, sobbing, "No. It's true. Our son was killed in action. His plane was shot down." They sat down and the Hills told them all that they knew.

"What kind of arrangements are to be made?"

"Well, the message said the body will be sent home. We will have to wait for further instructions. Lily, we just wanted you to know, first."

Lily felt faint. She sat down on the sofa. Margaret was hugging Mrs. Hill, now both women were crying. One for her dead son, the other with a dread and knowledge that it could have just as easily have been her son.

Lily was in a daze, unable to process the muffled voices still talking in the living room. Lily's heart was broken.

Kate could hear the conversation from where she was reading. She laid her book down and leaned forward to grasp every word, learning just which man had died. When she heard it was Johnny Hill, she looked up toward heaven and a tear rolled down her cheek before she could rub it away with her sleeve. The sun shone brilliantly through the library window and reflected on the statue – a bust of David – from the museum in Florence, Italy. A beautiful room in a lovely house was filled with sadness.

The funeral and the days following were a blur of emotion. Lily spent most of her time in her room, rereading Johnny's letters. It was her first tragedy and one that she had to endure without Tom at her side. Days turned into weeks, when Lily's brother Jack came to her and urged her to leave the house. Lily finally listened to him. "Lily, life isn't about waiting for storms to pass, another one will always come. It is about dancing in the rain."

Lily graduated with little fan fare and went to work full time in the law offices of Barnes and Barnes while studying for the bar. They were happy to have her working fulltime at the firm, not just summers and school breaks.

When Lily returned to work, she became very quietly involved in the war efforts. One snowy winter weekend, she joined in a peaceful protest in Washington, D.C., carrying a candle around the White House. It was a silent, but glaring protest to the war. She pulled her scarf over her nose, trying to keep the wind and snow from her face. The snow had picked up and a bitter cold front was settling in when Lily heard a woman's voice calling out to her.

She looked over to the kiosk where a lady was selling candles. Did she know someone else had joined in the protest march, she wondered. It was Maryanne Cranston from St. Mary's convent school. She stepped out of line and warmly greeted her friend. "Gosh Maryanne, it is a long way from Wisconsin."

"You bet, and many events later. Are you married, any kids?

"Not yet, how about you?" They each asked the usual summary questions. Soon, the women went back each to their positions, one selling candles and the other walking in protest.

Now the youngest Arnold family member, Jack, had joined the Navy. Jack was always considered "the youngster." His mother, Margaret, would brag about Jack to her many friends. One might have thought he was her favorite child, the way she bragged about how he looked in his uniform, how well he got along with the men, which aircraft carrier he was assigned. She listened for any news regarding the USS Coral Sea CV 43, The Yorktown or whichever carrier he was assigned. However whenever he was on leave, Margaret would tease him about being worried about her little boy. The family took it all in fun.

Jack loved his both parents and especially his mother. After a while, Lily did not keep to herself completely. Although she was still heartsick with grief, she learned it was better to work through it and do something constructive to keep busy. She met her dear friend Martha who joined her in some of her extra circular activities.

After work and on Sundays both Lily and Martha would teach first aid, or recruit blood donors for the Red Cross. They also helped at the Boys and Girls Club. They felt it most important to continue services that made them feel important and patriotic. Helping with blood drives for the military and caring for the children of military families made them both feel they were of some use to their county. It kept Lily too busy to think about her loss. Volunteering had been part if the Arnold family's social life. The Red Cross in particular seemed to fit Lily's need to help with the war.

Lily felt the decisions she made were not all negative, whether it was not joining the nunnery or allowing her father to make her college choice, but losing the man she dearly loved was most difficult.

Still Lily had other tribulations waiting for her. After she passed the bar, Lily began work at the Law Firm of Smith, Anderson and Jones. She felt sure that of these days it would included the name of Arnold, too. Lily seemed to relish her cases. She was getting a fine reputation in law, and spent a great deal of her limited free time volunteering at the Boy's and Girl's Club.

One morning the rain was falling, the wind was only slight, but blowing the rain enough to keep the windshield wipers going. Nothing could make her feel sad today. Tom was finally home, she had a good job, and finally felt a little more like her old self. It was a distance to the office. Lily enjoyed driving herself to work.

Usually she parked in an open parking lot and enjoyed walking the short distance. With the rain maybe I'll park in the parking garage thought Lily. Lily was surprised to find the parking garage almost full of cars.

"Guess I'll have to go up a couple of levels," she said to herself. She had spent several minutes driving around looking before finding a spot, yes, one way back in the row. Oh, well even a short walk would do me good. Let's see, oh, yes, level 3 and row N, I'd better mark that down so I don't forget where I've parked she thought. The garage was a bit dark since it relied mostly on the daylight and particularly sunshine to show the way.

She heard other cars and people's voices. She saw a group walking to the stairwell and relaxed. She had to hurry to the office; clients might be arriving so she picked up her stride and soon found herself running down the stairs.

Once in a while, a client would get angry if he or she didn't understand the Judge's ruling, but usually Lily could explain it making the client less angry or upset. Today, it seemed like everyone was calling with complaints or angry comments. The rain kept Lily in her own office rather than back and forth to the law library or the court house. Being cooped up and on the phone most of the day was tiring, but at last the work day ended and at five o'clock the personal day would begin.

Lily placed the various folders in the file drawer and reached for her raincoat and purse. There was a basketball game at the Boy's and Girl's Club and Lily had promised to be there on time to help. She looked at her watch. She quickly took the necessary papers, ones she must study for the next day and put them in her briefcase. With her purse in hand, she walked toward the parking garage, went up the stairs, in a hurry to get to the game. As she got to the third floor of the parking garage, she began to look around for the "N" section. It would be so much better when she had a numbered space.

This time in her haste, Lily threw caution to the wind, not particularly noticing other cars or people in the garage, and fumbled for her keys.

It was darker now and the rain had almost stopped. It was surprisingly quiet on the 3rd level. "Oh, where did I put them?" She reached for the door handle while balancing the other items in her arms. One began to fall, she started to retrieve it. She started to turn around when she felt the blow to her head, the items strew about, and her purse came open.

Someone from behind had struck her hard, her slim body first leaned against the car door, then very slowly slid down the door onto the cold, dirty cement floor. A boot came crashing into her ribs, she was kicked again and this time it came directly in the face. Lily could feel the blood oozing from her head. She lay in a pool of her own blood.

She began to wake up and looked through the bandages to see that she was in a hospital. "It must be Memorial Hospital," she thought.. Her face was so badly bruised she could barely open her eyes, and besides a cut lip, her nose was broken. She took a deep breath and held it, oh, how her ribs hurt. What a head ache and now she could feel casts on both arms.

Someone driving out of the garage had seen her laying on the cold cement floor and called the police. They found some of her identification and recognizing the name, called the Arnold house and informed the family. Margaret, Lester and Jack came immediately and sat in Lily's room waiting for her to stir. The medication allowed her to sleep for several hours. When she finally became awake her Mother was leaning over her.

"What a mess. Our lovely Lily looks like a broken heap under the sheet," claimed her mother. "Our prayers have been answered. Lily is alive."

"It will be a long while before she will be healed enough to come home," said Jack,

"Lily, Tom is waiting for you at home," her father said. "When you are ready to receive calls, he will telephone you. Kate sends her love."

"Thank you Dad"

Lily learned that it was a woman from one of the doctor's offices that found her and called the police who rushed her to the hospital. During the months that Lily was recuperating she tried so hard to think why or who could have done this to her. Was it the man on the phone earlier? No he knew that he couldn't have full custody. Was it the man who was being sued for fraud? No he wasn't that upset with the verdict. Then who? She felt she herself had never cause harm to others. And yet she daily thanked the Lord that she was found in time and her bruises and breaks would eventually heal. She was alive and safe.

Homecoming was great for Lily, even with all the bandages and limping, she loved being back in her home, back in the Huntington Beach house with her family. Although mature enough to have her own apartment, what was the purpose? She could save money and had everything she wanted right here. She was safe and secure in her family's home and safe is a good feeling. Tom is as helpful as ever, well as much as he can be. Lily is always Lily, still his little sister.

Chapter 8

THE SUN'S RAYS SHONE in from an open window and fell on Michael's paper, as he glanced up quickly to look at the time. The rest of his Grover Public High School classmates were bent over their desks, working busily on their writing. It was a cultural rich group of students, and many, like Michael, were striving to attain high grades and make their parents proud. The teacher, old enough to have adult children, was dressed in a plain brown skirt and a green sweater set, and flat brown shoes. She sat erect at her desk and suddenly looked up as a shrill sound grew in intensity. Several students dropped their pencils and covered their ears at the sound. The loud speaker made a screeching noise and then quieted for for the familiar voice of the principal, Mr. Furtado.

"Good morning students," The room went quiet for a moment in anticipation. "We now have the results of the student who has sold the most advertisements for the year book. That winner will receive a prize.

Michael held his breath, "Oh please let it be me."

The voice came clearly through the loudspeaker, "And that winner is Michael Lopez in homeroom 213. Congratulations

Michael. You can come to the office and receive your gift certificate. And a big thank you to all who participated."

Michael's winning smile brightened the room and the classmates began clapping and praising him. Young Michael was so thrilled that the principal of the announced to the entire student body that he Michael Lopez had won the competition. Michael was the number one salesman for advertisements in the class yearbook! "Wait until I tell Mom, won't she be proud?" he thought to himself. He was on the yearbook staff, and well known as outstanding student. He was a peer tutor in the library, and the other students knew they could rely on him. When he took on a project or an assignment, it would be completed in proper time and proper order.

Michael was careful to stay in the top ten percent of the class. It was important to him. Early in life he understood perseverance. Getting good marks was a learned behavior, something Eddie never understood.

Michael Lopez, Jr. and his brother Eddie were as different as two brothers could be. Although their looks were similar and it was easy to mistake one for the other, that's where the similarities ended. They had begun to grow apart when they went to school. Michael loved everything to do with academics, while Eddie loathed school and only passed his classes so that he could play sports. Michael became very proud of his scholastic achievements He was good at everything he endeavored.

One particular Sunday, he returned from church to find the front door open. He walked in to the living room and could see his father standing in the dining room holding the Sunday newspaper in his right hand. His father's face was closed angrily; his lips pursed and glancing about he saw Michael.

"Michael come in here" the demanding voice was his father.

This son was not usually summoned in such a manner. Eddie sometimes was, but not Michael. Something must be terribly wrong. As he entered the dining room, he looked at the rug near his father.

"Michael, look at this! How could you behave in such a manner, now clean it up." Michael looked at the rug. His father continued, "That was your mother's new vase full of flowers." It had been knocked over and broken. There's even water on this new Oriental rug." Michael looked dumbfounded at his father's accusations. He kept quiet and listened to him rant on.

"Even after you clean it up, Michael, that is not the end – there is another issue. That vase cannot be replaced. How could you do this and not even tell her?"

Michael started to say something and then stopped short.

"I've questioned your sisters, both Nancy and Mary. I had Eddie in here. I could see he was surprised at the mess, too. When I questioned Eddie he said you were responsible for this, and Mary agreed that it must have been you. Now what have you to say about it?"

Alarmed to think that anyone would accuse him, Michael stuttered, "But Dad, I didn't do it, I didn't even know about it." His father continued in a very solemn voice, "Eddie said you were fooling around before you left for church this morning and knocked over the vase."

Michael was getting very frustrated and very angry. "No Dad, I didn't. Why do you believe Eddie over me? Eddie is always up to something and often lies about it. You know I tell the truth. Dad, how can you take Eddie's word over mine?" questioned Michael.

Dismissing his young son, Mr. Lopez concluded "Son, enough, even Mary agreed with Eddie." Angry and hurt, Michael promptly began picking up the pieces and clearing the floor of the broken vase and flowers. He was able to rescue the flowers and went to the kitchen to find another vase. Michael placed the vase of flowers on the table and quietly walked away. His quiet anger did not go away. He was humiliated and his pride was hurt.

Michael went to his room, the one he shared with Eddie. His stomache hurt and he stewed over the events all night. "Eddie damn him, had convinced Mary to lie for him. Eddie is very convincing whenever he wants to be. But I didn't think Dad would buy into it. And then Mary, who should know better, actually enjoys helping Eddie out of trouble. Same old crap, nothing ever changes with those two. I just can't believe Dad thinks I did it."

Eddie and Michael had shared a room since he was born. They had twin bed, ones that were "bunk beds when they were smaller, now Mother tried to treat them as older young men. Each had his own chest and a small table with a mirror. Their Mother had shopped carefully waiting for the sales and purchasing the more masculine spreads and curtains. The oak floors were clean and polished with small scatter rugs by the beds.

Looking around upstairs, Michael saw Eddie was nowhere to be found. He went to Mary's room only to find Nancy sitting in the only chair. She had placed the crochet covered pillows on top of the ruffled printed spread. The room was very tidy. When Michael asked for Mary or Eddie Nancy answered, "I don't know where either Eddie or Mary are, who ever knows where they are,"

Michael returned to his room; and sat on the bed, his thoughts led him to a plan. "I'm going to show them, all of them. I'll make them feel sorry. I just can't believe Dad would even think I would do that. Especially to Mom, she is always so good to me. They all will be sorry for blaming me."

The telephone was in the dining room. Michael quietly looked to see if anyone was near enough to hear him. He lifted the receiver. No one was on the line. He dialed the number carefully and soon the phone was ringing at his friend Norbert's home. . Yes, he was home,

"Oh Norbert what are you doing? Oh yes, well, I was wondering if I could come over. Yes now, and do you think your folks would mind if I stayed over night?"

Norbert replied happily, "Yes, you can come over, and well,

sure you can stay over night". Norbert's parents were not strict at all. In fact his father worked out of town and his Mother was busy with her volunteer position at the library. So, that meant no one paid attention the Norbert's new roommate and friend Michael, no one but Norbert's grandpa.

Grandpa would telephone Norbert every now and then, while keeping an eye on his young grandson and easily figured out how things were going for the lad. The boy's parents were pleased to have Grandpa spend time with their son.

Norbert's grandfather had a small restaurant and Norbert helped out there after school. The first day following school Michael went along with Norbert and helped put the dishes in the kitchen. They would clear the tables, wipe them off and place clean tablecloths on each table. Michael enjoyed the project and liked Grandpa's comments about being "good boys".

Michael thought he had a good plan to make everyone feel sorry, so he would profess to have a toothache. Norbert and Michael showered the next morning and dressed for school, Michael wearing some of Norbert's clothes, made their own breakfast from cold cereal, Wheaties, the Breakfast of Champions. While Norbert's mother usually slept late, the boys got ready alone. This was good. There were no extra questions from anyone regarding Michael staying over. After they were out the door and on their way to school, Michael realized they are going past the café. He began his plan, "Oh Norbert, I cannot believe this tooth ache. I don't think I can go to school."

Michael confessed to Norbert about Eddie and the broken vase, but not about the plan to stay away from his real home and make the family feel bad for accusing him of something he didn't do.

"Mickey, what are you going to do? You can't go home now, can you?"

"No, but I can help your Grandpa."

Norbert shrugged his shoulders, "Mickey I've got to hurry so I won't be late for school."

"I'll just go back to the cafe, your Grandpa won't say anything, will he?"

"Naw, I don't think so" answered Norbert.

Michael knowing he didn't have a toothache and thought I won't be bored working at the cafe. It is fun helping out instead of going to school.

While this was happening at the cafe, Maria was preparing the evening meal. She asked both Mary and Eddie to come to the kitchen.

"Have either of you seen Michael this afternoon?"

Eddie answered, "Aw Mom why do you worry so about your kids?" He began to pull the tie on her apron to tease her. She felt in no mood to be teased.

"What about you, Mary?"

"What do you mean, Mom?"

"You know what I mean…I understand that Michael cleaned up the broken vase and the mess in the dinning room. The mess I think someone else made. Michael hasn't been home all day and it is now evening."

Nancy entered the room and began putting the dishes aside to place on the table. "Nancy, do you know where Michael is?" Nancy quickly spoke up, "I heard him on the phone with Norbert and I think he was invited to stay over night." That seemed like a strange thought to Maria,

Always the children asked for permission to be away for a night. She went into the living room where Michael, Sr. was sitting reading the Sunday paper. He enjoyed his chair which matched the sofa. The table lamps were each on the side of the sofa. Maria had her chair too, where she sat and did her hand work, while she rested.

"Do you know why Michael is at Norbert's?"

"No, I haven't seen him since I scolded him about the flowers and the vase."

"Oh no, Michael, why? I don't think it was our young son…"

"Well, it appears so, and both Eddie and Mary said he did it."

"I still doubt it."

I'll send Eddie over in the morning to see what is happening. Let him stay overnight, he enjoys Norbert."

"Fine, now come to supper, please."

With a deep breath, he rose from the chair, hugged his wife and followed her to the kitchen. Maria was concerned but acknowledged her husband to be the head of the house. "So we shall see," she thought.

Michael continued his story about the toothache, but Grandpa was suspicious about the story. Late the next afternoon, Michael's parents saw him at the Cafe. He had a white starched apron too large for his young body, and carried an arm load of dirty dishes, on his way to the kitchen. Neither his father nor mother said a word. They waited until he was near them.

Michael looked up when he heard the familiar voice of his mother. He glanced at his mother and met her with a sheepish smile. He didn't look at his father, but it was his father who spoke directly to him. He immediately recognized the clarity of direction when he heard his father's voice.

"Michael my son, put the dishes down and come home now."

Michael knew immediately with his father that "now" meant right now.

He placed the pan of dishes on a nearby table and reached behind him and untied the apron, placing it on a near by chair. All the time, he kept a steady stare at his father.

Before Michael could say a word, his mother spoke in a soft voice, "Come home, Michael." Michael was both pleased and yet surprised that both his mother and father were there. They came to rescue him from his foolishness. What a relief. They did not seem angry, just stern. Boy that was a stroke of luck he thought.

Michael looked up at Grandpa. Grandpa smiled and nodded brushing his jacket as if there was a need to brush it. "Grandpa, they want me to go home."

"Yes, Michael you better go with your parents. A good son you have there." he said to his parents.

"Thank you, now we shall take him home," his father replied.

"Thank you Mr. Riccardi for your help" Maria said as she reached for Michael's hand.

The ride home was quiet. Arriving at home, Michael's father went to read his paper and Maria went to the kitchen. Michael followed her.

"Mom, how did you know where I was?"

"Oh, your sister Nancy overheard your telephone conversation with Norbert, and when Eddie went past the cafe, looked through the window and saw you there. When you didn't show for the dinner that evening your father said it was best to let you realize the mistake you're making. I wanted to get you then, but your father said no. After a few days, Maria said she was certain young

Michael had learned his lesson and they both agreed. His mother said, "Now you are home. Michael, don't ever do that again."

"Okay Mom, you can count on it," replied Michael.

Home was wonderful, and his room looked better than ever; the plaid bedspreads, navy blue pillows, white curtains, and a shinny wooden floor. Each son had their favorite poster on their side of the room, mounted on the wall. Those few days away were now behind him. Michael sitting on his bed, shoes off, glanced up as Eddie came to the doorway. The door was open. Eddie leaned in with one hand on the knob and a silly grin on his face asking "Did the old man pay you, Mickey?"

Michael jumped up but Eddie put his hand out "Mickey, I'm sorry, really I am...no, no I am sorry." Eddie was apologizing. "This was new" thought Michael.

"What the hell were you two thinking? I ought to knock the crap out of you." said Michael

"Crap? don't you mean shit, huh Michael?

"Want me to?" as Michael slid off the bed.

"No, and Mary is sorry, too, but you know Dad. He would have exploded if he knew it was me."

"You know that, so did Mary."

"Mickey, please just leave it alone now. It is all over, just let it be because as mad as Dad was..."

"I thought he would beat the crap out of me right then and there."

"You deserved it! You owe Mom a vase, don't forget it and Eddie I'll let this one ride, but you owe me and I won't let the next one ride, just remember that. Michael scowled as he shook his fist at Eddie. "Both you and Mary, I mean it. Okay? Okay?"

"Yeah, Okay." replied Eddie.

Actually Michael was just glad to get home and forget the whole thing. "It's good to be home. I'm not really cut out for the cafe business. Sweeping the floor isn't that much fun." But this wasn't the end of Michael's angry foolishness. There is much more that will come this. The hardest lesson Michael is about to learn.

In the two days of Michaels's absence from school, he had missed the state exams.

"Michael I'm sorry, but there is no make up exam allowed," claimed Mrs. Ramos, the homeroom teacher. Michael, who was once in the top ten percent of the class, now had slipped to the upper middle of the group. They had been told for weeks that the state exam was a major part of their grades.

"Please, Mrs. Ramos, tell me what I can do so I can pass. How can I make up the exam?"

He was not about to talk about the non existent toothache; that worked for Norbert's grandfather, but he knew it wouldn't work with Mrs. Ramos. She didn't take any excuses.

"Since we are near the end of the school year, I'll have to think of something the principal will accept. The only thing I can think of is a research paper. I think Mr. Furtado might accept something like that, especially since you have good grades in all your classes. We'll see" Mrs. Ramos told Michael.

"Oh, please ask for me. I will do anything! I must pass," begged Michael

The paper was okayed with the understanding it would not bring the grade all the way up, but enough to pass. With great determination, he ended the semester with a good mark, but not the usual excellence. Michael learned a most difficult lesson about taking matters in his own hands. He learned it was better to accept life as it is, rearranging it usually doesn't work.

A sentence here about patience To foreshadow Title?

Patience is important

Chapter 9

MICHAEL'S DUTY TO COUNTRY was over and he returned from France. The military pay was not great, but one always had some money in his pocket. Now to get a job ---

Once he was settled back in at home, Michael's father said, "Son, you've had a couple of days to rest and now it is time to earn a pay." The very next morning shortly after breakfast, Michael put on a new suit and went to his Father's dealership. The suit looked nice, and even felt good to be a civilian again, thought Michael. The dealership had grown while he was away. It was much bigger. There were three women working there, a larger supply of automobiles and updated equipment. He was proud for his father.

Michael Sr. was well organized and had a steady flow of customers. He would make room for his returning son. The first day in the Office, Michael was getting acquainted with the usual paperwork when he began to wonder again just where was Eddie and why wasn't he working for our father.

"Dad, I've only seen Eddie at dinner, he was out before breakfast. What is he doing?

"You might as well know. Eddie is a big shot, he eats breakfast in the restaurant these days. Whenever I catch him at home long enough to ask him questions, he avoids giving me answers and simply says he has business elsewhere." Without any more details Michael Sr. simply stated Eddie had lots of business elsewhere. Michael quickly understood.

One evening Maria was serving dinner. In her gentle way she would tease Michael about his steak dinner. Maria had a wonderful way of maintaining good rapport with all the family members.

"Michael you have been home a while now," she said to her son.

After dinner Michael helped lift dishes and was alone in the kitchen with her. Not knowing where the conversation was going Michael answered her,

"Yes Mom."

"Well," she paused, "I don't see you dating anyone, maybe I'm wrong, but I don't think so."

"No Mom, you are right. I haven't anyone in particular I want to call upon."

"What about your old girlfriend Patsy?"

"Oh, I heard that Patsy went on to college and is now engaged."

"Oh, I didn't know… and what about Roseanne?"

"Roseanne," he said, not knowing what else to say, "how is she these days?"

"I hear she is most available and such a nice girl."

"But Mom, I think she likes Eddie."

"So what? We both know Eddie is too busy with his business to be bothered with her."

Maria spoke most gently pushing Michael to call upon Roseanne.

Maria knew it was time her son found a suitable partner and why not among a family friend. Maria knew Roseanne since she was born, and her fine family. Maria also knew that even if Eddie seemed to like Roseanne, he would not make a good husband. Roseanne deserved a good husband. Michael would make any girl a good husband. He was a family man. And Roseanne would easily belong to this family thought Maria.

Michael understood the relationship Eddie shared with her, so he tried to dissuade his mother. She, not knowing about Eddie's true feelings said Michael must call upon her. Michael finally agreed knowing Eddie would understand.

Michael had taken most of his college courses upon his return and was enrolled in the last two courses to receive his Business degree with a major in Marketing. Roseanne was finishing her classes to graduate that very same day as Michael. She was receiving a degree in Elementary Education.

Chapter 10

MICHAEL WAS IN HIS room thinking, "Mom and Dad have been really great to me. They haven't asked me for any contribution towards the house, but it is time to get my own place. I am earning a salary now. The day after graduation, I'll find my own apartment." He looked around at his books, knowing it was about time to put them away.

The telephone rang. He quickly picked it up to answer it, noticing an unfamiliar name showing and wondering how the party obtained the number.

"Hello"

"Hello, Michael?"

"Eddie, where are you?"

"Michael you don't want to know."

"Eddie what is wrong?"

"Listen Mike, I need a couple of thousand dollars, right now."

"Okay, Eddie – but what does this mean?"

"I'll see that you get it back, I need it now though. Listen just bring the money tomorrow before noon to Norbert's grandfather's cafe."

"How?"

"Put it in an envelope and place the envelope in a book. Someone will pick it up for me.. And Mikey – "

"What Eddie?"

"Take care of Roseanne for me."

"What do you mean?"

"You'll see, just do it for me, please!"

The phone went dead. Michael immediately knew it was important and that no one must know about the call or the money.

Michael's graduation day arrived and both families attended the ceremony. Cameras flashed and everyone was in the pictures not only once but twice, so it seemed. It wasn't Texas A&M, but The University of Texas was close to home and allowed Michael to schedule work and attend classes at the same time.

The Lopez and Rodriquez families planned a lovely celebration, both families attended. Both houses were in the same neighborhood. The Lopez back yard was prepared with lawn chairs, a large table with a checkered table cloth laden with home cooked dishes prepared by both families and lemonade for the children. The men shared wine. The families were proud; their children were the first row of college graduates in each of the families. They knew what it took to raise "college kids". Everyone was there, twenty- three of the two families and a few close friends.

Mary and Nancy's children were happily attended to by the grandparents. "Grandma's darlings" they were called. Music and dancing on the porch was included in the merriment. Roseanne seemed so happy, and truly beautiful. Michael found it so easy to watch her and her winning ways. She enjoyed everyone's children.

The party went on until the sun set. People began picking up the dishes and collecting the paper plates. Soon you could hear the cars starting and people saying their goodbyes. Following the celebration it became a quiet early summer night. Roseanne went outside and sat on the back porch steps. Michael had picked up some of the disarray and while in the kitchen, he went to the stove and felt the coffee pot. It was still very warm. He filled his coffee cup, opened the refrigerator, found the cream for his coffee. He was feeling quite mellow. He looked through the screen door. Roxanne heard him, turned and noticed his standing just inside the door.

"Want some company Roseanne? It's a beautiful evening, isn't it?"

"Yes, it is Michael, and wasn't that a lovely celebration?"

"Want a chair?" he asked.

"No, thank you. This is just fine." Her face was partially hidden in the shadows.

Michael went out and sat beside her on the step. They sat quietly out on the back porch, enjoying the cool of the evening.

"Michael, do you ever hear from Eddie?"

"Why do you ask?"

Michael knew he couldn't tell anyone, not even Roseanne.

"Are you certain?" she asked again.

"What is the matter Roseanne?"

"Nothing."

"Come now, this is Michael... you can tell me."

Roseanne began to cry, putting her hands on her face. She was quiet for a moment. Michael was surprised at her reaction. He listened as she began to talk.

"Michael, about a month ago, Eddie saw me after class and I went with him. You know we have cared for each other most of our lives. I spent the weekend with him."

"Oh no, Roseanne." Michael was surprised. He looked straight at her, she at him.

"Yes, Michael, and I think I am pregnant. I haven't told any one, and I haven't heard from Eddie. I can't take care of a baby! Michael I don't know what to do," she pleaded.

The frantic look on her face told the story. "Roseanne, don't do anything just yet. Let me see what I can do." He couldn't believe that of all things Eddie had done, he could let this happen. Michael thought of many probabilities, but only one sure possibility.

Chapter 11

ICHAEL SAT IN THE usual place holding the same book.
Norbert's grandfather now had a new manager. Doug
kept filling Michael's cup. Watching his watch, Michael ordered
a sandwich, laying the book in a very conspicuous place on the
table. Michael had been spending his lunch hour in this same spot
for nearly a week, hoping he would find Eddie here again. He was
not disappointed.

"Hello, Micky."

"Eddie! Finally!"

"Shh... Not so loud." Eddie adjusted his shoulder gun under
his suit jacket. "How are you Mikey? And Mom and Dad? I'll have
some money for you the first of the month, in fact all of it."

"Eddie that isn't why I'm looking for you, it's Roseanne."

"Mike, you know this is no life for her. She is a great girl, but
you know me...."

"Eddie, she is pretty sure she is pregnant and I think she is
considering abortion. You know that is out of the question."

"Oh, come on Mike - and what do you mean 'out of the
question?'"

"Yes, of course it's out of the question. That isn't the way we were raised. You should marry her."

"Mick, you are the marrying type, not me. You marry her!"

"Me, why me?"

"Why not? The same DNA, well, almost" Mike, with my blessing and I'll take care of you.. Mom and Dad will never know the difference. Think about it Mikey."

On the way home, Michael was still mulling Eddie's words over and over in his mind. Michael had wanted a home life and a family life. And Patsy was no longer in the picture. Roseanne was lovely and both families knew each other well. There were many positives in uniting the two families. And to keep Mom and Dad's grandchild in their family was the most important issue.

The very next evening Michael telephoned Roseanne.

"Hi Roseanne."

"Oh, hi Michael."

"How is everything? How are you feeling?"

"Oh Michael everything is fine. It was a long day at work. Being a bank teller isn't all that great. Lot's of time on your feet."

"Well as long as you count the money correctly...right? Michael said jokingly.

"Yes, that is right."

"Well, Roseanne I thought I'd go out to dinner Saturday night and really was hoping you could come with me. Would you be available?"

"Oh, just you and me?"

"Yes, I thought it would be nice and we could talk."

"That *would* be very nice, Michael. I could use a good friend. What time?"

"May I pick you up about 7:30? I thought we'd go to the Olive Garden. Is that okay with you?"

"Yes, Michael I shall look forward to it. Thank you."

"Ok, Roseanne, see you then."

"Well, now I've made the first move to what has to be done," Michael thought as he hung up the telephone. "I hope the rest goes as easily."

Seven o'clock arrived and Michael was at the front door. He rang the bell. Roseanne quickly opened it. Michael was very pleased to see how lovely she looked. She was wearing a light green dress, buttoned down the front with a light weight white sweater. She had white beads and a gold bracelet. He recognized it as one Eddie gave her for her fifteenth birthday.

She invited Michael in to the living room. It was very similar to his parent's home. Her mother was watching television. She looked up. "Oh hello Michael, and how are you? And your mother?" Michael replied just as Roseanne picked up her purse and indicated she was ready to go.

He helped Roseanne into the car. They kept the conversation casual as they drove a ways across town. Michael parked the car, and the couple walked to the front of the restaurant. Once inside, they were quickly seated and took their time in ordering. Michael laughed when they both ordered similar pasta dishes. They nursed their drinks as they waited for dinner to arrive. As they discussed the day and various friends, he couldn't help but notice how many things they had in common. They both were careful to avoid comments about Eddie. Michael knew what he was thinking, but Roseanne was unsure of what or why the evening was going. She did not ask, only wondered.

When Michael returned Roseanne to her home, he hugged her good night and thanked her for making the evening so pleasant. He wanted to be both somewhat casual and very polite. Then he asked if she might be available to attend a dance the following week. Both agreed on the time. Michael left for his parent's home feeling quite accomplished. As he drove to his parents home he thought, "That went well. I have the second date lined up, too"

The weekend of the dance at the Navigators Club went very well. They found a table close to the dance floor and enjoyed the "Mel Tones" playing. The couple watched the dance competition teams and listened to the band. When it was open dancing Michael turned to Roseanne, "Would you like to dance?"

"Yes, thank you, as she took his hand and went on the dance floor. They danced well together. Michael continued his pursuit of Roseanne. All the time he was considering what it would be like to being married and have a family. He liked the idea. They began to see each other regularly and look forward to their time together.

The following week was the Junior League's social, then the Comedy Hour and a dinner dance. Michael's only concern was the time frame for the courting period verses Roseanne's physical change. When they danced, he held her close to see if she felt the same. At first he kissed her cheek when he said good night, before long, it was a full kiss and soon he felt he was on the right road.

"Roseanne, would you mind if we stop by the park?" Michael asked as they were leaving yet another dance.

"No that would be fine."

It was a beautiful park, a full moon, and only a few couples walking around. Michael held Roseanne's hand and they soon found a bench. Michael put his arm around Roseanne and kissed her gently.

"Roseanne, I very much enjoy being with you."

"I enjoy you, too Michael. It has been like a dream, the attention, and the fun. The flowers you sent to my office made the entire staff talk. I've never been so happy.

"Thank you Roseanne, but I want to ask you something. Please think it through before you answer. Would you consider...well, will you marry me?"

"But Michael, this is kind of awkward considering, well, you know what I'm trying to say."

"Yes, Roseanne I understand, and I will be the best husband and father possible."

"Oh Michael, I cannot believe you would do this. Are you sure you want this? Really sure?"

"Yes, Roseanne with the understanding that this baby would be known as mine to all people --- forever."

"But, what are you trying to say? What about Eddie?"

"Roseanne, I've thought a lot about this - there can be no Eddie in the Michael Jr. Lopez family, just you, me and our baby. With those conditions, will you marry me?"

"Are you certain you want me and the baby Michael?"

"Oh, yes Roseanne, very much."

She reached for him, and embraced him and let the tear roll down her cheek. "Michael, I shall love you and our baby. Yes, Michael. Yes, yes, Michael."

The next week, Roseanne was happily showing her fellow employees the beautiful engagement ring Michael had given her. Both the Lopez and Rodriquez families were thrilled. Roseanne's mother couldn't believe it was Michael she was marrying, but said nothing to her. The couple decided they wanted a small wedding as soon as the arrangements could be made.

The flowers were beautiful, the music flowing, all was lovely as Michael opened the side door of St. Martins' Chapel near the suburban park in Dallas, Texas. "I think I can do it," Michael thought to himself. "I really think I can do it. No, I know I can do it, and with God's help it will work out just fine."

His lovely bride stepped out of the car and she picked up the heavy skirt of her bridle. She smoothed it and looked over her right shoulder. As she looked she saw a car. It was slowly driving past her, in front of St. Martin's, a new black Mercedes with a driver. She caught a glimpse of Eddie in the back seat. He smiled, nodded and his lips said "good luck" as if acknowledging Roseanne as the bride then drove on. Her heart raced, but she knew what she had to do. She went inside to finish her preparations..

Fussing with her hair, Roseanne's mother smiled, pleased that it was Michael and not Eddie, yet totally unaware of what her daughter was thinking.

"Yes, it will be fine. I'll do whatever it takes to make it a fine family. Michael is a wonderful man. I love Eddie, but I shall learn to love Michael. I know I can do it."

Roseanne made a beautiful bride, wearing her Mother's gown, let out a little to fit her growing waist. She walked down the aisle on the arm of her father, and her bridesmaids, all three dressed in soft pink, walked behind her.

The priest said the traditional vows. "Dearly beloved..." Michael kissed his bride at the familiar words, "I now pronounce you husband and wife." The priest paused, they turned to the congregation and he announced, "And now, I present to you for the first time, Mr. and Mrs. Michael Lopez Jr." Michael looked at his bride and thought to himself, "and family."

The reception was held in the community room of the church, where their families and friends gathered and to enjoy the merriment. Michael's brother-in-law, Jacob, was the best man and he toasted the couple. Following the reception, the couple stayed at the Sheraton and the next day, they flew to Miami for a few days.

Back at the dealership, during his break, Michael laid the local newspaper down and picked up the telephone. He dialed Rosanne at the bank where she was working.

"Rosanne, remember the house on Roosevelt Street, the one we always talk about when we drive past? You know, we said all it needs is a white picket fence to be perfect. Well, I was looking at the paper today and saw it listed in the Dallas Morning News. Yes for sale."

"Ok, well, I called Regal Realtors and asked for Liz Brown, the realtor listed in the paper. She is going to come by at lunch time and take me over for a quick look at the place. She said that the house was recently updated. I have to work this evening, but why don't you call Liz. Here, I'll write her number down and you can give her a call; have her take you over to see it later."

"Michael, you are wonderful, to think we could actually own a house?"

"Look, I'll call you back after I see it and if it is as good on the inside and if you like it, then give her the okay I'm sure we can swing the cost. I'll talk to Dad about a bonus for a down payment. When I hang up, please go to your friend Jerry in the mortgage department and see if the bank can give us pre-approval."

"I'll go see Jerry right now and then I'll call Liz. I'll talk with you when you get home."

When Liz arrived at the dealership, she and Michael went directly up to Roosevelt Street. The houses that lined the street were all well kept, neat yards, some with picket fences. The area was also not too far from either of their parents. As Liz began her pitch, Michael only half listened.

They entered the front door; the living room - dining room combination was fine, nice hardwood floors, one bathroom, but three bedrooms. As Michael looked at the smaller bedroom he thought to himself, "That's for my new baby". Liz noticed he lingered a bit, "Mr. Lopez, do you have children? she asked.

"Soon" he replied with a smile. He took a glance at the kitchen and knew it would be fine. The previous owner was very handy, perhaps a landscaper or painter he thought. He told Liz he wanted to have his wife see it and if she approved, he was interested in the purchase price.

Roseanne was thrilled with her inspection of the house. She called Michael to tell him, she wanted the house to be their home. She hung up the phone and said to herself, "Hmm, Mr. and Mrs. Michael Lopez, Jr. at 731 Roosevelt St. Sounds nice."

The wedding, the honeymoon, the house and soon the baby, it was all going so fast. Michael and his wife purchased a lovely house that only needed a family and a picket fence.

Roseanne was a happy wife and also enjoyed the sociability of her job. The other women shared recipes, and comments regarding their families. As time went on, her co-workers teased Roseanne about how tight her skirts were getting. She began to show that she was with child. They were delighted and thoughtful as the months rolled around regarding her condition. She enjoyed their teasing.

Michael was extremely helpful while working with his father and enjoyed helping his lovely and now very pregnant wife. The time had come for Roseanne to leave her banking position and spend more hours resting; the baby was growing. Her co-workers at the bank held a baby shower after hours, delighting her with the darling gifts of baby clothes.

Michael would tease her. "Do you want pickles or ice cream?" Michael accompanied his wife to the birthing classes, doing all that a husband and or father must do. Roseanne was most grateful that she was so busy with the house, her doctor's appointments and Michael, she seldom had time to think about Eddie.

Then the possibility of a little vacation appeared. Notice had arrived at the dealership regarding a convention in Chicago. Michael Sr. wanted Michael to go. He called Michael into his office. "Michael there is an important convention for us in the auto industry. Your mother and I can't go, but we need to be represented. I thought of sending Louie, but you would better understand the information and really be better at representing us."

Michael hesitated, "What about Roseanne?"

"Of course, take her with you. I'll send both of you. Well, think it over."

"I'll talk to her tonight Dad and see what she says." Michael seemed pleased with the idea of a going to Chicago for a few days.

Chapter 12

Rubbing her swollen stomach, she was noticing that the new pink over blouse hardly covered it anymore. Roseanne had been standing, but now reached for a kitchen chair to sit for a while longer before helping Michael prepare the evening meal. Michael was very careful to have the right diet for his pregnant wife. The "not too much" diet included not too much salt, not too much sugar, not too much fat, all the foods in moderation. Roseanne delighted in her husband's care and concern.

Texas's warm weather was not easy for a pregnant woman, but Roseanne seldom commented on it. Michael enjoyed being the head of his home and would soon be the head of a family. Roseanne was using a folded paper as a fan and had her feet up on a kitchen chair. He was eager to talk to her about having a few days off and what might be their last chance to have some alone time.

"Dad called me into his office today. Usually, he and Mom go to the auto convention. This year it is in Chicago and he doesn't think Mom is up to going, so he wants us to go."

"This trip to Chicago would be wonderful," he continued. "Dad thinks it would give me that extra self confidence. At least that is what he hinted at when he told me about the convention. He is probably right."

"What do you think? Roseanne, this would be like a vacation for us, fancy foods, and a fancy hotel - I'm certain you would like it."

"I think it sounds like a great opportunity. It's nice of your father, but really, Michael, you have earned this trip to Chicago! You deserve to attend this convention, but Darling I don't feel well enough to travel."

"I'm not leaving you here! Honey, you will feel better once you leave this hot weather for some cool weather. Honestly, it will be good for both of us. Five days in Chicago will be great. Please consider it. I told Dad I'd see what you said and tell him tomorrow."

"Sweetheart, if that is what you want, I will be happy to go with you, swollen feet and all." They both laughed and Michael hugged his pretty wife. Later that evening Roseanne telephoned her mother.

"Guess what, Michael and I are going to Chicago. I know, I've never been there. Yes, next week, I may need to shop, but I will need you to help me pack. Great Mom, I'll talk more about it tomorrow...good night." She hung up the telephone and turned to Michael. He smiled and went back to his book.

Michael quickly found their seats and placed the luggage overhead.

"I'd like to sit by the window, if you don't mind."

"That's fine. Here let me help you with the seat belt."

"Here is a small pillow if you'd like to rest."

"Thank you. If the flight attendant comes, I'd like some water."

"Of course."

The flight to Chicago was long but good, not the least bumpy and Roseanne settled down and was able to nap for some of the trip. Although the baby was very active, making her uncomfortable, she never complained.

When the plane landed, Michael was careful to see that Roseanne was not rushed.

They left the airport and he ordered a taxi. It was a short taxi ride to the Ambassador Hotel. Michael pointed out the various scenes of interest and the tourist spots. They both were very impressed with the scenic route around Lake Michigan.

Once inside their hotel room, Roseanne settled on the large bed for a nap while her husband unpacked their things. Roseanne yawned and soon was asleep. Her sleeping time was frequently cut short whenever the small darling inside of her needed to stretch or turn about. The baby was gaining at the normal rate which increased the pressure on her back. Turning over was difficult but sleep was most comforting.

Michael called room service for some tea and wrote her a

note—Tea will arrive at 10:30, love Michael. Then he hurried down to the first meeting of the convention.

The handouts were near the door. One of the attendants was handing them to the men and women as they arrived. Michael looked for a seat close to the stage. He sat down next to a rather large man. The man introduced himself, they shook hands and then speaker was just going across the stage to the podium.

The applause was resounding as the CEO of Chrysler Industries was introduced as the keynote speaker. However Michael was distracted, thinking about the changes which would soon take place in his life. Things seemed good and soon the baby would make a family for them, the Michael Lopez family. "Ladies and Gentlemen"....

Chapter 13

"IT IS SO NICE having breakfast with you Dad."

"Yes, Lily, I enjoy it too."

"But Lily, what is this about your going back to work - isn't it too early?"

"No, Dad, the doctor agreed it is best for me. I'm physically and mentally I'm fine, too. I'll probably always be a bit afraid when I'm in certain places or areas, but I can live with that."

Lily was eager to get on with her life, but honest enough with herself to know that the attack was going to haunt her in some ways for a long time.

"Oh Dad I wanted to tell you, the firm is sending me to Chicago to sit in on a conference. It is something to do with automobile dealerships and the new lemon laws."

"Well Lily that sounds great! It will be like a mini vacation for you. Chicago is a fun city. And it is time you get out and have some fun."

Lily was ready for some fun and the Ambassador was just the place. She phoned her friend at work to let her know she had arrived safely. "What luxury! I think I'll have a nice hot bath and a short nap before dinner tonight. Yes, the dinner meeting is in the Washington Suite. Fred usually sits next to me. He is good company. Yes, his wife is so nice. Well, I'd better hang up. Bye for now."

The days and the sessions went on in the usual style and Fred and his wife were great companions for walks, sightseeing and a late night brandy.

Late one afternoon during the break, Lily stepped into the ladies room. She immediately noticed a lovely young lady slumped over the counter near the sink.

"Are you alright?"

"I don't feel well. I feel faint."

"Let me get the hotel doctor for you."

"Please do…" she said, her voice becoming weak.

"When are you due?"

"I'm eight months… Please hurry!"

"I'll be right back. Don't worry; I'll stay with you until the doctor arrives."

After finding a staff member to summon the doctor, Lily returned to wait with the young lady. When he arrived, Lily began to leave and return to the conference. As she was opening the door, an anxious gentleman inquired about his wife.

"Oh, she is with the doctor, just inside the lounge area." He looked at Lily. Some how he thought Lily looked familiar. Where had he seen her before? "Roseanne where are you?"

Lily explained which door and began to walk away. Michael

thanked Lily for her help. As she turned the corner, Lily thought she had met him before, but couldn't remember. The conference was enlightening and they flew back to California pleased with the trip and eager to share their findings with the office.

"Wasn't the wedding lovely, Lily?" her mother asked as she offered her more coffee.

"Yes, Mother it truly was. And it was so good to see Robert and his family there. We don't get to see enough of him."

"Well, he has lived overseas for so many years now. If his service with the Whale Project keeps getting funded, they will continue to stay there I'm sure. But Lily, enough about everyone else, I want to talk about you."

She quickly continued her comments before Lily could interrupt, "Have you thought about getting married? When is it going to be your beautiful wedding we are discussing?"

"Oh, Mother, now don't start again. I don't have anyone special in my life yet."

"Well, Margo called. She and Howard have a friend, Richard Austin. I understand he is quite a successful businessman. They want you to meet him."

"No Mother!" Lily said cutting her off from any further discussion. "I don't want your friends or my friends finding gentlemen for me." She excused herself, a bit annoyed and left the room..

Lily called her friend Martha for a round of Saturday golf and a chance to catch up on life.

"So, tell me about your trip."

"Well, the conference was good and there was plenty of time to see Chicago. Fred's wife was very nice and they were good company. Oh, yes, and something so odd happened while I was there! There was a pregnant woman who fainted in the ladies room and I ran to get a doctor. When I was leaving, I met her husband. It was so odd, I just had that feeling we had met or knew each other. But Martha I cannot, for the life of me, remember when. Oh well… cest la vie."

Chapter 14

Los Angeles, California. Lily was thinking of how lovely and cool the weather is in the evening when the phone rang. It was Margo, she and Howard were on their way over. Twenty minutes she said. "Please Lily, we want to take you out for dinner." "Yes, we have a friend for you to meet. Yes, his name *is* Richard"

Lily was really annoyed. She genuinely did not want to be introduced to anyone. Her life was going along just fine. Her work and volunteering was just the right balance for her and she didn't want a relationship to change everything.

"No Margo, absolutely not!"

"Lily we are already on our way over-."

"Margo, I cannot believe you of all people are doing this."

"Just be ready, bye now."

Lily hurried to her room, still very annoyed, but brushed her blonde hair and put on some light pink lipstick. She quickly checked out the skirt and blouse in the mirror, smoothing a slight wrinkle in the back.

"I'll get it," she said as the doorbell rang.

Lily opened the door. Richard entered and said "Hello". Despite herself, Lily was very impressed with the presentation.

Well, maybe going out wasn't such a bad idea, in fact it might be a very good idea.

From that moment on Richard pursued Lily in a completely irresistible way. No matter what she said, he had the right comment or answer. No matter where they went, it was the most interesting adventure. It wasn't long before Richard became the love of Lily's life.

Following a rather splendid holiday, a van arrived at the Arnold home. It was full of flowers and plants. Richard had outdone himself again. Lily telephoned Margo to share the recent events and thank her for the thoughtfulness of introducing her to Richard. He was handsome, educated and wealthy.

Richard was known for some of the city's finest commercial buildings. It was not uncommon to hear references about his being an international contractor. To Lily, he was simply Richard. And Richard wanted to be known as Lily's Richard. Most of all he wanted Lily, and Richard always got what Richard wanted...

Chapter 15

"LILY YOU OUT DID yourself again. The wedding was absolutely beautiful. The church was so astonishingly beautiful." her mother said. "I know, both you and Richard wanted it simple and small, but simple made it so elegant. Even the celebration was perfect. Everyone raved about the food and the quartet. You are always so conservative in your dress, yet your Chanel gown was, well, very much a statement. I have to compliment you again. Richard must be so proud."

"Thank you Mother, and the wedding trip to Ireland and England was simple, restful and outstanding. England is one of my favorite places."

"Remember when you and Dad took us there as children?"

"Yes, dear. You said someday you would return. And so you did."

Richard had the realtor select three homes that he thought Lily might like. The Tutor styled house on the hill side made a reflection on the exclusive area. There was a lovely drive to the house. It was very impressive. The realtor praised the great finish of the various rooms. Each one decorated in perfect harmony. Four bedrooms, three bathrooms, and a very large dining room all very nicely decorated. .

"Oh Richard, how lovely!"

"Lily there is more." The second one Richard chose for Lily to consider was the high end contemporary overlooking the ocean. One could sit on the terrace and enjoy the view. The spacious feeling with the many glass windows and one wall nearly all glass brought the outdoors inside. The Realtor smiled while she watched Lily seeming to dance around the room. Richard walked into the room just then. He had been viewing the scene, almost smelling the ocean and its fresh air. He caught Lily's hand and pretended to hear the same music.

"Richard, it is wonderful"

"Don't decide yet, Lily. There is more."

Each week they were house hunting, Saturday was the perfect day. Seeing one a week allowed them plenty of time to consider the pros and cons of each property. It became the topic of dinner each evening. A selection from three outstanding properties was a delight.

The third Saturday arrived. This time Richard had Lily place her scarf over her eyes until they reached the street, rather the beginning of the lane.

"Gosh Richard, what no gates?" she said sarcastically, removing her scarf.

"Yes, it is rather ostentatious, but wait until you have had the tour. The realtor is waiting inside the house."

The drive was lined with beautiful poplar trees, a Federal Colonial style that was similar to Lily's parent's home. No sign of rain, Richard left the top down on the white convertible when he parked the car. Inside the front door, was a tiled foyer with dark wood work. Each room was comfortably large, and when they reached the dining room, Lily simply exclaimed how perfect it was. Richard smiled as he introduced Lily to the library with an adjoining study. Yes, the terrace was surrounded by lovely flowering bushes, the tennis court and swimming pool were very much like Lily's home.

Finally Richard asked "Well what do you think? Which house pleases you the most?"

Lily raised her eyebrow. "Richard, they are all so beautiful, and yet, so different. Which do you like the best?" Lily had gotten in the habit of referring to him before stating her thoughts.

"Lily, which one do you think would be the best to raise a family?" Lily hugged her husband, "This one feels most like home, our home." She preferred the beach to the mountains, so be it. They purchased the beautiful Federal Colonial home. One they could easily raise their children in. It had all the necessary luxuries. Knowing this was the one Lily preferred he asked "When will the house be available?

The realtor answered, "It is available as soon as you are ready for it."

It was a wonderful ride back to their apartment, stopping for a glass of champagne on the way. They drove down to the beach and took off their shoes and carried them as they walked along the water's edge. The sand was warm, the small splashes of water were cool. As they walked they were talking about the possibilities of their newly acquired home.

Lily was anxious to call her mother and explain in detail. Her father knew of the Malibu beach property. He commented that Richard had made a smart investment. They also liked the idea that Lily wasn't so far away.

Moving day arrived. The packers were scurrying between the apartment, and both Richards and Lily's former homes. With everything gathered, they moved the goods to the new home and began placing the furniture and personal items. Richard and Lily had contacted a well known decorator; they quickly decided on the style of furniture and put all in their decorator's competent hands. When they return from their two week trip to Hawaii they would be ready to settle in. Joshua had done his usual magnificent job and better than most magazine layouts. They were finally ready to entertain.

The card read, Mr. and Mrs. Richard Austin, cordially invite you to their home at 117 Stony Run… It was a great festive time and showing off their home to friends and colleagues was a delight. The Los Angeles Times reporter was most gracious in his commentary and the photographer captured the occasion perfectly. Following the party Lily immediately began making Richard most comfortable in the house they now called home.

Lily had taken a sabbatical from her position and was able to involve another parent in her volunteer work, so she was free to do as Richard and she decided.

Traveling was second nature to them both and they would often spend a month in Greece, Spain or England. One morning, just after breakfast, Richard said to Lily, "Look, I have to leave for Africa in a couple of weeks."

Without missing a beat, Lily responded, "You are simply too good looking to go alone, can you get two tickets?" Richard loved travelling with Lily; she was always fun and stimulating. She enjoyed all the sights and foods and spoke several languages.

Being out on safari in Africa had Lily breathless, being so close to the wild animals. Yet she was in awe of them and the beauty of Africa. To see the beautiful trees unique only to Africa, and watch the elephants gather for their annual trek. Watching the mother elephants communicating with their young was especially pleasing to Lily. After seeing Mt. Kilimanjaro in the movies so many times and then to stand and look up at it, watching the cloudless sky and warm sun would be vivid in Lily's mind for years to come. Although she wasn't interested in mountain climbing, she enjoyed seeing Africa's natural beauty.

Richard rejoiced when he obtained a club room on the train from Lake Victoria to Mombassa. Richard had read the history of building and this famous railroad. Its history included the man eating lions. Richard slept well that night on the train, while Lily wondered about those man eating lions. The African coastline with the warm waves splashing the sand was remarkable. Everyone could see they were a loving couple, but even Lily couldn't see what she was beginning to feel, something was missing.

Chapter 16

Back home in near by Malibu Beach, Richard and Lily held many parties with friends and relatives. The Austin family was thoroughly enjoying their home and their lives together.

One day, Richard looked at Lily and said "What is the matter?"

"I'm not certain Richard, I have just not felt well."

"Perhaps you should see a doctor?"

"Well, Richard, I think I'll wait another month first."

"What are you saying Lily? Are you..."

"I'm not sure Richard, but it is certainly time, right?"

No couple was ever happier. They enjoyed the pregnancy, the moments when the baby moved, the selecting of names, who to honor first. James was the paternal grandfather's name and Richard would be the father's name. If a boy, it was all settled. Margaret told Lily many times that she was certain the grandchild would be a boy.

And sure enough it was! As the time came closer, Richard insisted Lily have someone with her at all times. It was a good time for Martha and Lily to catch up on their recent events. Richard gave Lily a new Cadillac and had it delivered to their home the day she noticed the baby moving.

Lily's water broke and Martha drove Lily to the hospital. Richard reached the hospital room as the labor began to increase. Hours passed and Lily was finally taken into the delivery room. Martha stayed with Richard until Doctor Larson came down the hall. Richard had drunk more than enough coffee waiting for the news.

Within the hour, the doctor came out smiling and extended his hand to Richard. "Congratulations, Mr. Austin. You have a fine looking son. Eight pounds, seven ounces. Both Mother and baby are doing just fine. You will be able to see them in another few minutes."

"Thank you doctor, thank you." Richard reached over and hugged Martha, saying, "Now I am officially a Dad."

James Richard Austin's birth was quite an occasion. Tommy and Jack were busy calling themselves uncle and when they phoned Robert to tell him the good news, they asked for "Uncle Robert." Mr. and Mrs. Austin and Mr. and Mrs. Arnold were busy trying on grandmother and grandfather. Uncle Robert wrote his happy note. There were the cousins, too. And the parents, Richard and Lily were delighted to be just plain Mother and Daddy. What a happy time.

A year earlier in a city many miles away, it is a few minutes after midnight in Dallas, Texas.

"Michael wake up, Honey please wake up."

"Mmmm, yes. Roseanne what is it, pickles or ice cream?"

"Silly, no, I think it is time to go."

"Go where?"

"To the hospital honey, the hospital…" Michael threw back the covers and was on his feet in a matter of seconds. It was the day he had been waiting for. Within minutes, he had the suitcase in the car and they were on their way.

Dr. Osgood came down the hallway to see Michael. He looked very serious and Michael became apprehensive wondering what may have happened to the baby, and or could it be Roseanne?"

"Mr. Lopez."

"Call me Michael, please. What is it?"

"Your wife is having a difficult time. We need your permission to operate and save the baby if that becomes necessary. "Dr. Osgood, please save my wife and the baby, please." Michael pleaded.

It seemed hours had passed before Michael had any news. Michael's anxiety was so high. The sun was coming up, a beautiful morning. Dr. Osgood returned, smiling. "Michael you have a beautiful baby girl and your wife is doing just fine. It will be a few days before she will be up and around. That means you will be responsible for your daughter."

Michael breathed a sign of relief and then the impact hit him, he was a Father. No one would know he wasn't. Michael thought if it walks like a duck and quacks like a duck it must be a duck, and he certainly could become the greatest father around.

Both families were at the house when Michael assisted Roseanne and now "little Rosie" into their home. It was wonderful having them in an almost party like atmosphere. Well, that day anyway. And daily Roseanne's mother arrived as Michael was leaving for work. Soon it seemed as if her father had taken over the various needs. He put the crib together, and then repainted the porch. The grass was always mowed on time; the baby was bathed and asleep most of the evenings. Michael's mother baked frequently and sent dishes full of delicious goodies. And Grandpa Lopez would stop by on his way home, just to say hello to Roseanne and "little Rosie."

One evening, Michael had begun to feel as if their home was more like the bus depot, with so many family members and some friends coming to visit so often.

Later, Roseanne answered the phone and quickly hung up. Michael asked, "Who was it, sweetheart?"

"Oh, it was just your brother Eddie asking how everyone was. He said he tried to call your Mother and with no answer he called here. I told him she just left."

"Did he say anything else?"

"No, ah, well, he asked about "little Rosie.""

The next day Michael called his mother and explained how

important that he and Roseanne and little Rosie needed time to become a family. His mother completely understood and said she would talk to the rest of her family. Then Michael called his mother in law and asked her to understand that they needed some time to grow as a family.

That evening Michael held Rosie while Roseanne prepared dinner. He even gave his daughter her bottle of milk while holding her. It was wonderful being together with his family. As he was dressing for work, he thought about how he loved his job and his life.

"Roseanne, are the trousers to my new suit back from the tailor?"

"Yes, darling. They are hanging just under the jacket."

"Thank you." Michael finished dressing and tied his tie, admiring himself in the mirror. One thing that hadn't changed was his love for fashion.

"Oh Michael you look superb."

And he did until Daddy's little girl spit her milk all over his shirt and tie.

Chapter 17

"WHO PRESENTS THIS CHILD, Rose Maria for baptism?" The two names, Rose and Maria, one from each grandmother.

"We do, as godparents," said Norbert and Mary simultaneously.

Both grandparents were so pleased and proud of their darling granddaughter on this special day. Roseanne requested the prayer of St. Francis to end the ceremony. Her head was filled with the words, to be loved as to love; for it is in giving that we receive. It is in pardoning that we are pardoned...

Roseanne's thoughts turned to Eddie, who was not in attendance, and of course to Michael.

One year after young Rose Marie's baptism, another ceremony was taking place at St Joseph's in Huntington Beach. The family Priest began the service in the same ritual he had for so many times. Blessed be God: Father, Son, and Holy Spirit. Gathered around the baptism fount were the godparents and Jimmy.

"Who presents this child, James Richard for baptism?"

Tom and Jack's wife, Joyce, immediately answered, "We do as godparents."

Lily had hoped Sister Hildegarde would be able to attend, however she was most pleased that Sister Mello came in her place. Both families were pleased and proud of their adorable grandson on this special day. The entire Austin family was in attendance and many of the Arnold's were there. Richard and Lily were so pleased. Tom and Colleen had brought all three of their children, Sheila, Michael and Michelle, too. Robert and his wife and family brought flowers and gifts.

The service ended with Richard's request for the prayer of St. Francis of Assisi. Both Lily and Richard loved these special words, "to be loved as to love; for it is in giving that we receive." Lily and Richard reflected on the love they gave each other and how much more love they had for their little son.

For many years, many miles apart, the sun shone down on the two families, its radiance casting varying shades of light on their lives.

Chapter 18

DAYS TURNED TO WEEKS. Weeks turned to months and months turned to years.

"Jimmy come in now, it is time for dinner. Dad will be here shortly and we need to get ready for dinner. Darling, shower and put on fresh clothes. And please leave Murphy outside; be sure his dish is full of water."

"Come on Jimmy," she nagged again. "Hazel has made your favorite dessert…"

"Mom, I have baseball practice tomorrow. Please don't forget my uniform." At twelve years old, Jimmy had become quite the athlete; He was on the swim team and loved baseball. He and Richard attended Boy Scout meetings together and Lily saw that he was in Junior Choir. At Jimmy's fourteenth birthday party, they enjoyed paint ball. At fourteen, girls weren't quite in the picture for him, but by his seventeenth birthday, he had traded in his childhood activities for those of other young men.

It was a family affair. Jim's grandparents, aunts, uncles, and many cousins went to the club for dinner. Just as the candle lit cake arrived, a lovely young girl named Sherry led the group in the traditional happy birthday song. Jim was blushing about now.

He had acquired a great fondness for Sherry, the striking blonde daughter of Richard's friend Smithy. Following the gala event, Lily and Richard walked with Jim to the door of the club.

Outside, the parking attendant delivered the new red convertible to the door. Jim's eyes grew big as the attendant handed the keys to him.

"Mine? Dad? Mom? Oh, I love you both. Thank you," Jim ran down the stairs and prepared to drive off. What pleasure this child, young man now had given his parents.

Richard and Lily had continued to be successful and didn't want for anything. They often took off for long weekends, as they had when they were first married, but now they had their own small plane.. Richard was an avid pilot and enjoyed the freedom and privacy it afforded them.

Richard telephoned the local hanger to have the five passenger plane prepared for flight to San Francisco. It would be a quick getaway, just a long weekend, but with Jim so close to college age, there wouldn't be that many of these family weekends left. Richard had seen that both his wife and son had taken flying lessons, so the family was well aware of the dangers and could take over in an emergency.

The family arrived with light luggage and entered the plane. Richard was at the instruments and Jim next to him as his co-pilot. Lily made herself comfortable in back. She could listen to some music that she had obtained for the flight. It was only a four hour trip, and the plane was scheduled to arrive late afternoon.

Jim had forgotten his tennis racquet. Lily suggested they drop down before they get to the mountains. There was a specialty sporting shop in Oakhurst. Richard agreed and brought the plane down.

Immediately Lily and Jim hailed a taxi and were off to seek a new tennis racquet... Richard stayed back to speak with the mechanic regarding a noise he thought he had heard as they were coming through the clouds. The mechanic could not seem to find the problem, when Richard decided to take the plane up as a trial run to see if he continued to hear the noise. Yes, he definitely heard something and started down. The landing gear didn't drop down.

Lily and Jim heard sirens and saw the emergency vehicles fly by them as they headed back toward the airport. Richard was already on the way to the local hospital. When Lily and Jim arrived at the hospital they were met by the emergency room doctor. Dr. Matheson had to perform this terrible painful duty many times before. This was no easier. Lily and her son clung to each other sobbing.

The funeral was held at St. Joseph's Church in Huntington Beach area. The church where so many of the family events were held overflowed this time. Jim's many school friends offered their condolences. The reception was held in the home. Lily's friends from far and near hugged her and cried with her. The family was so close, thank God.

Lily and Jim were alone with their grief after the many relatives returned to their daily lives. Time passed slowly and painfully. Jim hated to broach the subject, but he knew he had to.

"Mom, school will start next month. I'll be a senior, then college. Mom I really want to graduate from the Abbey, like your brothers."

"But Jim, it is so far from here. It is in Rhode Island. I don't know…"

"Mom, going to the Abby will help me get into the college I want. I want to go out East. I want to go to school in New England. You did, Dad did. I know he would want me to go too."

"Well, Jim, I guess that means I'll have to make a home in New England."

Chapter 19

ROSE MARIE WAS A lovely child; she had grown more beautiful each day. Rose had met each of the developmental milestones at the right time, excelled at school, and was the perfect daughter to her parents. Time passed too quickly. One day Dad was saying yes to roller skates, and the next, he was saying yes to her playing basketball on the high school team.

Rose Marie had good coordination and had been on several city teams besides the school team. She was looking forward to her senior year and campaigned for class president. She even prayed over it. She won, by one vote. But she won, and that was what was important to Rosie. She was a winner, like her Dad.

Oh, yes, every now and then Uncle Eddie would find himself at one of her games. Usually unannounced Uncle Eddie would appear and always so happy. Rosie knew him as Uncle Eddie and was always pleased whenever he appeared. Many times he had a gift for her and if Michael didn't attend the game, Eddie would take Rosanne and Rosie for ice cream after the game.

Their lives revolved around family. Michael and Roseanne enjoyed the traditional family cookouts when his father would bar-b-que chicken, or Mr. Rodriquez would prepare a brisket and the grandmothers would out do each other with salads and desserts. Michael's sisters, Mary and Nancy would bring their families. And Roseanne's brother Steve and his family joined in the family fun. Once in a while Eddie would attend, always alone. It was a fine traditional family of three generations.

"Mom I'm tired of this piano. How many hours do you think I need to practice?" Her parents wanted her to take advantage of every opportunity, but Rosie just wanted to get on the telephone and talk to her girlfriends. After all, she was now 13 and had other things on her mind. Rosie didn't chase boys, but she was into the Drama Club and various other school activities. Rose Maria was an excellent student, just like her father. And now that her father has gone back to college for an advanced degree, she knew that is what she would do as well. College would be important to her, just like it was to her father. He understood her and was the best father in the world, according to Rosie.

Dad had been spending too many nights working late at Grandpa's office. Although Grandpa really depended on him, Mom would have liked it better if he came home early and spent more time with her. Michael was a good husband, good provider and a great man. He gave a helping hand to friends and relatives. Michael never missed his obligation to his church or his wife. Each weekend Michael would make or meet social plans to please Roseanne. They seemed to be a contented couple. And most of all Rose Marie adored her Daddy and Daddy adored Rose Maria.

It was a match made in heaven. Roseanne never regretted her decision to marry Michael.

Every once in a while, Michael thought of different government placements he might have. Maybe one where he could travel, have a supervisory position, something interesting and exciting. He just never mentioned it to Roseanne. They had it all, a beautiful home, lovely furnishings, good friends, a lovely neighborhood and most of all they were close to both sets of parents. They were able to have whatever they wanted and give their daughter the best. "Why upset the apple cart as the expression goes," Michael thought. "Anyway, who in their right mind would want to shovel snow in New England?"

Michael had been window shopping on his way home. It was Rosie's fifteenth birthday. He wanted to get her something special. He had been looking at a gold bracelet. Roseanne knew that next year would be a grand celebration for Rosie's sixteenth birthday, too. They had been talking about it and considering various plans for the celebration. Michael had been putting money aside for college, but this would be another expense.

Much to Michael's surprise, Rosie was at the door to greet him. "Daddy you'll never guess who came to visit us!"

"Who sweetheart?"

"Uncle Eddie! Mom said it was a surprise..."

"Isn't that wonderful?"

"Yes, darling, where is your Mother?"

Michael quietly put the gold bracelet away. It would be a special birthday gift to Rosie from him. He had the bracelet engraved with her initials. Something she would treasure forever.

Later that night as Michael and Roseanne prepared for bed, Michael said, "Rosie said Eddie was here."

"Michael I didn't want to upset you, so I didn't mention it."

"Has he been here before? Roseanne now tell me."

"Just once, when I was out with Rose Marie, she was only two years old. I was having lunch with my friend Michelle. Eddie came through the restaurant stopped by and patted Rosie on the head and said what a cute kid and walked away." Roseanne stopped, looking to see what his reaction would be before she continued.

"I'm sorry Michael that I didn't tell you before. It didn't seem important, really."

"Is that all? Is that all Roseanne? Rosie said you were crying when he left. What were you talking about?"

"Nothing really. I don't know what he wanted. He just showed up."

"Has he been here before? Have you seen him?'

"No, no more than you. I know you've seen him at some of Rosie's basketball games, too. He just comes and then leaves before the game ends Every so often he calls looking for your parents, but…"

"Roseanne, I am talking about Eddie seeing you."

"Oh, Michael, I would never do anything to upset our family,

Rosie's life." Neither slept well that night and neither spoke of it again.

But their relationship was never the same.

Father and daughter were looking at the prom pictures from the Junior Prom. "Sweetheart you look beautiful in your prom gown. And Levi is a nice looking young man.By the way, have you heard about any of your college applications? Your good grades will get you early acceptance you know."

"Daddy I know I haven't said anything about it, but..."

"But what sweetheart?"

"Well Daddy..."

"Well Daddy what, what is it Rosie?"

"Dad, I know you seem to have your heart set on my attending a school here in Texas, but I've put in some other applications, away from here. What I really, really want is to go to college in New England."

"Why New England?"

"Well, I just do, would that be all right?"

"We'll see sweetheart. But you'll have to promise not to run off and marry one of those cold New England boys."

"Oh, Daddy, don't be silly."

Chapter 20

"MICHAEL HAVE YOU EVER thought about moving somewhere else? Having a new life?"

"Why are you asking Roseanne?" he asked, raising his eyes above his juice glass. Breakfast had been quiet for months now. They had developed a wedge between them, only speaking when necessary, when Rosie or other family members were within earshot.

"Michael, we need to talk. We have to stop ignoring each other. We can't go on like this." She poured some more coffee and sat across from him.

I know that you have thought about a government position more than once. In fact, you've been thinking about it for a long time."

"Why do you say that?"

"Let's say I just know. I think you deserve to be happy. You've fulfilled your obligation to me, to Rosie. Maybe it's time for you to do something you've always wanted to do."

"What do you mean?"

"I mean I am releasing you from this marriage, from me," she said, her hand closing against the mug. "And Rosie will never have to know the truth."

"Roseanne, I don't understand what you are talking about. I know we've been having some issues, but…"

"Look, Rosie will be going off to college soon, flying out of the nest. She won't be back, or at least not for long if at all. We don't do anything together now…" She paused, and lowered her voice. "You don't feel the same way about me, Michael."

"Yes, so what?"

"Michael, I want a quiet divorce. I'm not holding you to anything, you have given me all." Roseanne looked at him, trying to see his reaction. "But now, don't you see? Now we can go our separate ways. Maybe have a second chance at love."

Michael moved uncomfortably in his chair, suddenly face to face with what he had known all along. "Roseanne has Eddie contacted you again?"

"Yes, I'm sorry Michael. I tried to make this work. And for a while it did, but…"

Chapter 21

"ROSIE, WHAT ARE THESE letters all piled up over here?"

"Oh, some letters from schools I applied to."

"What are they doing still here? Aren't you going to open them? Some look kind of thick – like acceptance letters."

"Well, I'm waiting for one in particular... If I don't get in there, well I guess I will have to go with one of these." *

"Which one are you waiting for?"

"I know you really liked Georgetown University, but Dad I have my heart set on Yale and you know if you accept a school with early acceptance, you own it!"

Michael didn't want to show her, but was he was concerned about Rosie being so far away. Well, now that circumstances had changed, he was free to Convincing his father would be the hard sell.

"Dad your granddaughter has her heart set on a school in Connecticut, Yale."

"That school is one of best in the nation. I love their basket ball team!"

"Dad, I have to tell you I am going to apply for some jobs in

refer to patience here

144

the Washington D.C. area. There's nothing for me here with Rosie on the East Coast. I need to be a part of her life."

"Son you will always be a part of your daughter's life," Michael Sr. said.

"I won't be so far away Dad that I won't see you and Mom often."

"I know son, I know."

Rosie had been so caught up in her own world of college applications and meeting senior requirements that she hadn't noticed how much her mother was traveling. She began to wonder why so many long trips, something had changed.

"Dad how come Mom is always going off on these long trips by herself? Has her job changed? How come you never go with her? You used to like to get a way together, don't tell me you are trying to make sure I don't get into trouble?" Rosie laughed, knowing how overprotective he was.

Michael didn't smile back. His voice choked out a response, one that was overdue.

"Well Rosie, there's something you need to know. Maybe we should both be here to tell you, but I'm tired of pretending. Your mom and I are going our separate ways."

"What do you mean, divorce?" Oh, no Daddy."

"Sweetheart don't you cry, we both love you very much. That's never going to change."

"Dad, I have to ask you something. Does this have anything to do with Uncle Eddie?"

"Why do you say that Rosie?"

"I don't know, it's just that she always acts so different around him. Like, whenever he showed up, she would be happy for days. Is that what's going on? Dad?" Rosie asked the question, but didn't wait to hear the answer. Her mind started putting the pieces into place. The late night phone calls that her mother would take in her room, all the weekend trips. No wonder her dad had been so quiet. She should have known…

"I'm sorry Dad. How could she?"

"Rosie, don't blame your mother. It was both of us. She loves you and that will never change."

Rosie was unhappy about the divorce, but somehow it didn't seem so bad since she knew Uncle Eddie. He would look after Mom. A few days later, the mail came. Rosie felt the thickness of the letter and then ripped it open, reading the first words carefully. 'We are pleased to inform you….'

"Dad! We are going on a trip to Yale campus! New England here I come!!"

Back in New England, another family was making great changes in their lives. Jim was showing his dormitory room to his mother, she seemed pleased with his attitude.

"Mom, I love it here at the Abby. Maybe it has a few drawbacks, like no girls," he said laughing. "But seriously, I can get early acceptance into college this way. If I went to another school, my grades alone wouldn't cut it."

"Early acceptance, why rush it?"

"Remember Sherry, the girl I hung out with over the last two summers? Well, she plans on attending Yale University, sooo..."

"Sooo - naturally you want to attend Yale University. Well applying early will give you a better chance, so I guess you better get applying."

"Mom did you get the house you were looking at?"

"Yes, I did dear! Right outside of Boston and just a few hours away from you. It's perfect. New England here we are!!"

Jim hugged his mother. As much as he tried to act like he didn't care, he knew he would really miss her if she wasn't within driving distance. California was too far away. She would miss him too ...especially with his dad gone.

Chapter 22

Maria called Michael Sr. into the kitchen, "My dear, let us have that second cup of coffee."

"Maria, that always means you have something to say."

"Yes, true, but this is something I should have said years ago," she placed a warm guava pastry near his cup.

"My dear what is it?"

"It's Michael."

"What could be wrong with Michael? He has been as near a perfect son any parent would want," he relaxed into the chair, suddenly relieved.

"Yes, too nearly perfect. I'm concerned about him. He hasn't been the same since…" she struggled to get the words out. "Well, I think he needs this new start. This has been hard on him."

"Maria, I'm way ahead of you. I told Michael he has my blessing several weeks ago. I have even hired Norbert's oldest son to give me a hand. Michael is training him now and he is just waiting to hear the details of his new job."

"Of course, he will never replace Michael, but somehow we'll make it."

They talked about the future and the past; Michael's impressive business sense that had put their company in the best financial shape it had ever been in. Because of his planning, his parents could easily retire. When the conversation turned to Eddie, Michael Sr. snapped.

"Look at our son Eddie; he puts *Eddie* first every time, wherever he is! Michael is different. He always thinks of others first. Don't you think I don't know how he picked up the cross that Eddie put down, and carried it like a real man all these years."

Maria looked at him in disbelief. He was confirming something that had been in her heart for a long time.

"Maria, I know, a father knows those things without being told."

"Well, my dear. So does a mother. I have always suspected this as well."

"So, maybe this divorce is going to be a blessing for Michael. He can have a new life, maybe even find love."

In a nearby chapel…

"Bless me Father for I have sinned."

Michael's voice was soft; he told the story of Roseanne's leaving and the legal decision. He did not seem to blame Roseanne, but he confessed to not doing enough for her, not caring enough. As the priest probed the confession, he learned the true story. With Father

Morales' insight and blessing, Michael left the chapel feeling like a free man.

Free of the guilt, free of the past, and most of all, free to love and be himself again.

Chapter 23

"CONGRATULATIONS MR. LOPEZ, AND welcome aboard. I hope you have enjoyed your trip to Washington DC." Mr. Wilson greeted him cordially, bringing him into the fold with a few easy words.

"We love it here. It is a big busy city. The buildings remind me so much of my mother country. My parents came from Salonika, Greece, a beautiful place, but the European buildings are large, too. Have you been to Greece, Michael?"

"No, I haven't Mr. Wilson, I was stationed in Paris for a while, and we went through the Netherlands and over to England."

"Some day, Michael you'll have to make the trip."

They had traveled down a corridor and had stopped in front of an office door. Wilson opened the door and they went in, sitting across from each other in a room that smelled like leather and coffee. Michael though he detected cigar smoke, but didn't see any ash trays.

"Now back to business. You will be in charge of our Boston Office, with a staff of five auditors, plus supportive staff. All your reports will be expected within ten days following an audit. Your specialty and extensive training as a CPA and Certified Fraud

Investigator is a vital part of the process. That's why you have to oversee every aspect of an audit. Your initials on each page of the report are essential." Wilson leaned forward to make sure he was listening to all the details.

"One of the men will be in touch with you tomorrow for your complete briefing. Oh, one thing you need to be cautioned about," he lowered his voice. "Gene Machado's ego. You will have to work closely with him, but watch out for him, he can be rather base, if you get my drift."

Michael nodded with just the right amount of movement. Too much and I look overconfident, too little, I look disinterested.

"He will be in your office at his own schedule, sometimes weekly sometimes monthly, just whatever works for him." Wilson stood up, stretching out his hand. "Okay, Michael Lopez Jr. we'll see you tomorrow at 9:00 AM."

"Wow does that man ever take a pause in his speech, he thought. Well, the job is mine. This is going to be an adventure all right. Now, for some pleasure. That secretary is cute and must know where the fun places are, someplace I can go to dance and relax."

Chapter 24

ROSE MARIE HAD SETTLED in at Yale University and loved school. She was carrying four subjects and doing well. With her background in Spanish she quickly accepted an aide's position to assist others in Spanish. Rosie, as she was known on campus, quickly fell in with the right crowd. Freddie was part of that crowd. He always seemed to be around to study with Rosie. He was a year ahead and knew what classes were good, and what teachers were the best.

Rosie's roommate Emma wasn't quite as neat as Rosie or quite as good a student. But she certainly was a good friend. Michael had warned Rosie about crossing campus late at night alone, but Emma and she were on the buddy system. They watched out for each other.

One evening while Rosie was dressing for a date with Freddie, she couldn't find the beautiful gold bracelet that she had so carefully guarded since her sixteenth birthday. She became anxious and then worried about the loss. Freddie wasn't concerned, perhaps it was just misplaced.

Several weeks passed and Emma seemed unconcerned about the missing bracelet. Then Emma remembered that Carol and her boyfriend had stopped in the day before the bracelet went missing. Rosie and Emma went together to Carol's room. Only her roommate was there. Rosie explained the loss and the value of the bracelet as a keepsake. When Rosie returned from class the following day, the bracelet was sitting on the dresser. Rosie carefully put it away. Emma had told Carol's roommate that Rosie's father was a fraud investigator and she thought that was a branch of the police.

When the summer came, Rosie went to see Grandma Lopez. They had a wonderful summer, but all too soon fall classes were beginning at Yale. She hurried back to make sure she had her books and the right schedule. As much as she loved her family, she had really missed school.

Jim Austin was a new man on campus. She had heard about him from a few people. He was very outgoing with a friendly, super personality. Although he was a good student, he was concerned about the Spanish class and was looking for a tutor. He hunted her down, pleading with her to make some room in her schedule for him.

"Dad you are not going to believe it. There is this really neat guy that I tutor in Spanish. I like him a lot, we've been spending some time together, you know, studying. But now, Freddie is acting like he's jealous."

It is nice having Freddie pay more attention to me, she thought. This new guy Jim is just a freshman. He is so interesting…

Chapter 25

EXCEPTIONALLY ATTRACTIVE IN HER new charcoal Armani suit and crème colored Carolina Herrera's silk blouse, and Ferragamo shoes, Lily leafed through a Vogue magazine while sitting in the reception area awaiting her meeting with John O'Conner. His secretary Irene smiled and extended her hand to Lily, greeting her warmly. They entered the offices of one of the principal owners. He stood up, holding his hand out to her.

"Mrs. Arnold, the head of our firm, Mr. Franklin Kincade, is a friend of long standing with your father. I understand they were roommates at MIT. Mr. Kincade was pleased to learn of your interest in our law offices," related John O'Conner.

"Yes, I've been looking forward to meeting you. I have heard wonderful things about this firm."

"Thank you. Lily, if I may call you by your first name, I see you have wonderful credentials. We have discussed your application and looked over your referrals. That said, we would be very pleased to have you join our Boston firm. Three days a week is just fine with us. Herbert will bring you up to speed with our policies and procedures. As you know, we cover corporations, estates and wills, divorces, injuries, both petty and major criminal cases and almost any matter that finds its way to our door. I'm certain the firm will be to your liking. Welcome aboard!"

"Herbert, would you show Lily around and introduce her to the staff?"

Herbert was a soft spoken gentleman who said he had held the title of new kid on the block fifteen years ago. Several of the offices on the floor were quiet since the attorneys were in court, so he quickly summarized the personnel and moved on. He seemed pleased to escort Lily to meet several of the other attorneys. He introduced her to Albert, a divorce attorney. Albert, a bit overweight, was married and had several children, all in private schools. Then next to Albert's office was Gloria, tall, thin, with a definite flair for fashion, large horn rimmed glasses handling accident and medical cases and finally to Cary.

Cary was exceptionally attractive, married and seemed the most friendly. She handled real estate. Lily seemed to feel at home when talking to Cary Lewis.

"Welcome aboard Lily, I'm certain you will like it here."

"Thank you Cary. Have you been here long?"

Herbert was leaning against the filing cabinet listening to the two women, looking back and forth as they were talking. He was a listener for sure.

"Well it seems a while, I guess some six or seven years now."

In a few minutes she had filled me in on her life and interests. I knew we would hit it off. "I have a wonderful husband, Craig, who is very understanding, and two adorable children. Well, most of the time they are adorable," she laughed, "A boy and a girl, the perfect family."

"What about you Lily?"

"I have Jimmy, just the one boy. He attended the Abby in Portsmouth, Rhode Island and is now studying at Yale. He has been the joy in my life. In fact he is what brought me east, his wanting to attend the Abby. The timing was good. There was just he and I, my husband passed away a while ago."

"Oh, I'm sorry to hear that."

"It's ok. Jimmy and I have moved forward as best we can. We have a new life now and professionally I use my maiden name."

"Well, it appears we shall be working together on some cases since we both will be doing probate work. Lily get your office situated and let me know if you need any help. Anything at all."

"Sounds great Cary, I'm looking forward to working with you."

Herbert walked her to her new office and allowed her to walk in first. She was impressed with the size of the room and immediately walked over to the windows. With one hand on the sill and the other on the glass, she marveled at the view. As Lily looked around she thought some very fine gentleman might have enjoyed the office and its decor. The draperies and furniture were elegant and would do to start, she thought. Later, however, she would put her personal items in place.

"Herbert, this is so nice, thank you for the tour."

"Lily you are going to fit right in. I have to get back to work, but don't forget my office is just down the hall, too."

A few weeks passed. Lily had been busy shopping to create the right décor for her office, meeting the other staff, and becoming acquainted with the caseload. After going over some of the cases they shared, Lily asked Cary out for an early dinner. "Oh, I'm sorry, Lily. This is the one evening that Craig has late police duty, which means I'm have to be home for the kids. Please ask me another time, though."

"I will. I have a home visit in the core section of the city anyway. Have you noticed it's getting darker earlier and earlier? Where did you park?"

"Oh, in my regular place in the parking garage. It's easier to pay the monthly fee than try to feed meters all day. Besides, I am very careful. I had a terrible experience once and learned my lesson. Don't worry, I'll be fine."

"Just be careful. Yeah, I have learned my lesson, too. I'm still kind of paranoid about using the parking garage, but I guess it's the best way."

The next day, Lily shared her parking garage experience, showing Cary her scars, and explaining the ones that didn't show. The women agreed to monitor each other and walk out together when they could.

Cary was also helpful trying to find Lily the right apartment.

She made inquiries and pointed out some of the areas that Lily might enjoy living in. Lily explained the short term lease she had on the present condominium and was looking for a comfortable house. She introduced her to Sue Davis who knew of a house right near her that was available. Sue, Cary shared, would be an excellent neighbor for Lily. Lily found the house very much to her liking. It was a one level ranch type, white with a blue roof and great landscaping and low maintenance.

After passing inspections and finishing bank paperwork, Lily purchased the house and soon obtained enough furniture to make it a lovely home. Cary was right, Sue was a great neighbor. Lily had found a new friend.

The telephone rang in the law office reception area. The ring was shrill but short. It seemed as though each ring became louder than the last. Jamie the receptionist was young; she made a practice of looking very professional, at least her perception of "professional". A dark suit designer type, small amount of makeup with her dark tresses pulled up and back. Jamie was too young to have gray strands; however one might think she would wear the same style through out her professional life. She always had a pleasant expression.

This time when the phone rang it was Mrs. Suzanne Davis, wanting to speak with either Lily or Cary. Jamie checked her telephone buttons, she favored the women lawyers since the men always gave the impression they were too busy. Cary's light was on, so her line was busy with the last call. Lily's button wasn't busy. Lily was available.

"Yes, Mrs. Davis," Lily's friendly manner and concern for the client was obvious. She would take time to listen to the client this Mrs. Davis liked as she talked endlessly. Lily didn't mind. It was all part of the job. Lily opened her office the door following the conversation, agreeing to this home visit. After all, it would be right next door to her new home. Not out of Lily's way at all.

As Lily left the office she informed Jaime of her appointment then hurried to her car. She thought about how wonderful it was to be outdoors on such a nice day and to get home a bit early while the sun is still shining is also very nice. When Lily arrived at the neighboring house, she rang the door bell. It took time for Mrs. Davis to come to the door. Mrs. Davis liked to be called Sue. She was walking much slower now that she had celebrated the ninetieth birthday. She greeted Lily in a most friendly fashion, then invited her in.

Mrs. Davis, sitting in her usual comfortable chair, pulled her sweater over her shoulder and ran her hand through her hair. She showed concern and stated she needed a new Will. Lily sat quietly on the stripped sofa looking around the room. It looked like a lovely picture of a former era. Everything nicely placed and not the least worn. Lily listened to Sue.

"You know Lily I am moving on in years. My children will soon be in charge not only my medical needs but the house and other things after I move myself to Heaven. Lily smiled at her comment.

"I am concerned about my lack of ability to continue caring for myself."

"I find that I am more forgetful as time goes on, even regarding my meals."

"So, I feel it's important that my children especially my daughter has the legal ability to not only care for me but help my sons with the disposition of my things."

Sitting in a nearby room was Sue's daughter Nikki reading a book she recently brought from the local city library.

Hearing her Mother speak, Nikki came to the doorway of the family room.

"Oh, Mother I didn't realize you had company."

"I walked to the library and returned just a few minutes ago." In fact I just started this book, a good mystery they say."

"Nikki this is Lily Arnold, my attorney. I want to update my will."

One could easily see Nikki had cheerfully cared for her Mother. It was obvious that her attitude was that caring for her mother was a pleasure not a duty.

"Now Lily, finances are not the problem. It would be a will for the division of assets. I want my two sons to share equally with their sister. You see they too come and care for me when their time allows."

After a long conversation, Sue and Lily came to a very desirable plan. Lily finished her tea, and took her notes to work up the results into Sue's Will. Sue wanted her children to know that she loved them equally. This Lily could do very nicely.

"When the document is drawn up, I'll go over it with you Mrs. Davis to be certain it covers all your stipulations." Thank you Lily, I'm so pleased you came."

Lily returned to her home, gathering the mail as she reached for the key. Taking the mail to the kitchen with her, she placed her purse on a chair and perused the various envelopes. When she came to the one from her lawyer, she stopped and tore open the envelope. She readily reached for the letter opener and read, "Case 247-Austin. …Sonny Barri …arrested for criminal assault …city parking garage. … no need to testify. We have concluded … case of mistaken identity… trial one month from this date… serve time for the assault." Lily began breathing easier. I had almost forgotten that, now I can."

Chapter 26

"HI DADDY."

"Hello Sweetheart."

"Dad, can I ask you something?"

"Whenever you start with that it usually costs me money, but yes..." Michael said laughing.

"I've been voted to represent the junior class and there is a leadership conference in Washington, D.C."

"What is it for? Leadership what?"

"It is a Leadership conference sponsored by the Congressional Young Adult Council."

"Wow that is quite an honor."

"It is to... wait, let me read the pamphlet. "... 'recognize and improve leadership skills and then use those skills to become a positive influence in your community.'"

"What do you think Dad?"

"Well sweetheart you certainly have a positive influence on me! Of course you can go. Just charge the expenses to me, as usual."

"Guess I'd better go over to Dr. Hill's office to let her know I'll be ready to go on Friday. It should be so much fun in D.C. Bye Dad!"

I wish Emma was around, I'd have her go with me. Oh, silly, get going. It's not that late and Dr. Hill needs to know ASAP. Living in Berkeley dormitory it is just a jaunt across campus to Sterling Library. Dr. Janis Hill's office is on the second floor of the library. She put her paperwork in her mail slot and turned around to go back to her dorm.

Rosie was hurrying along when she thought she heard something or someone. Her throat tightened. She had forgotten to tell anyone where she was going. Her thoughts raced. Should she act scared? She heard shuffling behind her and began to walk faster, not wanting to turn around and look, not daring to run. No! just act normal. Should she just run? No one was in sight, Rosie was really getting afraid now. She felt her heart beating through her sweatshirt and began to feel tears welling up when the person behind called to her.

"Rosie, is that you? Wait up, it's me, Jim."

"Oh, Jim, I was so scared. I didn't know it was you."

"What are you doing walking around campus alone at night? Let me walk you to Berkeley dorms."

"Gladly, Jim, Gladly, you are such a good friend.

Chapter 27

ANEW JOB FOR a new life, thought Michael. He showered, shaved, and carefully dressed for the first day at the Boston office. Which tie was not the question, it was more like which parking spot. Finally he found the closest one. I don't want to come in like a storm trooper he thought, but now that I'm the boss I need to prove to be the boss. Just the right balance of authority and camaraderie will set the tone. Nothing radical in the first year and he would be all set. He recognized his separate office from the general offices.

After a morning meeting with the staff, everything seemed to settle in. People came by introducing themselves and congratulating Michael. Work sites had to be evaluated and some staff reassigned with slightly different roles. Soon each day fell into predictable routine. Michael worked longer and harder than anyone else and it showed.

After 5pm one night someone in the office joked with Michael, "Don't you ever go home? You know, work can't be your whole life. This *is* Boston. Live a little."

Well, home was an apartment, comfortable yes, but not a place where Michael wanted to stay every leisure moment. In fact, he tried his back hand in tennis, but the schedule was not good. He didn't want bowling on Sundays, too much overtime for that schedule. What was there for him to do that would be a good social activity.

What is the matter with me, I love to dance and that schedule should work out well. Now where do these New England people go ballroom dancing? He got on the internet and found a place in New Hampshire. That wasn't too far. He made a promise to check it out. All work and no play…

The evening's event was very nice and the people were friendly.

A lady named Bertha seemed to be the best dancer. We talked and agreed to meet again the next week. This happened several weeks in a row. It was very nice, but Michael found a dance hall much closer and decided to give it a try. There seemed to be a nice choice of ladies who had taken lessons for some time and were quite graceful on the dance floor. One single lady, Michelle, was available for other evenings, too.

Michael and Michelle would share time at dinner, sometimes dancing in less favorable dance spots, sometimes in the more popular ones. Michelle was lovely, a good dancer, but not particularly receptive to any additional time. Michael enjoyed dancing and looked forward to the next time he could avail his self to the pleasant evening of dance. Michelle was nice, fun to joke with and good to dance with, but there was no magic between them.

The office was a different story. Gene Machado would drop in first infrequently and later more frequently. Each time Michael would make a fuss over him, making sure his ego was assuaged. Gene was never satisfied. There was always something that bothered him. Not anything that disrupted the order of business. The main office had always rewarded him with glowing praise. But Gene was totally different. Week after week, and month after month word would come to Michael that Gene was going behind his back to report some small item in a negative way.

Michael was annoyed about it all, but didn't want to get personal about the nonsense. So he would over look the comments. Michael knew his work was more than satisfactory and continued to keep up the standard he had set. Michael's staff had all improved themselves, personally and educationally, as far as Michael was concerned all was well in the office.

Chapter 28

"**M**OTHER, IT'S JIM."

"Yes, Jim. What is it?"

"Nothing, Mother. I was just walking on campus and decided to call."

"That's nice; you usually call on Sunday evening. Something up?"

"Yes, Mother, I just learned there is a Parent's Day or should I say Parent's Weekend coming up soon."

"When dear?"

"The first weekend in the month. Did you get the invitation? I wasn't sure with the move and all."

"No, actually I haven't gotten anything yet."

"Do you think you could make it?"

"You know I don't want to miss anything. Send me the information so I can make arrangements at the office."

"Thanks Mom, I love you."

My son is such a delight to me. He is really the only man in my life, other than my brothers of course. Well, then there is Dad. What am I talking about?

The weekend arrived, and so did Lily. Jim was delighted to

show her off. She was just as beautiful as she was brilliant. Lily seemed to know what to do and how to present her self in every situation and Jim was so proud. He graciously introduced her to his professors who immediately praised Jim's work. During those moments, Lily felt the move was worth it. She had a new beginning and so had Jim.

After meeting many of Jim's friends and it was nearly the end of the weekend, Lily asked Jim how his Spanish classes were going. Jim began praising his tutor, Rosie. When asked to be introduced to Rosie, Jim told Lily about her leadership trip and how happy she was that her Father was going to attend the ceremony and she could see him. Lily was pleased to hear such a warm comment. Jim did not always sound so enthusiastic about his other friends.

Chapter 29

IN THE LAW OFFICE, Lily had shown great responsibility to her clients and to the firm's owners. However she was spending all of her leisure time reviewing cases and volunteering either at the Red Cross or Child and Family Services. Every now and then she would take a weekend flight home to Los Angeles. Several of the male lawyers and principals of the firm would invite Lily out for a drink, dinner, the theatre or even a walk in the park. Lily always had a quick but witty answer in the negative. And to Lily, no means no.

One beautiful spring day following the church service, Lily heard a familiar voice calling her name. She was about to leave the building. Lily turned to see Norma, a friend who moved away from California many years ago. They hugged each other and made arrangements for dinner to catch up on old news and learn the new. Norma was excited to see Lily and after dinner she invited Lily to go dancing with her. She said since she moved east, it was an activity that helped her meet new people and enjoy her free time. Lily in her usual fashion half heartily agreed.

Norma didn't let it be, she called Lily twice more that week. Lily finally agreed to go with her and meet Norma's friends. It seemed easier to go and get it over. If she knew anything about Norma, it was that once she wanted something, she never gives up. So as the evening approached, Lily decided to pick out some clothes and make the best of it. She would be ready, but after this one time, she resolved not to get roped into anything like this again.

It is April 29, Friday, what a day it has been, thought Michael. The weather here in Boston is certainly cooler than back home. It wasn't easy finding this place. When they tell you that the entire area is simply paved cow paths, they aren't kidding. What time is it? Oh, so what if the dance has started. I like it better when I arrive to a full room. More chances of meeting someone fun. Now these gals who said they'd be here, let's hope they are. Norma is pretty responsible, so it seems. Hope I've found the right place. The Viking, yes, that sounds like New England.

Michael opened the car door. He looked around, and started in the club house. He was anticipating a pleasant evening. Michael had become a very accomplished dancer over the years. It could have been his career. His parents wanted their son to see the world through his own eyes. They were also accomplished dancers, but they wanted more for him.

His advanced college degrees and specialized training put his resume ahead of the class. His stint with the Marines and then being stationed in Paris opened his eyes to the world. He had done the right things in life and now Michael knew what he wanted and how he would get it. It had been a long day at work, heading up a field office for a quasi-governmental organization. Now he was ready for a long weekend of pure pleasure and relaxation.

Michael circled the room. From the right, his eyes were searching for the group he wanted to join. As he walked closer to the table where the four people were sitting, he noticed Norma was dancing. Susan jumped up to greet him. The others quickly joined in welcoming him, all but one. Somehow Michael felt he had seen her someplace prior to this particular evening. Where, I don't remember. Oh, well, I'll ask her to dance before the evening is over and find out where she is from. She sure doesn't look like Texas, though.

Michael could easily dance with each of the other ladies to the ballroom music. He loved ballroom dancing. His exceptionally friendly personality showed when and while he was talking with an acquaintance, Paul. He held perfect attitude while dancing, even with the most experienced of dancers. Soon Michael sat down with Susan between him and the very poised lady. Introductions were made.

Her name was Lily. And at that moment I knew I would date her. How, I wasn't certain, but I knew it as well as I knew my own name. She seemed somewhat formal, and yet exciting. Lily was refined in her appearance and mannerisms. Slowly as the evening progressed and after simple conversations with Lily, I asked her to dance. She politely refused. I continued to encourage her to dance with me. She continued to refer me to the other two ladies. I couldn't help smiling as I began to feel the chemistry between us.

She finally agreed. Not having danced for many years, she was most insecure and intimidated. Her shoe rubbed against my new shoes, but I just smiled. She quickly apologized, but I brushed it off, making sure she didn't feel out of place or uncomfortable. I continued to look at her while we danced. The chemistry became very strong; I wanted to bring her body closer to mine. I could feel the beginning of something sensuous, and yet I knew I could also easily frighten her away. Her speech was like her, elegant and refined. I knew then I wanted Lily. The dance ended, she smiled and thanked me.

I have gone to many dances through out my life. I have been with a zillion women. What was there about this woman I don't know, but I knew I was going to find out.

In careful pursuit...and it must be careful, I'll have her walking on my arm. Lily and me, how good it sounds. How good it feels. For the first time in my life I understood what it was between Roseanne and Eddie.

Chapter 30

"ATTORNEY ARNOLD'S OFFICE."

"No, I'm sorry. She is busy. Can I take a message?"

"Would you like to leave your name or number?"

"I'm sorry Mr. Lopez, you have called three times."

"Yes, I understand, but Attorney Arnold is very busy."

"Well, would you like an appointment?"

"Lunch? Hmm pretty sure that is out of my realm. Ok, I'll ask her. Your name again? Michael Lopez, Jr. – hold on, let me check with her."

"I'm sorry, she said lunch is out of the question today."

"I'm really sorry."

Lily popped her head out from her office to see if her secretary was back from lunch yet. "Helen, can you come in and get some of these files?"

"I'll be right in, Lily." Helen finished putting her coat and bag away and grabbed a box.

"You know Lily, you should get out more," Helen glanced at the half eaten salad. "How bad can this Michael guy be? He seems nice enough on the phone, and God knows I've spoken to him enough times this week!"

"I know, but I'd just rather be alone. Maybe I'm just not ready for all that yet. Here, take these…"

"Wait a minute, let me get the phone."

"Attorney Arnold's office."

"Yes, perhaps she is available now, lunch right? Let me see if I can locate her." Helen handed Lily the telephone and put her hand over the receiver, "Lily, I know you are busy, but you still have to eat sometime." She said, pushing it into her hand.

Lily frowned as she lifted the receiver to her ear. "Oh, Michael, how nice of you to think of me," she said, giving Helen an exasperated look.

"Yes it was a pleasant evening. You know I'm not a very good dancer though."

"Well, see I don't usually take lunch breaks and with the city so busy it would take too long…" she could tell her reasons were starting to sound lame as she struggled to end the conversation.

"Thank you for thinking of me Michael. Yes. Alright, I really have to get back to work now. Thank you again."

Well, this isn't working, thought Michael, but I'll figure it out yet. I shall have to think of something else. Oh, well, Mr. Machado is due to arrive soon. Ouch, I'll probably have to have lunch with him and listen to all the wonderful things he does and how important he is. Back at the office, the phone rang. Apparently, it wasn't lunch he was after, it was me.

"Look Gene I've been here almost a year now and our reports

show we are doing more audits than ever, finding areas of concern and offering solutions for many of these issues."

"What are you talking about? Our statistics are on point."

"With all due respect, what *is* your problem?"

"That is absurd. Do you hear yourself? Are you trying to make it sound as if I discriminate? This is down right foolish."

"Well, we are going to have a meeting with the whole team for this. I'm tired of the backstabbing. It's going to stop."

On the weekend, Michael decided to telephone Lily at home and make another pitch. He definitely needed a break from work. He hesitated at first, then decided he would try again. "Lily, I know you are busy at the office, but I have just a few questions to ask you."

"Michael Lopez? The same Michael Lopez who called the office this week?"

"Well, yes, but this isn't a personal matter. I am having a legal issue and you were the only person I knew…"

"Ok, well, what seems to be the problem?"

"Well, Lily, it is in the interpretation of this agreement…," knowing full well, she would think it was a business call. Maybe that would work. Well, now I at least have her talking to me. What is next?

Chapter 31

LILY HAD REESTABLISHED HER friendship with Olivia and Olivia's friend Susan. They continued to invite Lily to share social events. And Lily being Lily felt she needed to have some sort of gathering at her home. It would make it more like a home to see friends and associates in the house again. Jim had given her a waffle maker. Not because she liked waffles, but because Jim loved to be home from college on a Sunday morning have waffles in the morning. Lily could make simple meals an event. So why not do something as simple as having a waffle party for a few friends.

Lily knew she could serve eight people at the crystal topped table, but which eight. First she would invite Helen. No.Well how about Dave. No. Well first I'll start with Olivia, and her friend Susan, and oh yes, Michael Lopez. And list went on.

Michael couldn't believe it when he received the electronic message with her invitation. Of course the first evening he met Lily he had handed her his card. It was on the card. How simple this would be. I'll call Lily for directions that will facilitate talking directly with her.

Michael telephoned Lily with his acceptance and told her he

needed directions. After she completed the directions and he was off the phone. I knew I'd get to see her again, I knew it.

When Lily hung up the telephone she smiled. Something had changed in her. She thought, such a nice gentleman, and so handsome, too. I don't know what I gave him such a difficult time for...

Lily was busy sharing some conversation regarding the waffle party when Olivia offered comments regarding several guests including Michael.

"Yes, Lily, he is nice, handsome and oh, by the way he is very single."

"Lily you know he seemed interested in you when you two first met."

"Oh, Olivia, don't be silly He must see a zillion ladies. And I don't really date anyway."

"Come on Lily you must have thought about it when you invited him."

"No, not really, it just makes the right number at the table and you all keep mentioning him."

"Now Lily really, are you blind? He is so good looking and so nice..."

When Michael arrived, Lily opened the door. She thought, yes he is handsome. As Michael stepped forward he leaned in and kissed Lily on the cheek. It seemed so natural to kiss her, but he really wanted his arms around her, too. She backed up almost as a reaction. Again he realized he had to be gentle and go slow.

She was not used to male affection, except from Jim, since Richard had died. She was startled and simultaneously felt guilty. She wasn't certain how to handle the situation. Michael graciously commented on her home, making polite conversation. This pleased Lily as she took pride in the appearance of each room. Soon the other guests arrived. And the conversation flowed and the waffles were served and as time went on the guests were leaving.

Michael politely said good night as he left. This time Lily waited for the kiss on the cheek. She decided to think about the situation after everyone had gone. On Sunday, Michael called to make small talk. This time, Lily was pleased to hear his voice. He could feel the smile in her voice. He knew she was pleased to talk to him.

Monday, in the office, Lily was still thinking about his presence in her home when the work week began as usual with the telephone ringing. The following Friday the conversation was much easier. Michael telephoned to say he was on his way to the airport. He had to catch a flight. Lily teasing him, asked, "Are you going commercial or do you need my broom?" "You are funny," he replied.

He said he would call again when he returned. Lily smiled and said very little. Soon it was the middle of the following week, and Lily had agreed to have dinner with Michael. He arrived and they went to the Italian Garden for dinner and returned to Lily's home. Michael seemed very comfortable. Lily was pondering as to why Michael would show interest in her. She thought of the other women she had met since she arrived in New England. They certainly made themselves very available to him.

Lily very innocently questioned Michael about why he hadn't dated some of them. Then she pursued her question. Why did he single her out? He quickly answered, "You really don't know" Look at yourself, your clothing, your education, just you being you should be enough for any man. You are so different from the others."

Lily was speechless for a moment. She never thought that of herself. She quickly changed the conversation to various topics comparing their offices. The conversation was light. Then Michael sitting next to her, reached for her hand. She did not withdraw it. In fact it was rather nice. Light conversation continued. Time was flying fast and the evening was about to end. Lily stood up, signaling the lateness of the evening when Michael raised to his feet and holding her hand, started for the door. Then he kissed her good night. After that moment she didn't care why he seemed interested. Lily was just pleased. She kissed him back holding him momentarily. Michael left and soon called her from the car to compliment her on the evening.

Shortly thereafter, Lily telephoned Tommy. The time zone allowed her brother to be awake. She felt he talk her through what might become somewhat complicated. Lily couldn't figure out why she felt so guilty that she may have betrayed Richard's memory. Tommy assured Lily that it was perfectly permissible to date another man at this time. She had a mourning period that was way too long. It should end.

Chapter 32

MICHAEL'S BECAME A REGULAR visitor. He telephoned several times a week and would see Lily at least twice a week. Lily became much more of a free spirit. Michael enjoyed holding her close, kissing her and telling her how much he enjoyed being with her. Whenever he would tease her he would say, "Hey Sexy." Michael was in love. Why Lily and why this wonderful chemistry was happened when ever he was around her. All he knew was Michael felt wonderfully excited being with Lily.

As late afternoon became early evening, Michael was sitting on Lily's glassed in porch, enjoying the breeze and the Boston Globe newspaper.

"Please sweetheart, call the club and change the reservation to an hour later."

Lily returned to Michael shortly in a lovely but expensive silk dress. His smile soon covered Lily's mouth. The air was warm, his thoughts even warmer.

"Lily we better go now or we might not get there at all."

"Isn't that the point…?"

Weeks soon turned to months. When they were not with their own children, Michael was with Lily. Lily had only been intimate with her husband until Michael. Michael never asked, but he sensed it. Whenever they were alone, he would gently pull her into the library. She never said it, but he knew she was ready to make love. Every emotion inside them responded. His lips would curl over hers, and soon he nuzzled just below her ear onto her neck. He would say, "I will be gentle." And to himself he would question, "How shall I please her tonight?" Michael craved being with her and inside of her. He knew she would respond to him.

At the appropriate time Lily would slip into her robe. Michael knew her naked body was under the smooth cotton designer robe. When he invited her to sit on his lap, she knew how to place herself in the most seductive manner. He found her very delicate and very special. Lily enjoyed Michael, he was all male, strong, hard, and as she placed her lips on his shoulder she enjoyed the taste of his skin. Michael's hands were near her mouth, cupping her chin, so as to own her mouth, her tongue, her. Their expression of love was magical. It was as if they had only belonged to each other, never anyone else. And that magic belonged only to them.

Strangely so their children, Rosie and Jim, did not know of the relationship that was developing between their parents. And yet, the children spoke very warmly of their individual parents. Whenever Michael and Lily were with others their relationship never seemed to be a topic of conversation. It was their relationship and theirs alone. Michael was Michael and Lily was Lily.

Chapter 33

"DAD, PROFESSOR WRIGHT WOULD like you to lecture in his place because he has had something unexpected come up."

"You know, my class in Advanced Accounting and Public Relations. In two weeks. Dad, please try hard to change your schedule."

"Yes, I gave him your number."

"You know you could take a couple of days vacation for it, stay over and we could see something at the theatre, too. Please Dad."

"My darling Rose Maria, I can never say no to you. I will see what I can do. It's pretty short notice, but tell Professor Wright I'll be expecting his call."

"Thank you Daddy."

The class was exceptionally receptive to Michael's presentation and sent an unusually long thank you note. A local newspaper reporter came at Professor Wright's request and some of the student's comments were directly under a photo of the guest speaker.

A week later during an extremely busy day at the office,

Michael had a visit from Gene Machado. Most of Gene's visits were not terribly friendly nor were they planned visits. Michael would always take time to be polite and listen to Gene expound on his accomplishments. This particular visit was less than friendly. Gene was still angry about the last phone call and the more he expounded on the topic the louder the voices became. Gene showed very openly that he had become Michael's enemy. Gene left in a huff. Michael was unsettled the rest of the day.

Michael hugged Lily goodbye, checking on his ticket to Washington, D.C. he took his valise in hand and soon would be on the flight. Michael usually called Lily from the waiting room at the airport, this time, no call. Lily knew things were not good.

Michael checked into the Army Navy Club. It felt good to be in such grand surroundings and familiar ones. It was only two blocks from the White House. He had stayed there many times on his many trips to the company's headquarters.

This time he was to go directly to Mr. Wilson's office. Pressing the elevator button, He could feel the anxiety. It seemed forever for the elevator to arrive, finally three people hurried off, none familiar to Michael. He pressed the 6th floor button. His early morning coffee was not sitting well. Requesting a meeting with Mr. Wilson is not something an underling would easily do. To have to work under a supervisor who cannot tolerate you is not easy, and Gene had let it be known how he disliked Michael. The elevator stopped, Michael got off stepping on the thick oriental carpet. The Hallway seemed long; the name on the door seemed very sobering. As he opened the door the secretary smiled and acknowledged Mr. Wilson was waiting for Michael. He seemed friendly and quickly offered Michael a chair.

"Would you like some coffee?"

"No thank you."

"Rather nice weather we are having"

"Yes, and especially for this time of year."

Shortly thereafter Gene Machado entered the office. Today he was dressed in a suit. He acknowledged Mr. Wilson, and barely looked toward Michael.

Mr. Wilson had cleared his schedule for this meeting. It was important to the company for the staff to remain friendly to each other. Without summonsing, the secretary entered and was introduced to the others.

"Gene, Michael tells me in his last report that you two haven't been getting along..."

"Getting along? Michael forgets that I supervise him." he began, getting right to his complaints. "He continuously goes out on his own without any authorization. Frank, I'm sure you know about his latest antic, teaching a class at Yale without asking company permission. He has written articles for the Auditors Newsletter and frequently has his name in the local paper with his Letters to the Editor. There seems to be no end to what he does without permission. Unfortunately, he works for us, not the other way around."

"Gene do you feel Michael's extracurricular activities need to have prior authorization? Have any of these issues brought harm to the company?"

"Well, no, but how am I to know what he is doing? Especially if he doesn't tell me first."

"Does he do this on company time? Does he complete his duties and responsibilities within the company framework?"

"Well, no they are on his personal time, but then he does represent us."

"Now Gene do I have this straight? You are concerned that Michael lets the Accounting and Marketing classes at Yale University know where he is employed? Isn't that all he is doing?"

"Well, Frank, if you put it that way, I guess you are right."

"Since you are his supervisor, let's go over his responsibilities."

"Michael, you have a job description, please tell us, enumerate those responsibilities."

Michael cleared his throat and began reviewing the list almost as if he were reading it. The three gentlemen and a secretary with a steno machine continued the scenario of Michael's responsibilities.

"Michael, thank you, we have the idea that not only do you know them quickly from memory but that you do them with great achievement. This meeting has gone on for over an hour and so far I can only compliment Michael for all of the overtime he has put into the job Michael, thank you for continuing to keep the company name out there for others to respect on your own time."

"Thank you, Sara. That will be all for now."

"Gene - a letter of apology to Michael will be in order."

Mr. Wilson continued to compliment Michael on his work ethic. Gene did not look happy and again he reiterated that Michael was somehow disrespectful by giving a class at Yale University, disrespectful to him by not advising him first. Mr. Wilson and Michael quickly looked at each other.

"Gene you are out of order. Michael can do what he pleases on his vacation time. Send him the letter, and that is an order. Now the matter is closed."

Gene quickly got up, gingerly shook hands with Michael, then Frank Wilson and left. As Michael put his jacket on and prepared to leave, Mr. Wilson again praised him for taking his personal time to benefit the agency. Now he would return to his room. The sun was shining as he walked back to the officers club. The meeting was over. Gene was instructed to write a letter of apology to Michael for the record. Michael was pleased. Yet he wondered how this would really end. Knowing Gene, he wondered if he would lose by winning. He could feel a headache coming on. The only reason to come to Washington was for the meeting – a one hour meeting. This one hour meeting would change his life.

Michael stayed another two days to rest and have some much needed quiet time for himself. Returning to his room, he stopped to order a sandwich, hoping it would settle his upset stomach. Then he lay across the bed. He woke up, the room was dark. He lay there a few minutes. Still very tired from the stress of the issues and the concern about the future, he decided to shower and return to bed until morning. Hearing the vacuum in the hallway, he looked at the clock. Ten o'clock, time to get up.

The warm water flowed over his hair, down his face and back, around his feet and felt so good. He allowed it to continue for a few minutes. The towel was large and fluffy and wiped himself off, then wrapped it around his waist and plugged in his electric shaver. Michael always looked his best, like a man straight out of "Gentlemen's Quarterly"

He could almost whistle as he stepped out on the street. Looking both ways he hailed a taxi. "Appleton's please."

The restaurant was busy, but not particularly noisy. He ordered his usual, bacon, two eggs, wheat toast, orange juice and hot coffee. Michael enjoyed the morning meal with the local paper. He looked at his cell phone, no messages. Thank goodness. A walk in the park, reservations for a musical, "Jersey Boys" and no stress. A day to be thankful for. Oh, yes, and make a reservation for the return flight tomorrow.

Lily had not heard from Michael. She was concerned, but never intruded in Michael's space or personal issues. She felt that he would contact her when he was ready. She knew Michael would tell her when and what he wanted to share.

Before Michael boarded the plane, he called and left the message he would be back and take her to dinner. He knew he needed to share the issues with her, but was still reluctant. Was it real discrimination thought Michael or just jealousy? It was a strange victory for Michael. His supervisor Gene's visits were fewer and farther between. It was good on one hand but Michael wondered why and what was he up to now.

Michael knew that Gene could not be trusted. This type of man would find a way to continue his struggle against Michael. Michael never felt genuinely victorious, no matter how vindicated.

Two months later, Michael finally told Lily the whole story. After much conversation and Lily quietly listening and pondering the situation, she warned Michael to be careful of any actions he might take.

"For every action there is a direct and deliberate reaction, Michael. Do be prepared."

"I know Lily and that has me concerned. I shall have to be careful and make sure I have everything planned out just in case." Little did Michael know how the impact of that statement would haunt him.

The evening wore on and Lily called her private club for dinner reservations. Michael enjoyed dinning at the private club. They met many of their friends there, and yet they felt closer with out the entire public observing. Michael arrived; he hugged Lily and kissed her passionately.

"Michael, I've called for dinner reservations for eight o'clock; we can have drinks before, if you like."

"Lily you are always so thoughtful, but if you don't mind, I would like to skip dinner; I am simply hungry for you."

Chapter 34

L ILY TURNED AND RESPONDED, "Michael, I love you. Dinner is easily forgotten." And Lily responded in full.

Being widowed for several years did not stop her passion for Michael. She excited him and she knew it. She kissed his fingers and held his hand, and walked him down that very familiar hall to the room they had shared so many times. Michael knew Lily to be very reserved everywhere except during their love making. They frequently took turns deciding how the love making would be performed. This time Michael encouraged Lily to be a lady of mystery, to have a fantasy. One they both would remember.

"Michael this time you are my captive, I shall imprison you and tie you to the corners of the bed." She knew Michael would forget any problems or at least set them aside and relax with her performance and fantasy. Totally out of character she said,

"Darling, may I simply use these silk scarves and gently tie you to the four posters."

"Sweetheart, you may pleasure me any way you like tonight."

Lily gently tied a wrist, kissing his warm body, the hand and forearm slowly, then her warm lips rested on his taunt thigh. He breathing was deep. He began to relax. Her small mouth followed down his leg to an ankle. Her moist lips lingered. She tied his ankle gently to the foot poster. Lily's lips were warm on Michael's toes. She ran her tongue across his foot. It was easy for Michael to start breathing heavily. He already wanted her. His erection was in place.

Lily continued the same wonderful process on Michael's other wrist. When she came to his outer thigh she kissed it; then carefully she kissed his inner thigh. Michael was comfortably tied and wonderfully aroused. With her full body next to his, he could feel the dampness of her breasts as her mouth went across his chest from one nipple to the next. He longed to touch her. The ties prevented it. The erection ached. Lily put her face near Michael's ear, tenderly with his ear lobe between her teeth; she slid her tongue onto the lobe and into the ear. He turned his head and kissed her. She kissed his eyes, his cheeks and then his mouth.

Never before had he been pleasured so well. Lily knew him as no other woman had even known him. He was ready for her. He wanted her completely. She whispered in his ear words of love, her small tongue and warm lips caressed every inch, every nook or cranny of his well cared for body. Michael needed Lily and he wanted her. She knew what he wanted. Then Lily carefully untied him and allowed him to simply devour her. He touched the smooth skin of her throat. His fingers were strong but damp. He cupped her chin in his hand and brushed her lips with his as he took possession of her body. First he slowly and lovingly took her shoulders, arms and even her finger tips to his mouth and caressed them. Michael very slowly and carefully suckled her breasts. Lily's breathing was uneven. Michael knew Lily needed him. He kissed her abdomen and could not stop. First he gently kissed each thigh, outside and then as he began to kiss the inner thigh he could not wait. No woman had ever or would ever taste so wonderful. Michael knew they were one in thought, now one in body.

He was her Michael and she was his Lily. They slept in each others arms until morning. The haunting concern returned. The alarm clock shouted out the morning routine. As Michael was buttoning his shirt and tying his tie he spoke to Lily, "Lily if anything happens to us, I want you to go on in life. Promise me."

Lily smiled as she brushed her hair and didn't answer, but wondered what brought those thoughts. Was Michael her dream or fantasy? He had become the second man in her life and the only man in her future. She was oblivious as to his issues. In her world, changing jobs was not a major problem.

As Michael left for the day, he knew how much he loved Lily, but more than that, he knew how much she loved him. He knew she would change her entire lifestyle for him. This he could not have. He would hurt without her, but could not take from her.

His mind raced back again to the disturbing and angry voice he had overheard on the phone the day before. "That goddamn spic thinks he can run this agency, well I'll show that fucking Mexican a thing or two. He thinks I'm apologizing? Well he's got another thing coming. Not only will I get his job, I'll get him fired, too. That son of bitch should know better than to fool with me. A spic talking back to me…who the hell does he thinks he is?

Michael's ears were ringing. Being put down for work related issues was one thing, but being called a 'spic'? I haven't had that problem since I was a kid and that was when I lived near the Mexican border. I had no idea these kinds of things went on in New England. One of the reasons I came here was to be certain that would never happen again. Now what?"

As he thought about what happened, his emotions rose up again. He felt inferior clear down to his toes. His revulsion slowly turned into anger and rose all the way up from his toes. He was nauseous and his head was spinning. "I've never spoken Spanish around him or the office, one or twice to my Mother on the telephone, so when did he learn of my being of Mexican decent. God, I'd like to smack him in the face but now is not the time. He'll get his one of these days. When he is least expecting it, a court summons might serve better than a fist. Isn't that just what Lily was referring to when she said I could never trust Gene again? This makes me sick. I'd like to punch him in the nose, but that is just what he would like. That would be enough to get me fired. Then no one would hire me.

Michael had never been placed in a position where he was being watched and criticized all of the time. He knew it best to leave the firm before it got worse. This sort of black mark on his record could follow him and eventually destroy his life. Gene was vindictive and held the power to make his life hell. He telephoned his father. His hands were trembling and his head aching, but he knew he had to make the call.

"Dad, I have a major problem. I have to leave my job and I'm not certain what to do."

"No, I'm not a quitter. Why would I quit? Well my immediate supervisor is planning to fire me. I have to protect my record. I've had to face discrimination issues before, but this has gotten past the point of harassment. Court is the only place to take care of him."

Michael told the story. His father replied, "Son if he is plotting and name calling behind your back, it will soon be in your face. You may not be able to control your temper. That, you don't ever want to happen. I have a good lawyer; why don't you come home. We'll figure this whole thing out."

Michael paused. Lily would sense something was drastically wrong, but he really didn't want her to know what was going on. She was not the sort of woman who would be familiar with racial discrimination. Hers was a different world, a different life. No, he could never let her become a part of this issue, be hurt like he was hurt. He had to settle this first before they could begin to think about a life together...

"Ok, Dad. I think you're right. I'll give you a call when I've made my flight arrangements."

Chapter 35

THE TELEPHONE RECEIVER WAS warm in his sweaty hand. His voice was soft...."American Airlines, please."

He walked down the flight corridor, carrying a small bag. He knew he could always send for the rest of his things later. His mind was preoccupied as he found his seat, 27C, on the aisle. "These electronic tickets are great, he thought, "what a time saver. What did the flight attendant say?"

Oh, yes, fasten your seat belt and turn off all electronic equipment. Let's see, I'll have to make arrangements for my things in the apartment. I'll think about that later. First I shall submit my resignation in writing. Mr. Wilson will quickly understand, no matter what I use as an excuse. Gene the bastard will be disappointed that he didn't get to fire me.

What was the matter with Gene, anyway? Did he think no one could hear him on his cell phone? He talked so loud. I guess it was just luck that I was standing in the hall about to go into the supply room when I heard his tirade of discrimination and threat to fire me if I didn't resign.

Being Mexican brings all the unkind remarks to the surface. Racism is everywhere. Poor Eddie, here he was only in the second grade and being called a "dirty little Spic." He didn't even know what that meant. He had to ask Mom. All he knew was that the tone of the remark was nasty. He only wanted to play ball with the rest of the kids. Poor kid.

I remember how he cried. And Dad was so angry and wanted to go see the other boy's father until Mom quietly said it would only get worse. No wonder Eddie has taken a wrong turn in life. I didn't understand it until I wanted to join the Boy's Club and one of the bullies said, "We don't want any wetbacks in our club." I tried to tell him I wasn't a 'wetback', but he wouldn't listen to me. I kept yelling "I was born here just like you." But soon I could see no one cared.

Then there was the time I hadn't eaten meat and one of the guys said "You must be one of those "beaners" and everyone laughed. I knew immediately it was bigotry. Just because my Mom was a vegetarian, they thought it was a Mexican diet.

I'm glad Dad answered the phone. I had decided to go to Human Resources and resign, telling them I had decided to take a good position in Texas and that being closer to family was important to me. I somehow thought that type of racism, particularly for Mexicans, didn't happen in New England. Somehow Lily and I had never spoken about my being Mexican. She is from California where many Mexicans live and work, but the only Mexicans who would be in her social circle would be the hired hands.

The real reason I quit had less to do with me and more to do with Lily. How could I ever allow discrimination take place in front of Lily? Unless someone has been subjected to bigotry and hate, they could never realize how hurtful, disappointing and demeaning it is.

I had planned to marry Lily. Now marriage is out of the question. Her background and mine were so different. The only thing we had in common were our loving families. I could never subject her to such anger and nastiness. Maybe later I could send for her and she would consider moving to Dallas. No, I'd better wise up.

She would be humiliated being married to a Mexican. Being Mexican is one thing, but to be married to one - that might even be worse. God, Lily, I love you so much, I cannot hurt you. There is no way I can tell her this. Her thinking any thing is better than this. It hurts so much, all of it. I was so close to a good life and now this. It is too stormy for her. She deserves so much more.

Michael's eyes were welling up. He began sniffing and running his hand inside his briefcase for a handkerchief for his nose. The tears began running down his face. God this hurts, I cannot believe I'm sitting here crying. When I was a child my mother said, "Big boys don't cry." Well, Mom, this big boy does. I really loved my job and my lady.

A few more hours and I'll be back in Texas. Mexicans not only blend in, they outnumber the rest. Dad will be waiting. The hum of the motors began a rhythm. He lowered his head back to the head rest. The other voices blended in, and Michael closed his eyes. They were warm, he needed to rest. One upset after another, one decision after another, one hurt emotion followed another. By the time the plane was about to land, Michael felt more at peace.

"Wait until the seatbelt sign goes off before you stand up or reach for your luggage please," came the voice of one of the lovely flight attendants. Michael opened the overhead storage door and reached for his bag. He handed the next bag to the elderly lady who indicated it to belong to her. Walking behind her up to aisle he looked at his watch. He hadn't changed the hours to coincide with the time zone. The passengers were eyeing the crowd searching for their families; others were hurrying to the baggage claim department.

Michael gripped his bag and looked for the exit. He knew his father would be waiting for him in the car near the passenger area. Once outside in the warm sunshine, he began to feel more at peace with himself. He set the bag down and waited. Soon a new blue Buick pulled up and the horn honked, and Mr. Lopez, Michael's father reached over to open the car door for his son. He was home.

Chapter 36

Later that day, when the men were in the home, Mrs. Lopez shed tears of happiness to see her youngest son. Michael looked around the Lopez home. Everything was just as he left it. The living room was formal, with everything in place. Some of the antiques had been cared for so well that the wood shone as if they were new. Dad loved collecting antiques. On rainy Saturdays, he and Mom would spend time going to the various dealers. The long mahogany table they all sat at during their early years was still set up in the dining room.

Mother's fresh flowers smelled even more fragrant than he remembered. She placed a great value on flowers, especially if they came from her yard. One of the bedrooms had now become Dad's study, more like a library with all the books and book shelves. Yes, it had been a while since Michael visited them.

Mrs. Lopez smiled, hugged him, held him tight and kissed his cheek, "I know you and your father want to talk. I won't interrupt you until dinner is served."

"Dad, how can I be a man and do nothing? Gene was my immediate boss and was constantly throwing stones at my work. I didn't want to take things into my own hands at the office because

I knew I might regret it. He's vindictive and I need references to get another job."

"Son, what does your Lily say?"

"We haven't really spoken about it. Dad I don't think she would have any idea about being discriminated against, not with her background…"

"Oh, I see," Michael's father said, nodding his head slightly. Yes, he was all too aware of the dangers of racism, and understood it never touched the lives of some people.

"Dad, she is very much a strong independent person. She has her son and her work.".

"She even has family on the West coast. I cannot involve her in this."

"But I thought you said you two were in love."

"Dad this is something I must handle myself."

"Be careful my son, you can't fight the world alone. I know you take so much upon yourself. But don't ruin you life over it. We all have had to face it at one time or another."

"Those hypocrites, those bastards --- they are quick to say "God created man in his own image." How do they know God wasn't a Mexican? He hung his head, placed his arm across his face and cried. His father sat quietly and shed a few tears while watching his son struggle. Michael finally stopped, wiped the tears and blew his nose, just as his mother came to the doorway and announced dinner.

Maria was careful to prepare the foods that both her husband and youngest son enjoyed the most, followed by her best apple pie. The men didn't talk much during the meal, but it didn't escape Maria's notice that both plates were empty at the end of the meal. Neither man went into detail as to why Michael was home, but Maria knew her husband would inform her when they were alone.

The men went into the other room to talk, leaving Maria to wonder what their conversation was all about.

"So, have you thought about your next move?" Michael Sr. asked.

"Well, I thought the best solution is to leave that position and find another," he answered.

His father, smiling, replied, "Maybe this time near home? Your mother would like that. She hasn't been feeling like herself lately."

"How is Rosie doing?" Michael asked, changing the subject. After Rosie graduated from Yale, she had landed an excellent position with a firm in Dallas, not far away. Although Michael was always in touch with her, it was not the same as seeing her face to face.

"She is fine. Have you told her you were coming?" he asked. "I didn't call her because I wasn't quite sure...."

"No, Dad. I just wanted to get out of there so that I could

think clearly about what I should do. Being able to see Rosie is going to be the icing on the cake."

That evening when the house was quiet and Maria knew the details of Michael's problem, she could finally understand the pain in his face and the sadness in his voice.

maybe a last sentence
about patience

as his mother she
knows he will
patiently find
life's purpose.

Chapter 37

FALL IN NEW ENGLAND, the season of change. When the warm sun breaks into the cool, crisp dry air and the smell of dried leaves fills the air. The landscape seems to almost burst overnight from hues of green and brown to bursts of brilliant yellow, orange, and red. The foliage created beautiful pictures along the highways and even more colorful scenes along the winding side roads.

Lily enjoyed her drive home from the office. Her Lexus simply glided along and even with the immense beauty around her, she was careful not to become distracted. Remembering she needed to get come groceries, Lily pulled into the supermarket parking lot. She always parked at the end of the lot since it gave her a longer walk, one she enjoyed after sitting behind the desk most of the day. Once inside, Lily began collecting the items, only a few she thought. What else should I get…

Let's see, I haven't heard from Michael now for two days, he'll be calling and wanting a hearty meal. However I won't start it until I hear from him. Lily left the market and continued her way home, thinking about what might be on the menu. She pulled into the driveway, pushed the automatic garage door opener, and drove into the garage. Lifting the groceries out of the car, Lily thought, "Maybe he will call and want to go out to eat. It has been a while."

Lily entered the house, put the groceries away, and collected the mail from the small table in the hall. She checked the light on her answering machine. Lily ran to pick up the phone as it rang, "Hello, oh, yes Cary, thanks for the reminder of the early morning meeting at the office."

Disappointed, Lily went back to the mail, finding a note from her brother Jack. She reached for the letter opener and began reading about his recent vacation. Lily turned on the local news. The Mayor was telling about the ribbon cutting ceremony at the new addition of the library. She picked up a magazine and slowly turned the pages, looking at the telephone every now and then waiting for it to ring.

Now past the usual dinner hour, Lily went into the kitchen, and opened the refrigerator door. She stood staring at the foodstuff and then decided she'd better make a sandwich. She ate in front of the television, a new sitcom for company. When the phone rang, she almost dropped her plate racing for it before the ring stopped, but this time it was someone campaigning for a local office. Again Lily was disappointed. This wasn't like Michael to go without at least letting her know what he was doing.

Lily hesitated to call Michael, but decided to wait until morning and call his office then. She called home to California and spoke with her mother, then showered and went to bed. It was a restless night, and soon morning arrived. Lily decided not to call once she arrived at her office. However, each day seemed to be a near repeat of the first.

The first week, Lily kept listening for the phone to ring. The house seemed even quieter than usual, with only the noise of the television for background. Lily liked to have the voices and the news in the background. Other times, she would put on some classical music as background for a novel or mystery, still waiting for Michael's call.

Whenever the telephone did ring, she was disappointed that it wasn't Michael. Cary would call her on weekends and the Bridge Club gals frequently called her for a movie or lunch or dinner out. Sometimes it would be a neighbor who wanted company on a walk to the park.

She longed for his calls. She knew he had been upset about something, and was surprised that he didn't confide in her. Lily would sit quietly and rethink of their last few conversations. Had she missed something he said? She felt they were so close - what happened? She began to make excuses for him in her mind. There were times she listened and the phone wasn't ringing. It would be a ringing on television. Friends asked about Michael, not knowing what really happened. Lily found it hard to answer them.

Finally, after 18 long days, Lily felt it was time to take matters into her own hands and tell him no matter what was wrong; they would work it out together. She called Michael's private number in his office. The man who answered said, Michael Lopez no longer works here. There is no forwarding number. Lily was speechless and quietly hung up. It was hard to focus on her work for the rest of the day. She was grateful that most of the staff was either very busy or out of the office. They didn't notice that she was in shock.

She left work early and spent most of the evening crying in disbelief. Why? What could have happened? She couldn't fit the pieces together and needed to know how he could have just up and left without leaving a note, making a call. There had to be more to it than this. Maybe he was kidnapped or in some kind of trouble. Lily just wanted to find him. It was not her nature to be in strong pursuit, but at times she wished it was.

Chapter 38

OVER THE NEXT FEW days she caught herself now and then with a tear in her eye and a bit of a quiver in her voice. Was he wrong to leave with no closure, she didn't know. Lily missed his calling her "his cup of happiness." Or "What's for breakfast, sexy?" Lily was hurt and cried easily when alone.

Once he said to her, "The man you choose will be very lucky." Was that his way of saying goodbye? I thought he was teasing. Was that his goodbye ...she wondered.

Many mornings, Lily tossed and turned most restlessly and was reaching for the warmth of his body when she felt the cold sheet beside her and remembered. Coming from the shower recalling their bathing together, she would wipe a tear on the sleeve of her robe. She remembered oh so well when her soft hand reached for the handle and slowly opened the shower door – partway. Her foot would slide into the warm water, looking up - the droplets covered her face. He would reached forward and pull her lovely body to his. The shower water ran from his chest onto her breasts. His lips would find hers. He could feel the warmth and firmness growing between his legs. Oh, yes I remember she said aloud. Michael I need you ...where are you?

Michael where can you be? I need you. At night I close my eyes and try oh so hard to think what happened, what did you not want from me, how had I not satisfied you, oh so many questions unanswered Michael. Lily was so lonesome for him, often crying herself to sleep at night. Dreaming he was trying to get to her. Oh, Michael you are so much a part of me, what happened? With you I was so happy, so complete.

Chapter 39

OCCASIONALLY AT WORK, LILY had mentioned Michael when talking to Cary about different restaurants or events they had gone to. The Boston theaters were holding Broadway plays and that reminded Lily of times she and Michael shared. Cary very politely would ask about him. Lily was happy to talk about the fun times. Cary's office was only two offices away from Lily's.

The hallway was always quiet and the women could tell if the other had a client in or was on the phone before they would barge in. Cary's office was large with full windows on the East side. She had selected lovely expensive lined draperies to use when the sun was too hot or too bright. The furniture was more modern than most, some called it "Scandinavian style" with less upholstered pieces than most of the offices. Cary had a large pendulum clock on the wall and decorative pictures of country scenes. The room was efficiently arranged with two chairs facing the desk, frequently filled with clients. She was one of the first women partners in the firm. Cary was openly friendly and yet very professional.

It was near lunch time, close to one o'clock. Cary was still in her office sitting near the window at her magnificent desk, with a locked drawer for her private papers. The day was sunny, a bit chilly, but the window was opened an inch or so. Cary liked the fresh air instead of the circulating air of the offices.

"Busy Cary?"

"No, Lily, come on in."

"What's up?"

"Oh, my fax machine seems to be low on ink."

"Seeing that Cary wasn't using hers, Lily asked, May I use yours?"

"Of course, I don't expect anything until late afternoon."

While Lily was busy at the fax machine, Cary asked "What do you hear from Michael?" Lily didn't respond. Not wanting to sound aggressive, Cary leaned on her desk and arranged the flowers on the corner of the desk. Cary enjoyed fresh flowers and had them delivered each Monday morning from a local florist. She usually requested pink flowers since they would be the focal point of the room.

With the Oriental rug on the floor, beautiful draperies, blonde furniture and fresh flowers, it was an office to remember, elegant and classic. The board members and especially the chairman enjoyed having the offices represent of the caliber of lawyers behind each desk. "First class," he would say admiringly when he entered her office.

"Hey, Lily, have you heard from Michael yet? What about his parents? Does he have brothers or sisters?"

"Cary I'm sorry to say, but I don't know if he ever told them about us." answered Lily as she continued to add information to the fax.

Cary stood up, quickly commenting, "Come on Lily, he certainly didn't try to keep your relationship a secret, did he?

Pondering the question, Lily answered, "No, I guess not, but honestly, I haven't said much to my son Jim either."

"Are you almost through there? Come Lily, let's go to lunch; let's try the Season's Grill."

"Sounds good. You know, it has actually been many weeks now since I've heard from Michael. I can't lie, it really bothers me."

"Well, this will take your mind off of work and everything else. And why not? I'm buying!"

"You know Cary, Michael wanted to spend New Year's Eve aboard the Odyssey here in the harbor. Tickets were so hard to get, but I was able to find two and bought them as a surprise for Michael. Now with no word from him, I'm going to try to sell them back. It's supposed to be a wonderful yacht party, incredible food, dancing…" her voice trailed off. .

Cary just rolled her eyes and didn't comment. She had no use for someone who would treat a woman like Michael had. She didn't know much about him, but never imagined he was like that. They reached the restaurant and had a very short wait for a table. The grill was new and not totally discovered by the masses yet. After they ordered and the water glasses filled, Cary turned the conversation back to Michael.

"I cannot believe he just disappeared. Did you call the police?"

Lily shook her head no. "Cary if he wanted to be here he would be here, I firmly believe that."

"Lily," she continued. "Why aren't you angry with him? I don't get it. I'd be furious."

With tears in her eyes, Lily confessed, "Oh Cary, I could never be angry at Michael. He had taught me so much. He took the starch out of my collar, he taught me to believe in love. He taught me what love was, to know it, to feel it, and to believe in it. To me, Michael *was* love and yet…"

"Yet what?"

"One of the last things he said to me was to go on with life. Did he mean without him?"

Cary could tell that she had gone too far. She was afraid that Lily was going to break down right in the restaurant. "Look Lily," Cary said softly, looking Lily directly in the eye. "Michael knew about the pain you have had in your life. Didn't he know about your first love, John Hill and about your husband's plane crash? How could he give you even more sorrow?" Lily didn't answer. "You know Lily, I frequently go to a real kick-ass therapist. She says you need results not regrets. Maybe you should try her."

Lily smiled and nodded knowing she needed help with the

depression that was setting in. "Yes, Cary you are right, I've cried enough, I do need help to get through this."

While Lily was asking Cary some questions regarding her therapist the food arrived. Cary smiled and began to talk about her experiences.

"Well, once a month I have my group of girlfriends over. That's how I found out about this therapist. We talk things through, socialize, and have a great dessert. It is really good when you have friends who will listen and really care. We talk about different things. One of my friends, Sherry, works for a therapist. She talks very positive about it all. What I've heard from them sounds really good and might be something that will be a good fit for you. I'll tell you what I know about the sessions according to them."

"When Sherry was talking she was telling about her first few days in the office and told me about the conversation between them;

"Sherry, you are a great secretary and really help me bear the burden of this practice," explained the therapist. "I know that you can be trusted and of course you signed the declaration of privacy. But even without that, I have felt from the first you understand the ways of therapy. You mentioned you were in therapy when you were younger?"

"Yes, Doctor Grosart, I did. I had many sessions, all throughout elementary, secondary, and even my first year of college. It helped a lot," replied Sherry. Sherry told her that she had a problem with her brother always competing with her, and how she felt competitive with other boys.

She told her about the additional tapes from the library shelf.

The library was a distinguished looking room with many shelves, many, many books. Certain shelves were reserved for certain books, ones that Doctor Grosart could immediately put her hands on, others shelves held favorite novels and there was simply the spot where the many tapes lay waiting for use. Some tapes were new and some empty, others were filled with patients comments. It was the clerical aide Mary's job to keep the tapes apart, mark the used ones and place them in order. Each tape held a date and the initials of the patient. Doctor Grosart had instructed that the patients initials were to be placed in reverse order, thus adding to the confidentiality.

Sherry often told them about her job and Dr. Grosart. "I love working there, being an assistant to the world of mental health is certainly my ambition. One of these days I told the doctor, I shall go back to school and further my education. Knowledge is important, but in this world it also takes credentials to have a practice. Dr. Grosart not only holds credentials for family therapy, but especially children. I remember when she was the school psychologist – and she has worked the entire spectrum, even with the criminally insane. That I'm not sure I want to work with them, but she never gave me the impression that working with the criminally insane was a big deal.

"Well, Sherry," she said, "mental health comes in all sizes and all packages. Take that last client, she told me. It takes several sessions to establish a bond between us before the patient can become receptive to therapy. You know the oldest of therapy jokes. How many therapists does it take to change a light bulb? Well, the light bulb has to want to change first."

Lily enjoyed hearing about Cary's friends and especially about therapy and was still curious about the sessions. The women finished lunch and returned to the office.

Later in the week, the girls were meeting and Sherry, Helen, and Jane were discussing therapy again with Cary. Helen started the discussion. "Cary, my therapist didn't do much for me. She simply gave me the instructions and she had me do all the work. I see it this way. We pay them, lots of money and they give us nothing back. When my husband and I went to couples therapy she had us tell her how things were with us, you know. You would think that she would know how things were just by our making an appointment. They really are over paid for what little they do. First she had us fill our papers telling her how long we had been married, you know that stuff. All she had to do was look at us and she might have known that. Do we look like newlyweds, what a joke that therapy is. Really? Cary, it is just a stupid waste of money. Steve doesn't like me any better now that we have gone."

Jamie disagreed, "Well my or should I say, our couples therapy was much different. We gave her lots of background. We wanted her to know it was ten years for us, and the first few were really great. We wanted her to help us get back to there. So we told her where the turn seemed for us. By the time we got to the third session, things were already taking a turn for the good.

She pointed out the turn was when we decided that our role was just Mom and Dad. We completely forgot ourselves as individuals and stopped see each other in our personal way, our personal life, if you get what I mean. Boy did she straighten us out, but for good. And are we ever thankful. That Doctor was certainly a lot cheaper than a divorce lawyer. And we are looking forward to the vacations that the hubby and I take without the children."

Just then, Cary's husband Craig opened the front door. He smiled at the group. He frequently came home during their gab sessions and sometimes put his ten cents into the conversation.

"Well, I certainly have different slants on this couples therapy. From what the girls say, we should stick to it," Cary said as she smiled at Craig

Chapter 40

CARY ASSURED LILY THAT Dr. Grosart also saw individuals. "You make me laugh Cary, and yet therapy seems to have helped many. I feel a little better about making an appointment, now. You are a dear and it sounds like your friends are, too. Thanks for the insight."

Cary had talked to Lily about the pros and cons of therapy. Lily thought about whether to make an appointment or not, she seemed to vacillate, but finally decided to go.

She made the appointment for March 14, Tuesday late afternoon at 4:30. When the day arrived for the appointment, Lily left work an hour early and drove directly to the large medical building. She saw the sign, parked the car. The parking lot was very accessible; it was a lovely sunny day and still warm for the afternoon. There were many cars, perhaps many people inside. The directory was near the door. A few steps to the elevator and the second glass door had the name Dr. Gilbert Grosart, Psychologist. Lily went directly to the receptionist.

As soon as Lily stepped inside the office, she saw a very happy smiling face in the very curly head of brown hair. It must be, yes, the name plaque said Sherry Harrison.

Looking at the list of appointments, and being aware that Lily, from Cary's office, would arrive on time, Sherry called Lily by name and handed her forms to complete. They smiled at each other with recognition, but wanted to remain professional.

Lily found the blue chairs quite comfortable and her pen from her purse. With the forms completed, she handed them back to Sherry.

Looking at her watch, Lily picked up a magazine. She wondered about the woman she saw enter the inner office. Appearing to look at a magazine, she remembered Cary's comments about the therapist. She wondered if most patients felt the way she did with a bit of anxiety. Lily was wondering about the woman who entered the private office.

Little did Lily know about the anxiety of others or she could relate to the other patients and what was taking place in the private office of the therapist.

The client was mumbling. Lily heard snatches of the conversation and then nothing. If she had heard what was going on behind that door, she might have known there were many types of sessions and many different responses to therapy.

"Well, we finally meet. Now what is it you want to see me about? You think you know what is wrong with my marriage? Well, okay, now get with it. Don't just sit there acting as if you know it all, well, what is it? What do you know, what do you mean? Well, let's have it. Well, come clean. I think these draperies are light blue. You have spoken to my husband. Well, was it he who said the marriage was on the rocks? Well, what do you think? I know I have do it all. Well, I get everyone up each morning, and well, I get the food on the table, and well, yes, I see to it they brush their teeth, and well, someone has to taxi them to their schools, well who else but me, he isn't going to do it. He has to go to work, well, yes, who else is going to make the money. No, I think they are grey. Well, what do you think? Well, I know more about this relationship than you do. Well, that is for sure. Now tell me, you think you are so smart. Well, how long have you be doing this sort of counseling? Well, do you find any results? Well, like actually being of help to couples? This furniture is nice..."

"Well, I'm here so let's get on with it. Well, what do you think? Yes, well I am a good mother, not a maid as you call it. Well, yes, some days I feel like it is maid service. And taxi service, and dog care service, and garbage take out service, and accountant service, and...Well, wouldn't you cry, too? Where is the dam tissue? I hope this doesn't take too long.

Well, what do you mean, what kind of a wife am I? Doing all that, well, what else do you think a wife does? Well, just what do you mean? I'm not a wife to my husband? Of course, well, that is what wives do, right? Well, what do you mean no? Well, you say he wants me to be a companion? Well, what do you mean? Well, what is a companion? Well yes, I sleep with him, if that is what you mean. Well, exactly what is it you are talking about? Well, yes, I dress appropriately. Fancy no. Well, no, I can't clean and cook dressed up. Well, yes, and I sleep in those old tee shirts, except when it is cold. Well, one must keep warm, well yes the sweat pants are mostly comfortable. No he doesn't gripe, like you insinuate.

What do you mean? Well, those nighties are not comfortable. Well, what woman told you that? Well anyway I'm not going to do that. What is the matter with you anyway? Well, you must have a dirty mind to say such things. We know what and when we want to do such things. No one is going to tell us we have to do that two or three times a week. Well, what do you mean? It is a biological rhythm of our bodies? Well, where did you ever go to school? Well, now, just like eating and sleeping? Well, you have to be kidding, huh? Well, now you want me to change my, what? Well, behaviors, now what do you mean? The way we do things? Well, how many ways do you want me to do that? Well, that makes me laugh. I have to make him think I like what? Well, my God, woman, what next?

Oh really there is a next? Well, I should have known. Well for what I am paying you, well, there must be lots of nexts.

Then Dr. Grosart entered the room. The woman cleared her thoughts and the therapy began. And soon the anxiety lessened...

Chapter 41

IN THE GENERAL OFFICE, the clock ticked loudly and rhythmically. The room's wallpaper was striped and the carpet seemed to match one of the bands of colors. All in all it was a pleasant room, certainly not over done. The chairs were neatly placed around the room with small tables and piles of magazines on each table.

It seemed as though time was going slowly, then Sherry called out Lily's name. It was her turn to enter the private office. It was her turn to relay her feelings. She had looked forward to the session, knowing full well she would not only become aware of her actions and feelings, but somewhat relieved after the session. She hoped her tears would soon stop.

Dr. Grosart's friendly greeting made Lily feel comfortably at ease. She had carried the magazine into the office, looking about as to where to put it, Dr. Grosart motioned to the nearby table.

She asked Lily as to why she came and what was it that brought her there.

Lily, you can highlight the issues or detail one or two, this will give me an idea of your problems.

"Dr. Grosart, I'm not certain where to begin"

"What ever comes to mind, Lily."

"First, I guess, I have concerns about dark public places. I was attacked in a parking garage and had a long painful recovery. Then I lost my husband in a plane crash. And now I'm suffering the loss of a friend. I continually cry whenever I'm alone at home. Not in public, just at home."

"What do you mean a friend?"

"He and I were very close, in fact I thought one day we might marry."

"Oh, I see. What happened?"

"I'm not certain, but he simply left me without any notice or explanation. And now I just want to be alone, not really, but I'm not interested in another man."

"Well, Lily. I can certainly understand your feelings. Let's begin...."

After the hour had passed the door opened and Lily walked out. Therapy is somewhat tiring yet Lily looked very relieved and more at peace with herself. The therapy appeared to be helpful. Lily made another appointment and left. She said good night to Sherry as she walked out and closed the office door behind her.

Chapter 42

LILY THOUGHT ABOUT HER therapy sessions from time to time. As more time passed Lily tried to rationalize that Michael must be in Washington, still troubled over the office problems. Then Lily became most foolish thinking that it was the fantasy love making that sent him away, or was it the time she cried out "I love you", in the height of passion. Michael couldn't have been upset over that. No, it had to be something else.

Michael was most solicitous of his parents, perhaps one was ill or even worse, and he was too upset to call. Lily, most embarrassed asked some of Michael's friends if they had received word from him. She realized it was wrong to have asked; they all looked puzzled and shook their heads. It was better talking it over with the therapist.

Months passed and Cary intimated that "another woman" could have entered the picture and perhaps Michael didn't know how to tell her. Gosh, maybe he was telling me that when he said he wanted me to go on with life, and I was too foolish to know it. Thank goodness for my work. It helps keep my mind in the right direction. And thank goodness for my therapy.

All of my life, I felt the man that wants me will come for me.

I cannot reach out to him. When the door of time and providence opens, then it is the right time. I'll leave it in God's hands. My son, my friends, work, and volunteering will keep me busy.

Twenty-four months passed and Michael had not telephoned Lily and Lily would not take it upon herself to interfere with whatever was troubling him. She cared and was concerned, but would not present herself without being asked, no matter how much she longed to be with him. And then perhaps Michael had met someone else as Cary suggested.

Meanwhile Michael had taken a position within his father's automobile dealership in Dallas, Texas. He maintained the financial department and was, by all accounts, doing an outstanding job. With some regularity, Rosie and Freddie would come home to see both Michael and her grandparents. Michael was always lending a helping hand to both parents, and enjoyed his role as Uncle Michael with both Mary and Nancy's children whenever they were nearby. He loved seeing Rosie and being able to share in her life.

There was always a dance some place in Dallas, too. And Maria urged her son to go and have fun. Try to meet someone, she would say. One day Michael and his friend Angelo Monteiro stopped for a beer on their way home from the dealership. Angelo had sold cars for Michael's father for several years. In fact he was rather good at it. Angelo knew the business well and became their top salesman several years ago. Now Michael, being the financial officer at the dealership, worked very closely with Angelo. Both men were single, very handsome and enjoyed the ladies. He had introduced Michael to Molly Woods several months ago and they became an item soon there after. Michael enjoyed her company and they were frequently seen at the various dances. Angelo asked Michael how the relationship was going.

Michael ran his fingers through his hair and contemplated an answer. Finally he spoke, "Angelo, Molly is a very nice person, she suits me in some ways, but…and there is always a but, she is hinting that we should marry. I know we have been together now for nearly a year, but I am no way interested in marriage. I'm afraid she will be very hurt, however the time has come that I must tell her and be honest."

"Michael be certain she isn't the one before you drop her. She is a nice person and comes from a very fine family."

"Angelo, she *is* a beauty. I love her long dark hair and she has a pretty face and a great figure, but I am not in love with her."

"You still think about the girl in New England? What's her name?"

"Lily."

"Have you tried to contact her in all this time?"

"No, she may have met someone by now. I was so upset about my job and the employment problems that I just left without saying anything to her. You know Angelo she came from a very upper crust family and you know me, we are just the common blue collar workers.

"I doubt if she even thinks about me now. But getting back to Molly, I guess it is time to move on." The men finished their drink and parted for the evening.

Maria, Michael's mother knew how much Michael enjoyed family life and wondered when he would settle down again. Michael Sr. and Maria both noticed Michael didn't have the spark he used to have. Michael explained the same thing to his mother. Yes, he had had dates with many fine ladies. Let's see, Joan, Karen, Diane, Millie, Margaret, Sarah, and now Molly, "...but Mom, none I want to bring home to you."

And Michael knew none could ever compare to Lily. Whenever he thought of her, he could smell her perfume; think of her soft skin, and long to possess her.

Chapter 43

IT IS EARLY SUMMER and the lawns are manicured and the flowers in bloom. Overhead, the sun is shining and the sky clear and beautifully blue. Very little breeze is blowing in this warm temperature. It is never really hot in Vermont, even in July, but pleasantly warm.

Sitting outside on the steps of the hospital and feeling the warmth of the sun, finishing their box lunch before returning to the ward and their patients are two young women discussing their status.

In this area, the patients were mostly here for broken limbs in the winter and back problems from falling in the summer. Being a registered nurse is good solid employment, but these young ladies are beginning to think more of their personal lives than their career.

"You know Roz this job here is okay, you know just okay. St. Anne's Hospital has a good reputation, but our night life sucks… really sucks. I've been dating Harry for two years now and it just ain't going anywhere. First of all he's a nice enough guy, but doesn't make any money. With him, I'd be just like my mother, sewing the kitchen curtains."

"I know," said Corrine, "you want someone who can buy the kitchen curtains. Not me, I want some one who can hire a decorator and have money left over."

"Ya, that would be the day. Wouldn't we all want that, but who can you find here in this dinky town? I think you are lucky to have Harry, I haven't had a steady since we've arrived. Now wouldn't that be nice, having a regular boyfriend?"

"I saw the advertisement for nurses in Dallas. You know Roz, we can move just about any where we want. We don't have to stay here in Vermont!"

"Yes, and don't think I haven't been thinking about it," said Corrine. "I told my mother I was going away to find a rich husband. She laughed and said, 'you think in Vermont?' You know she was right."

Roz lifted her arm, adjusted her watch, and noted it was time to go back inside for the afternoon shift. "Come on Corrine, let's get going. Say how about going out tonight? Maybe to The Red Rooster for a drink or two?"

Corrine stood up, brushed the skirt of her uniform, tossed the remains of her lunch into the nearby trash can. "Yes, maybe your bit of fun sounds good. I'm going to take another look at the employment list around the country. Maybe St Louis would be a good spot."

When the workday was over, the girls met in the employee locker room. "Corrine did you see the Job Opportunity list on the board? What a great selection of cities. What do you think of New York City?"

"You've got to be kidding. The crowded place, over flowing with taxis and people who don't speak English?"

"Come on Corrine, you know better than to say that. Let me borrow your hairbrush. We'll have to talk about it later, let's get out of here."

The ladies, who had been great friends since their college days, were looking very attractive and feeling very light hearted as they started off to the Red Rooster. Because they knew they would be working at the same company, they had decided to share the cost of a car. They settled on a four door Chevrolet, just two years old purchased upon arriving in Stowe, Vermont. It worked out very well, keeping their expenses down and allowing them to save their money. The plan also had an ulterior motive. Both women planned to to save enough to have a lavishly expensive wedding when "Mr. Right" came along.

Both their mothers had encouraged their daughters to be nurses and to further their experiences by leaving home for employment. When the phone would ring in their apartment, either woman would answer and enjoy a conversation with the other one's mother. It was a relaxed relationship all the way around.

A friend called out to Roz just as they were entering the café part of the Red Rooster, "Hey there, come on over and sit with us."

"No thanks, maybe later. We want to get something to eat, we just got off work.".

Corrine nudged her as they walked toward the back of the room, "Roz, why did you do that? You know that Harry will come a long about 7:30 or 8:00."

"So What?"

"Well, he doesn't like them and I don't want to be in an argument all evening."

"Maybe that's what you should do, then just break it off with him."

"Why would I want to do that? You know there are very few men around here."

"Then let's get out of town."

"And go where?"

"Anywhere there are rich men!"

"Yeh, right. Well, let's eat now….what are you going to have?"

Later the women were sitting in the bar area and Corrine was waiting for Harry. "Corrine, how can you stand it, that man is always late?"

"Oh Roz don't start in again…"

"Well he is!"

"I know, but can't you just be nice tonight?"

"Okay, I will be nice if when we get home you'll put some

serious thought into getting out of here. I mean out of this town and this state."

"Okay, okay. Look Harry's coming in now. Be nice."

The park was a good three mile walk. The flowers were pretty almost bouncing their heads as the women walked past. Corrine was dressed in summer slacks and a sleeveless blouse and Roz was wearing pale green shorts and a tee shirt, both in tennis shoes. They were walking briskly, not conversing, but focusing on their breathing and their pace. They had talked late into the night Friday and finally agreed this week they would give two weeks notice at St. Anne's Hospital. They agreed to take the following week and pack up and map out their new adventure. They were moving to Dallas, Texas. Employment was wide open and they had saved enough in the two years to split the money and each have their own apartment or even buy into their own condominium. The friendship was strong, they were very comfortable with each other. Although they would continue to travel together, they would establish separate quarters. Their main purpose in moving was to find a "Mr. Right", and hopefully a rich Mr. Right.

"Corrine, I'm getting tired of this traveling. Even if we stay a day or two in various cities along the way, let's slow the pace down a bit. We've gone from highway 91 to 95 and now we cut across to Texas."

"I know Roz, you get bored easily. Two or three more days and we shall arrive in our new city, Dallas. All this sunshine is great. I was getting a bit tired of the cold winters and cool summers of Vermont. How about you?"

"Yes, I've had enough of Vermont. I like the idea of the big city effect now."

The Sheraton Hotel at Market Center located on Stemmons Freeway near Market Center Boulevard was lovely. Swimming in the outdoor pool was most relaxing, the meetings with the realtor were fruitful. Before they knew it, each woman was decorating her new home and shortly they would on duty at the local hospital. But Corrine needed her own car.

One day at the dealership, all the salesmen were attending their usual Monday morning meeting when the door opened and Michael heard this lovely voice with a bit of an English accent. He quickly left his desk and went to the showroom. There was a very striking young lady, a wind blown disheveled blonde somewhat glamorous in a very appealing way. Inviting was the word one might use to describe her.

"Hi, may I help you?"

"Yes, I'm looking for a car, a new Buick, I think. I saw the advertisement and thought it looked a bit sporty." As she spoke her smile came through and framed her white teeth.

"And you are?"

"Oh, call me Corrine"

"Well Corrine, I'm Michael and the salesmen are all in a meeting, I can get one for you."

"Oh, can you help me?"

"Yes, I'll tell the girls in the office that I'll be out on the lot, excuse me for just a moment."

Michael returned, spend an enjoyable time with Corrine, selling her a new beautiful blue, sports model Buick.

When he finished the paperwork he had a complete inventory of her status, single, a registered nurse and footloose and fancy free as some would say. And he had a date for dinner the following Saturday evening. One could hear him humming most of the day.

Saturday arrived and so did Michael. He arrived sharply at seven o'clock. He looked around, evaluating the surroundings. It certainly was upper middle class. He rang the bell, shortly the glamorous blonde appeared. Corrine invited him in to see her lovely condominium.

Her new dog "Topsy" jumped about and Michael enjoyed him. Corrine offered Michael a glass of Merlot and they sat and exchanged light conversation. It was easy for Michael to see that Corrine had a flare for decorating and apparently enjoyed reading. There were many books, mostly mysteries and women's magazines. Following discussing the weather and their positions of employment Michael could see her coat on a nearby chair. As he reached for the coat he assisted her in putting it on.

"Here in Dallas one may need a wrap for the evening, but our weather isn't like New England."

The comment surprised Michael, "Have you been to New England?" he asked.

"Oh, yes, I was in Vermont for two years."

"How did you like it?"

"Oh, the spring, summer and fall seasons are great, but the winter was too cold for me. I enjoyed some of the winter sports, skating and skiing, but not a lot of that either."

And with that, the couple closed the door behind them, settled down in the car and was off to one of Michael's favorite restaurants. The restaurant was in a private club, The Q Club, one Michael frequented. It was as if his car knew the way, this lovely evening. The valet opened the door, taking his keys and the captain opened the door for the attractive couple. Michael was greeted as usual and quickly seated at his usual table. Corrine was taking note of the casualness with which Michael handled every thing. Corrine loved having her chair pulled out for her by the staff. Michael requested a staff member place her wrap in the coat room. Wine was ordered.

"Corrine you mentioned New England, My daughter Rosie graduated from Yale"

"Oh, how nice.

"Yes the graduation was quite an affair."

"Tell me about it, Michael."

"Well, she had invited her boyfriend Freddie, her mother and her Uncle Eddie to attend. We all came from different directions, but made it there. I had given her carte blanche for her outfits for the various affairs. She giggled when it came to the day. All that money for a dress and the cap and gown covered everything!" he paused, remembering her laughter when she realized it.

Her grandparents did not actually attend the ceremony since they were hosting a party for her back in Dallas. The party included all of her former school friends and of course the family members. A new red convertible was her gift. Her only disappointment was that Jim, a friend of hers from Boston, was busy with his exams and couldn't attend. Rosie had invited both Jim and another friend. I think perhaps his girl, whom I have never met. Rosie had met her on several occasions, and really liked her. Jim sent flowers and a note. Rosie considered Jim a good friend even if he was a year behind her in school." "So you see, I've been to New England, too."

"Michael, there is a great difference in Connecticut where Yale is and Vermont."

"Yes, I'm sure, shall we order?"

The evening went well and Michael knew he would continue to see Corrine.

Chapter 44

THE NEXT MORNING CORRINE was on the phone to her friend Rosalind. They had gone to nursing school together. Actually it was a college program at the state University in Indiana. Both enjoyed their career at the local hospital in Dallas.

"Roz, I've got one!!, I've got one!!"

"What do you mean, Corrine?"

"Rosalind. why did we choose Dallas to work in?"

"You only call me that when you are really serious. Oh, I don't know."

Yes you do! Remember our plan to get a rich one?"

"Oh, ya, that's right. Well who is it?"

"Remember the picture of the man that spoke to the Rotary? Well, I went to the Buick Dealership to see about a used car. And guess what…he was there and so I had to buy a new car. I wanted to look as if I were in his class. And it worked! He invited me out. So last night we went to his Club for dinner. It was sooo nice. I think he owns the dealership or is a manager or something."

"Great, did he kiss you good night or anything?"

"No, but give me time and I'll get him. By the way do you still see Henry?"

"Corrine, last night Minnie and I went to the Sheraton for a drink after work. We ere sitting at the bar and a good looking fellow started talking to us. He lives up north in Maryland. He said he owns a string of Italian restaurants and is here for a three day meeting of restaurant owners. He said he used to live here as a kid. I guess most of the family moved away after his grandfather died."

"Did he say his name?

"Yes, it was something like Norman, no, Norbert. The last was a real Italian one, I think it was Riccardi or something like that. I think it was "Norbert Riccardi and he said he had an old classmate still living here. They had had lunch earlier that day. You'll never guess what his name was. Michael Lopez."

"Really, small wonders. Gosh Roz, too bad a fellow that rich doesn't live around here.

"Oh, forget it, he was married and had kids. But boy was he rich. But as far as Henry goes, he is cheap. You know, but nothing there. I still pay my way."

"Roz you have to get someone else, Henry is just cheap".

"Whoops, there is the door bell. I got to go. See you later."

Chapter 45

IN ANOTHER PART OF Dallas…

"Hey Angelo, after church do you want to play a round of golf?

"Okay, I'll call the club and get us a tee time, how about 1:30? Okay, I'll see you there."

Michael's parents always went to the 10:00 service and sat next to Rosie and Michael. Rosie and Michael's attendance was almost as regular as his parent's. Following the service they usually went to the Buttonwood Grille for breakfast.

"Dad, you can have my extra toast."

"Thank you sweetheart."

"Grandma could we go to the new store, Lowes? This afternoon, please?"

"Of course Rosie, that is if Grandpa doesn't need us."

"No, no, you two go along. I've things to do."

"What things Grandpa? Read the paper or take a nap?" Rosie said lovingly. Everyone else laughed and the plans seem to fall in place.

Michael drove the super deluxe edition of the Buick convertible to the Club house, enjoying the admiring looks. He was almost on the golf course when he heard Angelo's voice.

"Hey, big buddy, get your clubs and golf shoes and I'll get us a golf cart. It is a good course and a long one. Hurry up."

"Okay, Angelo, give me a minute and I'll be right there."

"Angelo hung around the first tee talking to the foursome teeing off."Michael walked over to join him and soon they were teeing off.

"Good shot, Michael, but I think I can beat you today."

"Since when?"

"Well, I've been taking a few lessons from the pro here."

"Oh, how is he? Good?"

"Yes, I like him. You should give him a try. Your putting could use it."

"Yes, maybe I will."

"Angelo did I tell you about my recent date?"

"Oh, that's right. You stopped going out with Molly a while ago. So the well isn't dry, huh? Angelo said, laughing at Michael's constant stream of choices.

"No, no. This is a cute red head named Corrine, could be straight from Ireland."

"Nice huh?"

"Yes, but watch your shot or you're going to be in the sand trap." And the men continued the game for eighteen holes. They ended up in the lounge for a drink or two when Angelo revived interest in Michael's recent date.

"Michael, you say this girl is kind of cute, maybe she has a sister."

"No Angelo, I got the lowdown on her when I sold her a car."

"She bought it from you? I thought you were the finance man there."

"I am, but everyone was busy, so since she was so cute...hey why not?"

"Okay, so how did the date go? Did she ask you in?"

"No, of course not. I think she read a how-to book on first dates or something, but time will tell."

"Hey, I got to go. See you at the dealership."

Chapter 46

TWO WEEKS LATER, MICHAEL received a phone call at work. It was Corrine. Michael had not contacted her and he could tell she was concerned. Michael immediately understood and quickly asked to see her the following Saturday evening. He promised to call her mid week to formalize the plans.

Corrine happily hung up the phone.

After work, Michael had promised his sister Nancy he would stop by and talk about an anniversary party being planned for their parents. Nancy and Mary wanted to make it a grand time. Michael wanted to be certain that it would take place when Rosie would be home from school. Eddie paid part of the expenses, but didn't care about the planning. He felt the sisters could handle it. They could and they did.

The Theater Guild was presenting a stage play, Oscar Wilde's, "Our Town" with Matt Dillon in the lead. Michael purchased tickets and called Corrine to go. She was delighted.

The evening arrived and Michael rang the door bell. "Michael is that you? Come right up."

"Oh, Michael it is good to see you. How do you like my new dress? Nice, huh?"

"Yes, Corrine, but we'd better go, the play starts exactly at 8:00 and we will have a hard time being seated after."

During the intermission, Michael purchased a non alcoholic drink for them when he looked up. He was surprised to see someone he recognized But from where? She smiled directly at him. He smiled back and handed Corrine her drink. Corrine noticed the expression on his face and asked "Michael what is it? Who is that lady?"

All of a sudden, Michael realized who it was. He excused himself from Corrine and walked directly to the lady. "Hello, Nicole, how are you?"

"Michael I saw you, and would know you any place. You look the same."

"Come now, Nicole, it has been quite a while since we were in Paris."

"Yes, it has been more than a few years. Imagine seeing you here! How are you doing? Are you married? Do you have a family?"

"Nicole, I was married, and divorced now. But I do have a lovely daughter, Rosie. She attends Yale University in Connecticut.

"Oh here comes my husband now. John I'd like you to meet Michael. We met while we both were in Paris, way back then. He was a Marine and I work in the Embassy. Those were the days, many years ago, when we were young."

"Nice to meet you Michael, but I think the play is about to start."

John took Nicole's arm and started towards the aisle and Michael quickly returned to Corrine. When the play was over Corrine began talking about the last act of the play while Michael's eyes searched the crowd for another glimpse of Nicole. He thought of Nicole and wondered if he would accidentally meet her again. He wondered about her marriage, if she had children, was Dallas a vacation or did she live there. If he had only gotten her last name, Corrine is nice, but Nicole was exceptional, he thought.

Angelo and Michael were at the little bar near the park, not far from the dealership. "Angelo, I never would have believed it, I ran into a girl I used to date when I was just a kid...in the Marines, over in France, Paris to be exact."

"Michael you are the luckiest guy. Now you can replace that Lily."

"No Angelo. First of all, no one can replace Lily and besides she was with her husband. She sure looked great. What a great coincidence. I hadn't thought of her in years and there she was."

"Where did you bump into her?

"Oh, I had taken Corrine to a play and at intermission there stood Nicole. But her husband came out of the men's room and whisked her away. I never got any information at all. Oh, well, that is the way things go."

"Yes, I guess you are right."

"By the way how are things going with Corrine?"

"Oh, we've been out a couple three times I guess."

"Not a big deal though."

A couple of weeks later Michael need some shaving cream and stopped at the local drug store on his way home from work. He parked and entered the store. As he walked to the specific area he recognized John.

"Well, hello, John. Remember me? Nicole's friend, from the play?"

"Oh, yes, hello Michael, I guess we both need a shave." they both laughed.

"John I don't remember your last name."

"Oh, it is Dunnham, John Dunnham."

"John are you from here, here in Dallas?"

"No, we live in Ohio, Nicole and I are visiting my sister, she lives here.

"Oh, well before you and Nicole go back home, maybe my girlfriend and I could take you two out to dinner some evening.:

"Well thank you Michael, but we leave tomorrow and have plans for this evening. Did Nicole mention we have a set of twins, twin boys. One is in veterinarian school and the other is into electrical engineering. But one is Michael the other is Marvin. Nicole said Marvin was after my dad but Michael was after an old friend. Maybe I've just met the old friend.

Michael laughed and looked a bit flustered, but quickly said, "John, I doubt that it was me."

"I bet it is," Michael thought.

At the counter with their shaving cream in hand, the men shook hands and said goodbye. In the car driving home Michael thought about the coincidence of meeting Nicole. It was fun seeing an old girlfriend, but only one lady has my heart. I wonder what Lily is doing about now...

Chapter 47

"CARY, JIM AND I were talking about his graduation last evening. It is so nice to have him home, even if only for a little while. Well, we were discussing the graduation party. It hardly seems possible the four years have gone so fast."

"Lily it's so unfair that the graduation invitations are for parents only. What are you going to do with so many family members?"

"Oh, Jim's girlfriend, Sherry's parents are attending and have asked me to sit with them and since the party will be held back in California, that makes sense."

"Oh, at your parent's place?"

"Oh, no, both Sherry's parents and mine belong to the same club, so that is where we will host a joint party. I know it will be large, but that is what Jim and Sherry want. So why not?"

"It sounds great, I'm happy for you and the kids."

Later that evening Jim shared his news with his mother. "Mom it is no surprise to you that Sherry and I want to go on to graduate school. We have applied and have both been accepted at University of California, Berkley. Both of us will be in California's top school for Business Administration!"

"Wouldn't you and Sherry rather go to a school in the Boston area?

"I would be glad to since it is closer to you, but Sherry had promised her mom that she would return to the California area."

"Oh, I see. Well Jim you are old enough to make your own plans. And that sounds like a good one."

"Mom, I have one more thing to ask you."

"What Son?"

Well, - well, the next surprise is that I want to marry Sherry."

"Jimmy, that is no surprise to me at all. How wonderful! You two have been together for a long time, so it seems you both know each other and I'm sure it will work out for you both. You know marriage in this family is a "forever" thing."

"Yes, Mom I know, so does Sherry. That's one of the things we both agree on."

"What would you think of me giving Sherry your engagement ring?"

"Jim that is a great idea. I'll get it out of the safety deposit box whenever you like. Do you have a plan?"

"She knows about my popping the question, I thought perhaps at the graduation party, what do you think?"

"Great idea, but you might want to tell her ahead of time that it was my ring from your father. She may not like that idea."

"Good idea, I wanted to ask you first. Are you real certain you don't mind?"

"Son, that ring would have gone to your eldest daughter, that is if you should have one, so you can call it a family inheritance."

Jim put his arms around his Mother and hugged her, "Thank you very much."

The next day Jim was happily whistling a tune and carefully arranging his room. After lunch, Jim planned on talking to Sherry. She had gone ahead and was home with her parents. They had been busy talking about the plans for the party. The telephone broke into the silence. "It is for me Mom. Hi honey, how is everything?"

"Sherry, you know I love you and we plan to announce our engagement at the party."

"Yes, Jim, is everything okay there with your mom?"

"It couldn't be better. Sherry, I have to ask you something. Now it is okay either way, yes or no, it won't matter to me.

"What is it Jim?"

"I plan to give you a ring and announce the engagement at the party."

"Yes, we agreed on that."

"Well, would it be okay with you I gave you the ring that my father had selected for my mother. It is a beautiful three carat yellow gold ring. Now if you don't want it, it is okay."

"Oh, Jim" Sherry said in a very soft voice, and began to cry.

"Oh, Sherry, I'm sorry I'll buy you one of your own."

"No, no, Jim, I'm crying because I am so happy and proud you and that your Mother would like me to have such a beautiful ring, knowing how much it meant to her."

"Are you sure?"

"Oh, yes my darling, yes, yes. I couldn't be happier."

"Alright if you really mean it, then I shall give it to you when we announce our engagement at the party."

"Jim you are truly thoughtful, I love you"

"I love you too, darling."

Jim hung up the telephone and smiled thinking that he couldn't wait to share this conversation with his mother.

Chapter 48

THE WORKDAY HAD ENDED with Lily quietly letting the conditions of the will settle in her mind. Her car was garaged and since Lily enjoyed walking to the nearby park, the car would not be used for the rest of the evening. As she walked next door, she admired the neighborhood and her own house in particular.

The sun was still out, the sky so blue and a gentle hum from the cars covered the other street sounds. Lily looked at the yellow flowers near the door. She again admired her new Brahmin bag as she opened it and reached for the door key. Lily never tired of the feeling of stepping into the room with the sun light coming through the sheer curtains. It felt very much like home. Life was becoming much better. She was learning life is the dancer and she is simply the dance.

The next morning, Lily finished her coffee, after having dressed with her usual impeccable taste. She picked up her notes, turned the key in the lock, and left the house. She loved the drive to work, it was long enough to enjoy and short enough not to be late. Having her own parking space in the garage near the law offices was a real benefit. It was a quick trip on the elevator up to the third floor with the nice floating elevator music. Jamie, who always looked the same, was in the same good mood as every day. What a gem. She quickly and most efficiently answered each call, never a sharp or frustrated tone.

"Good morning Mrs. Arnold."

"Good morning Jaime"

"Busy day already"

"Yes, and I have a Mr. Hollander on the line"

"Can you take him, Lily?" She frowned, raised her eyebrows, hesitatingly said "Yes, ok."

"Who is Mr. Hollander, Jaime?" The question went unanswered.

Whenever Jaime called you by your first name, it usually had to do with a personal favor. Lily learned this early on.

"Of course, Jaime. Just give me a minute and then put him through."

Lily hurried to her office, hanging up her coat, shoving her bag in the closet, and she reached for the telephone.

"Good morning Mr. Hollander, what can I help you with today?"

"Oh, yes, this is about a lease on one of your buildings?"

"Would it be best if you make an appointment and come to the office?

"Bring whatever paperwork you have."

"Yes, thank you, one o'clock today would be fine. We had a cancellation yesterday, so that will work out."

If Cary wasn't so busy she could fill me in on Mr. Hollander. He certainly sounded impatient. Lily continued to answer the client calls throughout the morning and work on a draft of Mrs. Davis' will. Realizing she had worked through lunch and Mr. Hollander would soon arrive, she was riffling through her desk drawer when she found a small package of cheese crackers. Swallowing the last bite and a long sip of coffee she watched the door knob turn. It was Mr. Hollander.

"I'm sorry if I just came in, but the receptionist was out of her area and I saw your name on the door." Watching Lily wipe her lips from the crackers and coffee, he commented," Hope that isn't your lunch!" When she nodded, he said, "I'll make up for it next time."

Lily was somewhat surprised, but rather intrigued by the man standing in front of her desk. She stood up and extended her hand to his.

"Excuse me, I'm being rude. I'm Ron Hollander, and you must be Attorney Arnold." he said as he reached to shake hands with Lily. Her hand was soft and warm, yet she had a firm handshake. His eyes quickly surveyed the room, blue oriental rug, antique oak desk, classic books on the shelf, Steinbeck, one of my favorite authors, two hangings, one hanging of modern art and a nice rendition of a Picasso, ... she looks like money. A large room with plenty of space, a conference table and chairs, hmm…She must be a savvy lawyer.

Lily sat comfortably behind the desk with her legs crossed and both hands on the desk, peering directly at Ron. Lily consciously stayed very still, never adjusting her clothes or touching her hair when she was with a client or in court. Ron noticed that she was very attractive, but also extremely professional.

She began assessing Ron Hollander, taking in everything about him. Lily noted a very attractive man, well dressed in an expensively made suit, in excellent physical shape, balding, but with a wonderful smile. She noticed his hands, strong and neatly manicured. His Rolex glinted in the sunlight as he comfortably placed his hands on the chair arms. He was in command, she thought, relaxed, but in control.

Mr. Hollander paused, and Lily smiled back as she swept a lock of blond hair across her forehead. "Please sit down Mr. Hollander."

"Call me Ron"

"Thank you, you may call me Lily."

As Ron sat down he wondered, "Can a lady as lovely as this one also be as bright and intelligent as they say?" Lily's thoughts were very similar regarding Ron. He was handsome, tall, well built and certainly self assured in all matters, almost arrogant.

Ron quickly stated his case, "My building on Central Avenue has been vacant for a couple of months. My agency has located a new lessee and I understand that company has been difficult to work with. I need a lease."

"Ron, if the company is as difficult as you say," said Lily, "then you need an iron clad lease."

Thirty minutes later, his business was completed. All the while, Ron became most aware that Lily was not only beautiful, but amazingly intelligent. Ron remembered his friend Al suggested he employ Lily as his attorney, but didn't really let on about how beautiful she was. "I'll have to tell Al he must be blind," Ron was thinking as he completed the office visit."

Chapter 49

As soon as Ron left, Lily went to into Cary's office, eager to compare notes. She went back to Jaime and questioned her, but then saw Cary coming down the hall. "Hey, Cary, I was looking for you." Lily said. The two women went into Cary's office and Lily closed the door behind them. Cary started talking about the divorce case that was coming up. "This couple has been haggling over the property almost two years. I'm beginning to think they don't really want a divorce. Oh well, they want the service and that's what we get paid for," Cary said after taking a deep breath. Lily listened for a few minutes and started chuckling to herself.

"Now what is it Lily?"

"Tell me about Ron Hollander."

"What about him?" she asked. "Let's see, he is a good business man, about your age, widowed, and come to think of it, a ballroom dancer like you. I'm surprised you haven't met him at one of your dances."

"Really? No I haven't, but he seems very interesting."

Ron went directly to the construction site looking for Al. Stepping over the debris and fragments of the job, while trying to keep his footing he called out "Hey, where is big Al?"

"Al Sheffield? He's in the office trailer, I think"

Ron walked over to the laborer who continued to answer, "Otherwise he is out for a late lunch."

"Okay, thanks." Ron said, reaching for his ringing phone. Flipping his phone open, he could see it was Al looking for him. On the construction site the office is frequently a house trailer turned into an office for the supervisor of the job.

Al said, "So you went to the law offices?"

"Yes and why didn't you tell me about her?"

"What's to tell, you have to see her, and in action. Have you ever seen someone look like that and be that smart?"

"You're right Al and I'm going to date her if she is single."

"Hey wait a minute. What about Amazing Grace? That poor soul. You know who I mean."

"Why do you keep calling her Amazing Grace? There is nothing amazing about her."

"Oh, you've got to be kidding, Ron. Everyone knows when she is in town. She acts as if she is your one and only. Doesn't she know that when she is out of town you date and bed them all?"

Ron laughed, "Yes, you're right, Grace is amazing that way."

"But this Lily is something else," Ron said very slowly and somewhat thoughtfully. "This one is different."

"You can say that again," Al shaking his head, "but don't try funny stuff with her. She is out of your league and way ahead of you."

"Yes, Al, I believe you are right."

"That I know for sure. She is single, her husband was killed in a plane crash, and she has a son in college. I understand she seldom dates, but enjoys ballroom dancing."

"Well, that's interesting. I go to a lot of those dances. I've never seen her there before."

"Well, look around, I'm sure she goes." Maybe you're too interested in you know who. What's Amazing Grace's real name?"

"You mean Grace Carlson?"

"Yes, that's her real name. You keep telling me that for the last four years you have repeatedly asked her if she wanted to make your relationship in to a regular one…whatever you call it."

"Yes, and she keeps telling me 'Hell no!'" Ron laughed.

"One of these days, she's going to say 'Yes' and then what will you do?

"Probably run like hell. I'm not one to settle down, you know that."

"Well, you like playing with fire. I don't think this one, this lawyer lady is game playing. Then what will you do?"

Ron looked around the room, closed his eyes a moment and listened to his friend.

"No Ron, I mean it, you cannot seem to make up your mind. Do you want someone...the same someone in your life?"

Cutting Al short, Ron asked, "What do you mean, I've got lots of someones, and then I've always got Grace. Not that we are committed, but it works for us. We are together when we are together and with others when we aren't together...besides who cares?"

"That is just what I mean Ron, this woman is different."

"Oh, come on Al, they are all that way. I'd even bet you I can have her."

"Then what, Ron? Then you'll tell her it is just a joke? Well, good luck with that. Whatever you do...that's your thing."

"Don't worry Al, I keep Grace right where I want her. I've told her that she is the only one, sooo I have to be careful that she doesn't catch me with anyone else. She knows that I date others, but pretends I don't."

Ron leaned back into his seat and put his feet up, crossing them at the ankles. "Most of the time she is fun and laughs easily. But when she gets angry, watch out. She likes her out of town trips with her friends and runs right back to me. What have I to complain about?"

"Ron, you have dated many women since your wife died, maybe life is going to change for you. Who knows, maybe you and this lawyer will have more in common than just ballroom dancing."

Dancing in the Rain

Wanting to change the subject, Ron asked "Al, how is Linda?"

"Oh, the wifey is just fine. Now I've got to get busy. Think about what I said. She is a great gal from what I've heard...a real lady."

Ron precariously picked his way around the construction site and walked to his car. Later that day, walking in front of one of his owned buildings, he was measuring the actual space in footsteps. A store owner came out and began a friendly conversation wanting Ron to notice him. Ron acknowledged the book store owner, looked at his watch and was anxious to end the business day.

All the way home, he was thinking about the gorgeous lady lawyer. Ron was so busy thinking about her he nearly took a wrong turn. "Wow, I don't remember when I've done that before. There's something different about this one already."

Chapter 50

RON DROVE UP THE driveway to his house. He left the car in the driveway and opened the back door. His basset hound ran to meet him and jumped, happily wagging his tail and giving a soft bark as Ron reached down and scratched "Max" behind the ear. "Good boy, down boy, atta boy" Ron said as he reached for the mail. Stacking it on the credenza he left the keys as well and went directly to the liquor cabinet. Ron removed his jacket and loosened his tie, placing both on the nearby chair. Selecting a glass, Ron held it up to the light. The sun shining through the window was so comforting. He smiled as he poured himself a glass of "two buck Chuck" and took a large sip of Merlot.

He sat down in a comfortable chair, looked around the familiar room and closed his eyes for a short time. The telephone rang, startling Ron. "Wrong number. Guess it's time to get going. Well, I'll try the dance hall in Braintree. Maybe Ms. Arnold will be there and maybe she won't. There are some nice gals who can dance there anyway," Ron told himself. "A bite to eat, a shower, shave and now - what to wear? Ah, the pink shirt with the bold tie. Yup, that will do just fine." He finished dressing and admired himself in the hall mirror. Turning his mind to dinner, he pondering what he had to fix.

He looked around in the fridge and pulled out the roasted chicken. Ellen is not only a great housekeeper, but a really good cook. Who needs a wife? She takes care of me just like a mother and cleans the house. Roasted chicken and chocolate cake... He sliced off some of the chicken and made his sandwich, wheat bread, light on the mayo, a bit of lettuce and a large glass of orange juice. There, that will keep me for the evening. Unless some wee lassie wants to take me home and cook for me. He laughed quietly at the thought. But it probably won't be my lawyer friend. Now, time to get going.

Chapter 51

"WHAT THE HECK, THE sun was out and now it is raining. Some spring we are having." Ron thought as he backed the car out of the driveway. The sound of the rain on the roof of his Lexus was not comforting, nor the squeak of the windshield wipers. Even the hissing of the street water wore on his patience as the car sped along. The radio was soft, too soft to be in chorus with the cold rainy weather. Ron thought to himself, "Thank God the police aren't out tonight; driving in this pouring rain is bad enough. I've got to get new windshield wipers. These just don't keep the view clear. Trying to get to a dance before eight o'clock is a real bitch. Every time I look at this damn speedometer it is over 80."

The first dance of the evening is almost as important as the last, and I want to know if she is there. Of course, she'll be there, that is silly. At last, oh, damn the parking lot is full. I would think she might park on the side under the street light. Let's see, parking stickers on the plate from her building would show up. Oh, there it is, her Lexus right under the light. She is so damn smart doing that. It is safer for both the car and herself. Oh, yes, it seems to me that Al said she was assaulted many years ago and never forgets. How could some bastard do that to such a lady...?

As Ron reached into his pocket he thought, "Now what did I do with my money? Going to these dances was not expensive, but it all adds up." The music snaked out of the building. His huge hand pressed the latch on the massive door, easily opening it. Although his stature was impressive, he was surprisingly light on his feet and really enjoyed the dancing as well as the socialization. Just inside, the diminutive, middle aged cashier was standing, waiting to make change when necessary. She recognized Ron, smiled and exchanged pleasantries. He was hurried; however he enjoyed giving the impression of being in control. Cool man Ron with the ladies.

He walked into the establishment sensing the music warming the room to the delight of the dancers. The lights were dimmed in the room, the dance had started. "This carpeted area keeps the dance floor clean or so they think, but look at it now." He looked around at the various people sitting at the tables first and then spotted his usual place among the simple but empty tables and wrought iron chairs. Ron hung his jacket on the back of the chair. Some left their coats in the coat check; others placed it on the back of the chair. He began replacing his shoes with "dance shoes."

Ron was a pretty good dancer and attributed it to the smooth soft leather of his shoes. His eyes were checking out the women sitting, the one he needed to start the dancing. He casually appeared to look over the crowd of dancing couples. Suddenly, Ron spotted her dancing. He went to the bar and ordered a drink. He knew all too well how to play the part and appear confident. Sipping it first, then sitting it down he walked towards a woman nicely dressed in beige slacks and a not too tight sweater, rather tall. She appeared very pleased when he offered her his hand. They walked towards the opposite end of the dance floor, opposite of where Lily was dancing. Soon he was in her line of vision. He waited until she saw him, she smiled, and then he smiled back.

Chapter 52

"WELL HELLO LILY ARNOLD. What a nice surprise meeting you here. Would you like to dance? I believe it is a waltz."

"Yes, thank you."

Ron reached for her as they approached the dance area. As the music began, Ron thought about his partner, "I'm attracted to her. I don't know why. Or maybe I do... She fits in my arms, she dances better than most, and yet she seems to be so damn casual. I suppose it is all business to her. She will learn about my relationship with Grace, but not tonight. Besides, Grace won't be back for a while anyway."

The couple quietly danced, smoothly, so well, as if she were simply his shadow. That evening, the music and the good time came to an end all too quickly. "Lily would you like to dance again tomorrow evening? There is a good dance in Worcester."

"Perhaps, Ron, but if I go, I'll just meet you there. My schedule is demanding. I have enough paperwork to keep me busy and people keep giving me more." They both laughed and Ron walked Lily to her car. He opened the car door and helped her in. He wanted to kiss her good night, but didn't. He waited until she drove away, hoping tomorrow would come soon. Having to think ahead this much was new to him, but how he loved a challenge – and Lily was just the kind of challenge he loved.

Chapter 53

THE NEXT DAY IN the office, Lily was anxious to talk to Cary about the previous night's events. At first Cary asked questions about the dance. Good music? Good dancers? Much of a crowd? Lily answered each question anticipating Cary's next.

Finally Lily said, "Cary, you'll never guess who showed up at the dance - Ron Hollander."

"Really? Our Mr. Hollander?" Cary said with great surprise.

"Yes, and Cary he is a good dancer."

"Oh, you danced with him?"

"Yes, several times."

"Lily, I hope you won't mind me saying this, but I understand he dates and flirts a lot and has been known to date a certain woman."

"Oh, I can easily imagine that."

"Lily I understand he doesn't play for keeps, so be careful."

"Oh Cary, thank you, but I'm only there to have fun, so don't worry."

"You've dated so few men, I do worry about you."

Lily gave Cary a hug and started back to her office. "Cary I'm trying out my new slogan, 'Wish it, Dream it and Do it'. You know my job is my life."

"Yes, your job, your house and your son. Well, just keep your priorities straight and you'll be fine."

"I will, but I think it's time to wish and dream again."

Chapter 54

THE NEXT DAY AT the office a young lady appeared asking if there was an attorney named Lily. Jamie noticed something in her voice and demeanor which startled her. She had become an excellent judge of character, and knew there was something very serious going on with this girl. She got up off her chair and walked the young lady to Lily's door. A soft knock brought Lily's voice saying, "Come in." Jaime quickly introduced Miss Waters.

"Won't you please sit down?" Lily asked.

Miss Waters appeared quite young, perhaps even sixteen and many months pregnant. Soon the motherly instinct came forward as Lily asked her name and within a few minutes it became Lily and Donna. Donna didn't quite know how to tell her story.

"You see I am pregnant and not married."

"Oh, a boyfriend from school?"

"No, I went out with a service man."

"Oh, what branch."

"What do you mean?"

"Which branch of service, Air Force, Army, Navy, Marines, Coast Guard?"

The young lady quietly answered, "I think it was the Coast Guard."

Lily questioned her more than once regarding a detail to ascertain the information. Donna indicated that the father of the child she was carrying was a serviceman's child. Donna said she didn't know how to get in touch with him and wanted Lily's help. And yet Lily knew something wasn't quite right about it. Something more was wrong.

This type of work wasn't the norm for Lily's firm, in fact it probably was more of a social worker's job, but something didn't ring true. She questioned Donna for some time. Finally Lily posed the question, "Could this possibly be anyone else's child?" and Donna began crying.

"What really is the matter Donna? Why did you really come to see me?"

She handed Donna another tissue. Donna finally stopped her crying so Lily could understand her problem. "My step father simply won't leave me alone and my mother doesn't believe me."

"I don't know what to do."

Lily took a deep breath and sat back in her chair.

"How long has this been going on?

"For over a year now."

"And you have informed your Mother? Have you told anyone else?

"My best friend, Elsie knows and she looked up in the phone book and found your name. That is how I found you."

"Well, Donna we have some work to do. I certainly will help you as much as I can."

They talked a while longer and Lily told Donna to make another appointment. Lily sat back and took a deep breath. She needed to consult with a partner to find out the procedure for pro bono cases. "Wills, leases and now incest, only God knows what is next', thought Lily.

"Alright, Donna. I have to talk with my research assistant, Henry, and then I'll have some answers for you." she said as she handed her a card. "Call me. We need to get this resolved and soon," she said and got up and put her arm around Donna and walked her to the door.

As she drove, her mind began to relax and clear of the day's issues. The sun was going down, leaving the air slightly cooler. The leaves on the trees were rustling and the drive was rather quiet. "I have so much to be thankful for," thought Lily. "God has blessed me again. He gave me a wonderful childhood, a wonderful husband and son, and now a new life."

"Maybe I'll call the girls to play bridge tonight."

Chapter 55

THE FOLLOWING DAY IN Cary's office, once again she cautioned Lily to remember Mr. Hollander was a flirt and enjoyed the company of many women. "He may mean what he is saying at the moment, but may easily repeat the same words to the next woman the next day." "Please Lily don't get carried away with his attentions." Lily appeared to listen to Cary's words.

In her office, a mother and daughter were waiting. As Lily walked in, she closed the door behind her. Donna introduced her mother as "Sylvia Waters, my Mother".

Lily shook hands and took her positioned seat behind the desk.

"What is this all about?" asked Mrs. Water. "Donna insisted I stay out of work to be here today for this appointment. Is Donna in trouble or something?"

Lily didn't answer the woman, but instead turned to her client. "Donna how would you like this meeting to go? Do you want to explain to your mother why we are here?"

Donna started to cry, "I don't think she will believe me. She wants him to marry her."

"Well, Mrs. Waters, I am just going to have to be blunt with you. I'm sorry to say this, but your fiancé has been mistreating your daughter."

"What do you mean? They seem to get along just fine," she said, looking at first one and then the other. "In fact Steven acts like he is her stepfather already. What are you trying to say?"

"I'm afraid your fiancé is not acting like any kind of father. Do you realize that your daughter is pregnant?"

"My God, Donna, what are you thinking? What have you been doing, sneaking around behind my back? What boy did this?"

"Mother it wasn't any boy, it..." she looked at Lily, trying to get enough courage to form the words. "it was Steven."

Mrs. Waters slapped Donna across the face screaming at her, "What are you saying? What are you trying to do? How could you do this to me?"

"Mother it was him, not me. This isn't my fault. Lily, Ms. Arnold, tell her."

Lily walked around the desk to calm the situation. "Mrs. Waters, sit down. I know this is a shock, but what she is saying is absolutely true. This is why I thought it best to tell you here so you can have a chance to process these charges. You are going to have to accept it and will have to make arrangements to keep your daughter safe. I am about to have Donna press charges of child molestation and rape."

"Ms. Austin! I cannot believe any thing like this could happen." She fell back into the chair, shocked by the revelations. "How did this happen? How could this have happened...?" The color drained from her face as her anger turned to shock and grief.

Lily picked up the phone and spoke to her secretary, "Jaime, could you bring some water in for Mrs. Waters, please? Oh, and call and reschedule my 2:00, it's just a signing for a will. Push it up to the end of the day if you can, tomorrow if not."

Lily turned her attention to Mrs. Waters, "First, I urge the two of you to go to the police and press charges against your fiancé Steven. We must also discuss what to do about this baby and make some decisions regarding whether she will consider adoption. Then, you both will need some counseling. I suggest the Women's Center."

Mrs. Waters had listened intently, still trying to take it all in. She suddenly turned to her daughter and pulled her to herself, holding her. "Lily please help us with these decisions. I'm not sure either one of us is capable of handling these issues by ourselves. I know I'm in shock and poor Donna has been through enough. One thing I do know is – we are grateful you are here."

Donna, who had been quiet up until now, nodded, "Oh, yes, Lily, Ms. Austin, what would I do without you?"

"Fine, let's go together to the police station." The three composed themselves as Lily told Jaime why they were leaving the office.

When Lily returned to the office to finish the day, both Jaime and Cary hugged her. Lily was just grateful the girl's mother had cooperated and justice had been served.

Chapter 56

LILY HAD GONE BACK to her routine of attending weekend dances. Ron always appeared most delighted to see her. He seemed to be watching and waiting for her. He knew that she was most delighted by simply having the first and last dance. It was the "old fashioned" way to tell everyone who was your special lady. Both would dance many dances together and also shared dances with others during the evening.

Lily continued her membership with a private club and the local reciprocal club. The club sent out a newsletter type publication with monthly events. When the bulletin arrived, she noticed there was a holiday dinner-dance coming up; Lily thought Ron might like to join her. At first, she was concerned about inviting him. Was she making a "statement" she asked herself. Would other members think their relationship was something other than it was? She finally decided to call and invite him. He was delighted.

That evening Lily had selected a lovely red dress and carefully presented herself when she opened the door. The dress was just the right shade of red, slid over her slim figure and set off her blonde hair perfectly. She wore her hair in that semi-refined, carefree tousled look which became her. The door bell rang. It was Westminster Chimes, thus giving her time to reach the door as they stopped ringing.

When she first appeared, Ron took a deep breath. He wasn't surprised, since she usually dressed exceptionally well. This was more than exceptionally nice, however. He reached forward, gently pulled her to him and kissed her. The kiss lingered and she seemed to kiss him back. Ron was and looked extremely handsome.

"Come in my dear man."

He looked at her momentarily and as he stood before the chair. It was a very comfortable living room chair in soft shades of tan. He sat back as Lily questioned, "A glass of merlot?"

Ron nodded with a smile. Lily walked over to the wine rack and selected the bottle that she thought he would enjoy the most. Ron immediately reached for the bottle and walked to the kitchen. Opening the drawer, Lily proceeded to get the opener and handed it to Ron. She had earlier placed the wine glasses on the counter. Ron poured a sample taste, swirled it, looked it over and carefully tasted the wine. His expression showed his approval.

"Lily, you always select the best."

She smiled, reached for her glass and toasted, "To us and ours and them and theirs." Laughing, they both tasted the wine. Soon they were enjoying a second glass of wine.

Lily had the table at the club reserved. She enjoyed having a special table, one she usually requested. It was distanced from the body of the dining room so they could both participate with any activities in the room, and yet carry on a comfortable conversation. Looking up at the large grandfather clock, they realized it was time to leave her home for the club.

"Here sweetheart let me help you." Ron helped Lily with her coat and gloves. As he handed her gloves, he smiled and in a very fatherly voice, "Now don't lay these down somewhere and forget them."

She giggled and reached into her evening bag for the door key. Lily liked to have a single door key in the bag, not those attached to the car or her office door. She handed the key to Ron who locked the house and then drove to the club.

Once there, Ron was introduced to the various members and pleasantries were exchanged. Then he noticed a gentleman whom he was certain he knew, Howard Hunter. Lily and Ron walked towards Howard when Howard recognized Ron.

"Well Hello, Ron. Nice meeting you here. It has been some time since we were at camp together." Howard nodded at Lily. "Lily did you know Ron when he was an Eagle Scout?"

Lily smiled, looked at Ron and back to Howard, "Can't say that I did. So you two were in Scouts together?"

"No not really, just a regional summer camp. But we had one helluva good time."

Soon other couples came up and there were many pleasant hellos. After they were seated and enjoying another glass of Merlot, the maître de announced a buffet of delicious food. Shortly afterward, music for ballroom dancing filled the air. It made for a happy evening.

As the evening ended and the last song was played, Lily took Ron's hand and they started for the door. The attendant was signaled and the car was returned from the parking lot.

The evening was cold, but not windy, just comfortable with their warm coats. As they stepped to enter the car, Ron put his arm around Lily and kissed her firmly on the mouth. She parted her lips and Ron knew their relationship had grown. He helped her into the car and then carefully drove to her home. When they arrived, Ron helped her out of the car and walked her to the door, she handed him the key.

Inside the house she slipped out of her coat, laid her gloves down. The room was warm and she had left a small light on. The light was dim but showing enough to make the room appear as if there were lighted candles. Ron removed his coat, then his tie.

Being a good hostess, Lily started for the wine rack when he pulled her back into his arms. He began kissing her, first on the lips, then the ear, neck and soon his lips were near her breast. He carefully slid the straps to her dress off her shoulder. Her hands were on his hips. He kissed her breast. She took his hand and they walked down the hall to her very feminine bedroom. He pulled back the covers on the bed very slowly. He sat on the cool white sheet trimmed with eyelet trimming and very fine percale, almost a satin finish. Ron had Lily standing directly in front of him while he carefully removed his trousers and shorts.

He was now fully erect. Her dress did not require a bra, so he let it fall to the floor as he kissed her body. He placed his hands inside of her silk panties and slowly lowered them as his lips soon followed. The warmth of her body and smell of her perfume radiated towards him. She could feel the cool sheets as he gently laid her in the bed. Soon he kissed her breasts again and gently was inside of her, soft moans, warm kisses and great sweep of wonderful heat filled them both. The light was dim, but he could see the soft curls around her face and the smile on her lips.

The feeling was like the first year of his marriage. He knew she was satisfied and soon would be asleep. He was capable of satisfying both of them more than once. Then resting next to her warm soft skin was like magic. He fell asleep as she had. It was a most relaxed wonderful sleep. It was a short time later when he awoke. She stirred.

"I'm going to leave now" he said. She nodded and soon fell back to sleep, a very deep sleep.

It was a long way home. The drive was slow. A few hours of sleep and time to think things through are what he needed. Ron had told his friend Al that he would have Lily and he did! But somehow it didn't feel like a victory. "I don't think I'll share with Al, not this one. She sure does make one feel they have to run out and buy her a ring. Well, that's not me. Hmm, I wonder what it would feel like if I did? Wonder what she'd say or do? She's probably like all the rest in the end. Oh, well. But what a night!"

"It is best to go slow with Lily under the current situation, and I don't want her to think it was anything more than a usual night of sex." he said to himself as he held his morning coffee. The coffee was hot and black, just the way Ron liked it in his two cup Gevalia machine.

"I don't want her to think the sex was anything extra, hmm wonder what is the way she would know it was meaningless. Usually if I don't pay attention to the lady, whoever it is, they get the message loud and clear. He questioned how he would do it. Throughout the day he thought about Lily. It was a lady he thought he could just shake off like the others. The picture of her blonde tousled hair on the pillow as she fell back to sleep was stuck in his head.

He got home and began to read a weekly article he enjoyed, but he found himself unable to focus. He tried to re-read the article to no avail. Restlessly turning the pages, he finally put the paper down. Instead of words, Ron found her picture still in his head. Throughout the day, his thoughts kept going back to her. I can almost smell her perfume. Why can't I simply close the door on her? Maybe I should close the door on Grace instead.

It is great that Grace spends so much time away from here. I haven't told Lily about her and I don't want to. God, too much to think about! Yeah, I should let God figure it all out.

Chapter 57

LILY HUNG UP THE receiver and swiveled her chair around sideways. Her thoughts turned to Ron. She knew he would call again. She thought to herself, "I'm not going to mislead him. I need to let him know I have traveled a long way over many unpaved roads. I learned early in life that even if I have pain, that a relationship doesn't solve everything. Yet throughout my marriage, I had a great life. There is always room in a heart to love again, but it has to be right. It has to be honest."

The weather was warm and the late sun shone through the curtain of the well furnished kitchen. Ron enjoyed preparing dinner; a skill that he had honed throughout the years. He had an oven stuffed roaster which would be fully cooked at the same time as the scalloped corn, Caesar salad, and double stuffed potatoes. He had stopped at the bakery for a lemon chiffon pie to complete the meal. Ron also had a flare for decorating the table. He had called her knowing when the meal would be ready to serve.

Shifting from one foot to another he waited for the ring on the other end to stop. Anxious for her reply he was most direct. "Lily my dear, I've been busy in the kitchen preparing this great meal. I hope you are free."

He was so pleasant on the phone. Lily dear.... Hmm, an invitation to dinner? I simply could not refuse if I wanted to. One thing she could say about Ron, he was on outstanding cook. Beside that, I'm hungry and tired of eating alone. No, I'm certainly not going to refuse and he sounded so... tender somehow.

She opened the second drawer of a nearby wooden chest where sweaters were neatly folded in layers of twos. Lily liked having an organized home as well as an organized office. Well manicured fingers slipped under the second pink cashmere sweater; light in weight yet warm enough for the weather. Closing the drawer and placing the chosen cardigan across her shoulders, she tied the sleeves in front. Reaching for her keys and clutch bag on the kitchen counter she walked back through the room to leave. Soon the back door was closed and locked by turning the key. Behind the wheel of her Lexus and on the road, her thoughts continued.

Somehow Ron seems to have mellowed lately. His demeanor seems different. I'm actually looking forward to being with him. The hum of the motor did not interfere with her pleasant mood nor did the red lights. The car turned to the driveway.

Standing near the window looking out wearing a funny apron over the tan pants and blue shirt, Ron held a wooden spoon, all for effect. He liked to hear her laugh.

"Oh, Ron, so now you are a great chef?" she said, breaking into a smile.

"Only for you my dear, only for you."

"Thank you and oh - that food smells delicious."

"Right this way my dear."

Reaching for her sweater, it was easy to pull her towards him. The kiss was warm and welcoming. Entering the dining room she stopped to admire the table. The place settings were Lenox silver rimmed plates rested on the Irish Linen cloth with white textured cloth napkins and sparkling silverware. The crystal stemware sparkled with D'Oro Moscato wine reaching the fullest part of the glass. Short stemmed white roses covered the rim of the mock Boch Delft dish in the center. Lily's five feet two inch frame was erect as she turned and smiled at Ron.

He pulled her chair waiting for her to grace the table. The food was carefully placed and soon they were toasting the evening, "To us and ours and them and theirs!" quickly followed by "and to the host." As the last fork was placed on the dessert plate, Lily turned to Ron,

"That was truly a wonderful meal."

"It was simple but for you."

Ron took Lily's hand in his, "Come sit with me in the living room."

His arm across her back, he walked her to the sofa. The six foot three inch frame was comfortable in the classic sofa. Lily snuggled up to him on the sofa. Knowing what he wanted to say, and yet not quite how he would say it, his eyes seem to search the room, his hand on her arm, he raised his eyebrows and began to talk.

First his voice was soft. She turned her head in surprise at his unusually gentle tone. He cleared his throat and asked about her day at the office followed by questions about Jimmy, her son. Her answers were simple and direct. When he asked her about what she wanted out of life, she thought for a moment and answered, "What I want in life? That is an easy question."

Easy, yes, but coming from him was surprising. He never seemed to be too interested the future, his or hers. She sat there with his arms about her top with dark brown silk slacks and bare feet in her loafers. Her blonde shoulder length hair fell softly over her light brown lamé sweater. He gently kissed her hair, and then moved it to kiss her neck.

They had been seeing each other now for several months. She no longer thought of Michael whenever she was with Ron. When he posed the question of what she wanted in life, Lily answered Ron, "The kind of love I want is true love, not just physical or romantic, just a man that accepts me and all that I have been, all that our life will be and whatever has been in our lives…and it is okay for what won't be part of our lives," she continued. "Many people see the world differently; I see it not as a threatening place but a loving place. In other words, the freer I am with my feelings, the more those feelings will be returned."

Ron hugged Lily, no words were spoken. Ron took her hand

and together they walked up stairs to his large inviting bedroom. One could feel the tremendous energy in the room. He undressed Lily first and she gathered the sheet over her warm succulent body as he undressed himself. Soon he had devoured her. The hours pleasured both and soon they were asleep.

Chapter 58

A S SHE ENTERED THE house, the telephone was ringing. Lily ran to reach it before it went into the answering machine. No luck. She could hear a familiar voice. At the same time she noticed there were three messages. Three? Hopefully not about to work.

Well, let's see, the first one ...Ron Hollander, the second one... Ron Hollander and yes, all three wanting to know if I plan to attend the dance. How persistent. Hmm....he is getting more interesting. Let's see, where did he say it was? Oh, yes, Worcester. I'll have to look on my computer to see how to get there. Mapquest is a great thing! First, some nourishment and a shower, perhaps my white blouse and a dark skirt. Oh well, why not, I like to dance.

Lily always maintained herself well, manicures and pedicures, hair neatly trimmed, and she always wore the latest style even in something as simple as a blouse. She freshly arranged her simple hair style, refreshed her makeup and put on that tiny whiff of Chanel. Feeling a bit hungry she reached for the potato chips, "just a few" she said to herself. "Oh yes, the vegetable soup, a cup and one of those great French rolls. A cool glass of milk and one, just one cookie. As fond as she was of oatmeal raisin cookies, she limited herself to one at a time.

Then off to the dance. It was nice of Ron to notify her where it was and then met her there. It seemed a good arrangement. This arrangement soon became the way of life for both Ron and Lily. They would meet at several dance places, Dedham, Newton, Braintree, and South shore. Each time they shared many dances, some fun loving swing and some close slow dances. Ron would walk Lily to her car at the end of each evening, and after a respectable amount of time, kissing her good night. As much as Lily enjoyed the relationship, she would pull back at times. Being so reserved surprised her, too.

Months passed and soon a year had passed. The telephone extension in the kitchen was ringing. Lily ran to answer it wondering if it were her son only to hear the usual familiar voice. "Oh, I'm sorry Ron, but tonight is 'girl's night out'. Please go on to the dance and enjoy yourself."

Rather than being put out, Ron was kind of relieved to have a break. Meeting at the dance was the usual, but going alone wasn't bad either. "There are several new gals I haven't met," he thought. Ron still enjoyed being Ron.

It was bridge night with the girls. Lily didn't have time to bake for the girls and had stopped at the local bakery and selected the special of the house, apple pie. Naturally she stopped at the market to be certain there was plenty of ice cream on hand. It was now shortly after 6:30 PM.

Soon thereafter, Cary arrived. She and Lily gave the friendly hug. The girls seemed to enjoy playing cards especially bridge. Pat and Marilyn arrived and the game began. 'One heart' was Marilyn's opening bid, followed by her opponent's 'Two Clubs'. The bidding ended with a 'Small Slam'. And the girls squealed with delight.

The game ended around 10:30 PM and the dessert was being served when the phone rang. It was Ron wondering how the game went. The women all looked at each other and rolled their eyes acknowledging the conversation between Lily and Ron. Shortly Lily hung up and Lily's friends bid her good night. It had been a fun evening.

The girls had no sooner left when Jim called. Every week like clock work, Jim called to report on the happenings at Berkley and this week was no exception. He always closed the conversation on a positive note, telling of his friend and the activities. His mother was important to him. But now he was engaged and about to be married. One more year in graduate school and then Jim and Sherry would be married. A great looking couple and they were already devoted to each other. What more could a mother ask for?

Chapter 59

THE NEXT EVENING, THE phone rang. Lily was in her room sorting the sweaters when she heard it and ran to answer the call. She wasn't really expecting any one and was a bit surprised when it was Ron.

"Hello Ron, gosh I haven't heard from you for a couple of weeks." "Yes, I've been busy, too." Oh, I don't know." "Well, okay, see you there."

Lily had hesitated, then decided if she had nothing better to do, then she might as well go to the dance. She slipped out of her navy blue Armani slacks and soft blue cashmere sweater and slid into a comfortable soft brown dress. Sorting sweaters can be done at any time, she thought. Looking herself over in the mirror, she nodded at the sight. Lily seldom wore frilly dresses, ones that were ruffled, off the shoulder, or straps. She preferred the classic style which accented her slim body and her choice for this evening was chic, yet feminine.

It was still cold outside, especially at night. She was actually looking forward to the dancing. Lily warmed up her car, then carefully backed out and touched the garage door button to close the door. She hoped the highway conditions were good. She drove carefully watching for pot holes made each winter by the salt and snow on the streets. Lily enjoyed the drive; it gave her time to hear some music. Forty-five minutes later she arrived. Turning into the parking lot she noticed a lot of cars tonight. That would mean a nice crowd of ballroom dancers.

Looking for a place to park she noticed a spot under the street light. She thought it looked pretty safe and well lit. She looked and saw several others walking towards the door where the dance was being held. She got out and locked the car, hurried cross the street and soon was inside. She received a friendly greeting when she paid for the dance.

She left her coat in the coat room, and proceeded to a table of newly acquired friends, Norma, Rosalind and Maryanne. The girls all exchanged personal comments and any bit of news since they met at the last dance. Lily looked around. The music started. One of Rosalind's friends asked Lily to dance as soon as the music started.

Ron was not in sight when the music started, but another gentleman Bernie asked Lily to dance. She was delighted, but somehow she wondered why Ron was not there since he had called her. "Oh well, who knows why, maybe car trouble." Before the first dance ended she looked over and he was dancing with a tall brunette.

As Ron danced he thought, "She always seems to have a partner, one after another. I'll dance with her soon, but not too soon. I don't want her to think I'm too eager. I'll keep my back towards her and pretend not to see her. Yet she always seems to know what I'm doing or thinking. If I'd just get it over when I first come in, she wouldn't stay in my head so long. Who am I kidding? I haven't gotten her out of my mind since that night. Enough already!"

He finished his dance and looked around carefully avoiding her, but making sure he saw her. "What the hell is with her, she seems happy all of the time. No one can smile like that all the time."

When Lily saw Ron dancing with others and not acknowledging her, she immediately connected it to the sexual encounter. "He wants me to think lightly of the sex. Well, I guess he just might be exactly the kind of person Cary told me he was."

She maintained a neutral expression as she danced, one that matched the expression on his face. "I guess it didn't really matter to her. That isn't the usual response, but I guess I'm learning that she isn't the usual gal."

It was the sixth set when Ron walked directly over to Lily. She smiled as if she hadn't noticed him before.

"Yes, I'd love to dance" she said, smiling a special smile for him.

He took her hand and went to the dance floor. He thought to himself, "After that night together I will act as if it never happened, very aloof. I don't want her to think we are a 'couple'. I'm not ready to commit to anyone. Besides, he thought, people who don't know the difference still think that Grace and I are together. I don't think I'm ready to mess that up yet."

The next day, at her regularly scheduled appointment, she was let into the inner office. Ron did not know that Lily had therapy. When her session was over, she put a great deal of thought in the therapist words. Lily had surprised herself; she thought her session would be all about Michael or herself.

Instead it was more about Ron Hollander. When Lily explained that she had heard about his long term dating of many women, the therapist explained why some men intentionally do just that. It allows them to play a role, one they feel comfortable with, over and over. Usually in their childhood they did not feel a strong commitment with their parents, therefore they are uncomfortable with any commitment to the opposite sex.

"This could easily be your friend Ron," Dr. Grosart explained. "That is a generalized motive for some men's lack of commitment, but men have various reasons for their actions. Now there are other men who have totally different roles and ways of thinking and behaving. There are some men who have a history of involvement with married women, or simply women who have a strong attachment to other men, women who cannot control their emotions. They are either possessive or demanding or cruelly castrating."

Dr. Grosart continued, "This gives these men a thrill like

no other thrill. Kind, thoughtful women bore them and any uncomplicated woman who tells them she loves him simply must be defective in their eyes. We professionals watch this type of behavior and easily see the influence of parental relationships.

"But what about the married woman?" asked Lily.

"It would not be unusual for the husband of the woman to want her to have relations with other men, then come home and tell him the complete details. The three of them are satisfying themselves. They react as if no one is being hurt or unhappy with the situation. It is a small part of … or kinship to voyeurism." Dr. Grosart paused to let his words sink in and then continued.

"However, Lily, that situation doesn't sound like your friend, so don't give it another thought. It sounds as if your friend doesn't plan any long term relationship with you or any other single woman, at least not you."

This was all new to Lily. Her session was soon over. It was too much to think about, perhaps later. Thank God her Ron wasn't one like the therapist described. But she realized too that he wasn't the type to commit, just like Cary said.

The next week, while at the dance, Lily was reminded of the therapist's comments while dancing, knowing she must keep her own emotions in check. Few words were spoken between them. Last week he was indifferent, but maybe this week would be different.

Ron came to Lily after a few dances. "Hello my lawyer friend."

"Hello, Ron."

"Would you care to dance or is this one taken? It is the waltz."

"Sure. I'd like that. My favorite is the waltz."

She extended her hand and he led her to the dance floor. She gently placed her left hand on his shoulder and he carefully took her right one. He was close enough to feel her legs against his. That wonderful euphoria came over him. He had tried to not recognize it, but it was simply there.

She and Ron danced close, their bodies reacted as if one. They danced through both pieces of music without a word. When the set ended, she smiled, feeling very happy and in control.

"Thank you."

"And thank you, said Ron."

He thought, "Her smile inferred she would enjoy being back in my life again." Ron suddenly thought he better make a move. "It is better to have loved and lost than never to have loved at all. I can never remember who said that." he said to her with a shrug and a smile.

She smiled and simply said, "Thank you." but was confounded by his behavior.

Ron noticed she danced several more sets with others. Thinking the evening would soon be over, he stood very close to her, not knowing if she would dance with him or not. Surprising himself, he thought with most women I'm very sure, but with her I never know. Reaching over and placing his warm hand on hers, he asked her once more to dance.

Near the end of the set, she coyly said, "I'm the best thing that ever happened to you, and you know it." She might have been kidding, but he knew she was right. "Maybe I can commit this time. It feels good, but a bit scary."

Ron's mind was racing on the way home. I've had two loves in my life, two marriages and the both ended tragically. Dating is easier and safer. They are just a series of events and I don't have to know what is next with them. With her, she just acts as if life is going to be good no matter what.

I hear her saying, "Enjoy life and play to have fun." Then there is her other comment, "Only God knows what He will do next." I wish I could be so sure of life, of what I was going to do next.

Chapter 60

Lily was standing in the Davis' living room "Mrs. Davis, I think the will is ready the way you indicated. I shall plan to be in attendance at the reading as you requested. Now let us review it now to be certain it is correct.

Do you want me to start the reading, or is there someone else you want to have here also?"

"No Lily, please read it. The house is quiet. My children are due home soon. Lily this will is for their benefit, so if one of them comes home while you are reading it, it is okay. I treat them all equally. The same way I love them." Lily read it in total. Mrs. Davis was delighted.

"Lily make an appointment and I will come to the office to sign it."

"I can bring it to you here at home to sign if you like."

"No Lily, I will come to the office even if I have someone bring me."

She knew how determined Mrs. Davis was and how she took great satisfaction in doing it her way. Lily left Mrs. Davis' home only to go next door to her home.

The sun was shining and there was a bit of snow still on the ground. Snowmen of varying types looked out from across the street and the children were shouting and laughing. When she reached the front door, she couldn't help but admire her shiny door knocker. It was a very rare New England style and unusual to find anymore. Lily's wreath was a seasonal one with pinecones, acorns, holly and pieces of the fir bushes adorned with a multi colored ribbon.

Lily reached into her bright red Brahmin bag. It was a bit expensive for an everyday bag, but it worked well with so many outfits. She had various ones to match or coordinate with her other coats. The door key would be in a side pocket on the bag. She reached for it and was ready to place it in the lock, when she noticed the door unlocked. At first she felt surprise and then fear set in. Why was the door unlocked? She remembered her way of always checking the door whenever she left the house.

"Should she push it open or just call someone first?" she wondered. She carefully pushed it open, listening for any strange sounds. .

"Mom! I've been waiting for you!" shouted Jimmy. "Anything to eat around here?"

What a wave of relief she felt. Lily hurried to give him a hug. Nothing like a son in the house to make her heart beat fast with pleasure.

She prepared the lamb chops and green beans just the way he liked them, and had a slice of lemon pie ready, too. Once the meal was ended, they continued the happy chatter until Lily finally got up, taking the plates to the sink to rinse. Jimmy removed the remaining food stuffs and placed them in the refrigerator. The dishwasher was loaded and turned on. They continued their conversation above the din of the machine.

They talked eagerly about their current lives. "Boy, Jim this is certainly different from our California life, but I'm enjoying it, and making the most of it."

"Mom, you could fit in anyplace. How do you like your job? Is it demanding? And how do you get along with everyone in the office? I bet Grandpa would be pleased with you. What do you hear from my uncles?" he asked.

"Okay Jim! Enough questions," Lily said jokingly. "Give me a little time to answer."

Lily was pleased that he was concerned about his grandparents and uncles. She always felt family was most important and stressed this with Jim in his early years. Lily's answers were satisfying and then she had her own questions, mostly about how his studies were going. He talked of his friend Rosie and of course his wonderful Sherry. Lily had heard many stories of Rosie and how great her father was all throughout each home visit. Soon the evening ended and Jim was to return to college the next morning. A short trip home, but he was glad to get to see his mother.

When Jim was ready for bed, he called out, "Good night Mom" and she answered

"Good night Jim."

The next morning, Jim's alarm went off, and Lily could hear the shower running. She had prepared a bowl of fruit, his favorite cereal and some hot chocolate. Jim was home again. He quickly finished the meal and hurriedly put on his coat and stocking cap. His youthful smile, bright white teeth under a shock of blonde hair was a delightful sight. "See you soon Mom," he said as he hurried out the door and drove away, off to school again.

Chapter 61

ON LILY'S WAY HOME she was thinking, "As soon as I unpack the groceries and get the house in order, I'll have the girls over for another night of bridge. It is nice to have a regular girls night out," thought Lily. "The weather is getting warmer and the girls don't mind getting out in the evening."

It was so nice hearing from Jim and how well he liked graduate school at Berkley. I'm certain it is not only the school, but Sherry that is making life so wonderful for him.

Maybe I'll give Tom a call and see how things are with him. He is such a great brother. I really miss not seeing him so often. Our telephone calls are good. Hmm, I wonder how Jack is doing, now that he has decided to make the Navy his career. Maybe while I have a few minutes I'll write him a letter.

Lily brushed her hair off her forehead and reached for the desk drawer to get a pen and paper. She took a few pages of paper from the box of personalized stationary, then sat back and thought of her brother Jack as she began to write. Dearest Jack,...

Jack always felt that serving his country was his calling. As a very handsome man, he had his choice of ladies. And with his generally happy attitude, Jack was content to serve aboard the aircraft carriers, but being at sea made him the most comfortable. He loved to tell her about his experiences with parachuting and the "free fall". Jack was always one who loved adventure. The navy was a good choice for him. He was a man's man, yet one the ladies like.

Like any young man, Jack soon fell in love with Joyce. She fit the pattern of a "Navy Wife", and as the children arrived, she seemed to handle each and every situation while Daddy Jack was aboard first one carrier then another. He served aboard several.

The twins, Doug and Steve arrived and the Austin family was delighted. Later Troylyn arrived and the rejoicing was even greater. Those three darling children were followed by two more, both adorable boys, Tommy and Jack Jr. Jack had a lovely family, and a fine career as a Navy officer. Being stationed at various bases around the States, he would fly home to see his parents and siblings as often as time allowed. Jack loved his family and they loved him. He always shared many of the fun stories about the children. He had promised many times to visit Lily, but duty always seemed to call. Lily said she understood, but nevertheless, she would have loved to have his company. The years had flown by and his children were now mostly grown up now, like her Jim. Where did the time go?

Lily tried to fit in as many details of her life in New England as she could, telling him all about her work and some of the more difficult cases she had taken on. She wrote about Jim and Sherry and asked for pictures of his family. Lily shared how she had a nice social life in Boston with new friends and plenty of dancing. She didn't share anything about Ron and didn't answer his question about Michael. That life was over.

Chapter 62

RON LOOKED AT HIS watch. He enjoyed his Rolex, it had been a gift from his friend, Al. Al liked nice things and was good about thanking Ron with expensive gifts. One of Ron's clients had needed a substantial amount of work done Ron had led him to Al's company. Al profited quite well, so he thanked Ron with the expensive thank you gift.

He squinted his eyes, trying to read the time in the bright sunlight. Ron turned around shading his watch and then adjusted his eyes and noted the time was nearly five o'clock. Enough for one day, he murmured. With a deep breath and a bit of a sigh he quickly remembered Lily was having her 'girls night out' "Hey why not?" he thought. As he walked to his car, parked at the street meter he saw a ticket. "Damn it anyhow!!! He reached for the ticket, "Oh, shit, it wasn't a ticket just an advertisement. Thank you God. I've enough tickets to last several years."

The car was warm, he rolled down the window and adjusted his seat belt and started the car. Another was waiting for the parking spot. "Back up and wait, Mister," he muttered with the window up. He pulled out on the street. It wasn't as crowded driving as usual. He reached for his sun glasses, nearly hit a dog running loose in the street, then quite angry, he swerved the car and soon got on the highway. It took less than 30 minutes to see his house and park in the driveway. Don't want to put it in the garage just yet, I might want to go out. He walked around the garage to the back door.

With key in hand he opened it. Max came running. Max was owned by a wealthy lady in one of his buildings, and when she moved Max was just a puppy, she didn't want to be bothered with him, so she saw Ron and quickly decided to give the well cared for, expensive dog to him. Max quickly took to Ron and the two enjoyed their company. Having been inside most of the day, except when the cleaning lady let him out for while and put him back inside when she left. Max needed to get out for a while. Ron spoke to Max as if one were speaking to a child.

As he entered the kitchen, he noticed Ellen his cleaning lady had been there. She was good about having every thing sparkle and plenty of ice water in the refrigerator

"Oh, peanut butter cookies on the counter, nice. "

"The phone was busy today, the message light is blinking. Oh, well let's see the mail first." Ron picked up the mail right where Ellen put it on the small antique table in the hall. He had asked her several times to place it on the plate sitting on the counter, but had finally given up. The hall table would have to do.

He sat in the overstuffed chair, kicked his leather loafers off, wiggled the toes and placed them on the matching foot stool.

Furniture all selected by a decorator, supposedly to match his personality. After the house was complete and the decorator gave him the grand tour, he most assuredly kissed her, opened a bottle of Merlot and after several glasses, she accommodated him in the bedroom on the new satin bedspread. He explained when it would be time to redecorate, he would call her.

"Nice only three letters, well one is a bill for work on the car. The brakes needed adjusting and the oil changed. Bill's garage did the 'loaner' bit and afforded excellent service, all of course for a generous fee.

Then the Cancer Fund's second request. He thought, "Did I sent a check or not? Well I'll look into it later," and oh, yes, a hand written address on this letter. Hmm it is from Grace. Well, let's see she said she was going with a couple of cousins to Switzerland and then end up in the Bahamas. Cousins she calls them, but it appears she has only male cousins and as usual, only one shows up for the trip. Oh, well what do I care?

He examined the envelope for some time, then reached for the letter opener. It was usually in the drawer. As he slid the instrument under the stamp and across the envelope, a single sheet of paper dropped out. It read, "I haven't been able to reach you by phone, so thought I'd better write. What have you been so busy about? I hope it's not another woman! I will be in Miami on Friday. Where shall I meet you? The Country Club? Let me know. I miss you. Are you planning to go the Islands with me? I need to know.

Can't wait to see you.

Miss you,

Grace

Oh, Shit! Today is already Wednesday. I'll have to call my secretary. I'll need the weekend at the Quequershan Club. Let's see, an American Airline ticket down. Now what will happen, well, let's see. I can call Lily from wherever I am, she'll just presume it is business. That part is easy.

Almost noon on Friday, in sunny Florida, Ron began to climb out of the pool. His hairy chest and strong arms are well suntanned. He stepped near the lounging chair and picked up the fluffy white monogrammed towel. The bikini clad waitress placed his gin and tonic with ice on the napkin next to his chair. She grinned as he smiled at her. "Her boyfriend must be nearby," he thought as he put the cool glass to his lips. A few minutes in the sun and his swim suit will be dry. His experience and sunlight was soon interrupted by a familiar voice.

"Well, Hellooo Ron, my big wonderful lover"

He opened his eyes, looked at her and stood up. "Hello Grace"

"Is that all you can say after two months?"

Ron smiled. Grace had a sharp voice, and frequently did the "Bette Midler" act with her hands. Her hair was various shades of red, some darker areas and some almost blonde. She appeared rather short, but actually was 5'2" and would try to conceal her slightly full figure with loose clothing.

Her very crinkled curly hair was medium length and the one piece red sarong bathing suit was mostly covered in a white terrycloth robe. Ornate thong sandals completed the ensemble.

She reached to hug Ron, he embraced her. She shrugged and pulled a lounge chair near his. "Hey good looking, order me a drink, too, will ya?"

He signaled the waitress. "Sure, sure." Within a few minutes she had the same drink for Grace. Grace thanked her and turned to Ron,

"Did you give her a big tip?"

He smiled at the waitress and said, "Put it on my tab will you doll?"

Grace began her never ending chatter about the trip she just returned from. Ron was not the least interested, but accommodated her with a small question now and then. The sun went under a cloud. Grace looked directly at Ron. He was watching the girls in the pool. "Let's go to your room. I assume it is 371. At least that's the one I changed in. Ron turned, picked up his book, smiled and nodded.

Once inside the room, he reached for her, untied the neck strap and dropped the suit part way. Grace stepped back, "Hey wait a minute!"

"Now what?"

"I want to know what you've been doing while I was away."

"Who in the hell cares? Let's just get with it," he said as he reached for her.

Wide eyed she said, "My cousin Dana said you just use me."

He frowned "What the hell, we use each other."

"I got a call saying you've been seeing some bitch named Lily. Is that true?"

Ron immediately got angry. His eyes opened wide, he pursed his lips, but unable to control the anger in his voice.

"Look Grace, you travel all over with men telling me they are your relatives. I don't believe they are relatives, in fact I've never believed it, but that never stopped you or me. But now I think the time has come, Grace you are either with me or not."

"Well, Ron, you have asked me several times and I always said 'Hell no!' Now I say 'yes', and you say 'Hell no', right?" He didn't answer. She knew that she was right. He had no future plans with her.

"Well, come to think of it, Ron, I've had enough. I had Dana wait for me at the Holiday Inn. You can take your little bitch and stuff her. How do you like that?"

With that, Grace began changing her clothes. She slipped out of the bathing suit in to her panties and lined white slacks lying on the chair. She fastened her bra and then reached for the pink top. Ron didn't say a word while she was dressing. Then he, too pulled on his pants over his shorts, and his cream colored shirt. While buttoning it, he looked straight at Grace. She looked directly at him.

"Grace this it is, you leave now, you don't come back to me."

"You've got that just right Mr. Ron."

Grace stuffed her belongings in the small case and slipped into her white mules. She placed her hand on the door knob and threw the hotel key on the floor. She turned toward Ron, saying, "This is good bye and good riddance Ron. It was fun while it lasted. Dana wants me full time." She paused for effect and then, "Ron you should wake up sometime!" and slammed the door behind her.

Well, that worked just fine. Now I don't even have to make a decision, she made one for me. I'll check out and get a cab back to the airport, and be home before Lily realizes what happened. She may not know I was gone at all. Oh, well, Grace, it was fun while it lasted… he thought.

The following weekday after returning from the Grace fiasco, Ron telephoned his friend Al at his construction company. The office on the worksite is a small house trailer pulled on the job used as the offices. Inside, the desk had three telephones, each with a separate number. Ron knowing which one Al used for his personal calls dialed it. Al was sitting in his office chair, jeans with a paunch over the belt line and a once white tee-shirt with the company's name and logo on it, an elbow on the desk looking out the window and thinking it must be time for a cigarette when the personal line started ringing. He looked at his Citizens' watch with the stainless steel band, hung up the original line and answered the personal line, glad to hear Ron's voice on the other end.

"Al --- want to go for lunch, I'm buying"

"No Ron, not today, I don't have time. But, why don't you come on over here and bring a couple of subs. We can have lunch here. Hey, make mine roast beef, will ya?"

Thirty minutes later Ron showed up dressed in jeans, leather belt with a large buckle, open necked shirt with a long sleeved sweater underneath and expensive cowboy boots picking his way through the construction site carrying a large brown paper bag. He sat across from Al and placed the paper bag in front of them. "Okay, two roast beef subs and extra pickles," he said as he handed the sandwich to Al.

"Thanks you lug. New boots?" Al said as he took his sandwich out and began to unwrap it,

"Yeah, my last trip to Arizona" Ron took the bag back, pulling out some chips.

"Hmm...nice. So what's up?"

"Nothing special" he said pulling his sandwich out of the bag and unwrapping it.

"Like Hell…you only come over or call when you've got some shit on your mind and don't know what to do." Al said with a mouthful of food.

Taking another bite, Ron said, "Yeah, I guess you are right and you guessed it right about Grace... or 'Amazing Grace' as you call her. She got fed up with me and had some guy named Dana hanging on....somehow she got wind of me and Lily and it pissed her off." Ron leaned back in the chair, putting his boots up on the desk.

"Yeah, some friend of hers, I don't know who, a blabber mouth told her. I don't really care any more."

"What are you going to do? asked Al while wadding up the empty paper and wiping his hands on his shirt."

"I'm sort of thinking about making Lily full time." with a softer voice

"Full time? You aren't thinking about marriage are you?" he asked with a wide eyed and a questionable look.

"No! Geez, hell no! But Lily isn't the type to keep this up without some kind of significant change in our status," he said throwing the leftover papers in the waste basket.

"Significant? What do you mean?

"A ring! God damn it! What did you think I mean? It may be the longest engagement in history, but at least she'll be satisfied."

"I think you are playing with fire Ron, don't do it."

"Yeah, you're probably right."

"Ron you cannot seem to make up your mind. Do you want someone, the same someone in your life full time or not?"

"Yeah, I know you're right, but I'm closer to Lily than ever before. I feel… different about her."

"Really???"

Looking to see which line was ringing, he said, "Hey Ron, sorry, I've been waiting for this call…I have to get back to work. I'll catch you later"

Stepping outside the office, Ron muttered "Oh, shit I wanted the name of his jeweler to save some money. Oh, well, I'll think of it, he thought as he stepped over the boards laying in the way and picked his way back to the street and his parked car.

Chapter 63

MICHAEL STOOD FRAMING THE living room doorway in Corrine's apartment. His six foot two physique gave him the appearance of a male model. His skin and completion was firm and tanned which made his black hair noticeably wavy. His yellow shirt, blue and white striped tie, Gucci belt on beige silk trousers and loafers gave him a total appearance as one of Gentlemen's Quarterly men.

Corrine's 5'5" and slim waist looks even taller adorned in a sheer white tank top layered with a matching cardigan over black crepe wide leg pants. Corrine's constant begging had become commonplace to him.

"Corrine, I know you would like for me to stay here every night, but as I've said a hundred times it isn't possible."

"I know, I know, but Friday night is better than nothing," she said as her eyes welled up.

"Sweetie don't go crying, that is silly. I get up early every week day so it is simply impossible for me to be here when all my clothes and personal items are in my apartment."

"You could move them here, I've said that before."

"Corrine, I usually stay over following the late dance at the

Country Club, and we sleep late Saturday before I leave for the gym. Isn't that enough for now?"

Michael I didn't tell you to move in, but why can't you stay the second night, Saturday night, too?"

"I know you have. I cannot stay over Saturday night

"I always go to church Sundays with my parents and Rosie when she is in town, that is simply a must. Come on, now. Let's stop this and relax. It is Friday and getting late. Where would you like to go for dinner? Your choice."

"Michael it is raining outside, why don't I make us something and we stay in?" He was listening to "Lionel Richie's 'Once, Twice Three Times a Lady'. Michael suddenly said, "Corrine honey, we could go dance in the rain."

"Honestly Michael you say such dumb things. We can dance right here in the living room while it is raining outside, that can be your dance in the rain."

"Have it your way Corrine."

Michael couldn't help but think about what Lily would have replied. He was sure it would have been simply a sweet smile as she reached for my hand. She would have stepped out of her shoes and let the clothes fall on the way outside. It was just a few years ago when the rain was gentle and inviting. Lily liked the rain and loved the idea of dancing in the rain. What a beautiful dance... There is only one Lily and it is only her who dances in the rain.

What was the song Lily and I danced to, oh yes, "Once, Twice, Three Times a Lady."

Oh, well back to reality, Corrine isn't Lily. That's for sure. Michael shook his head and needed to get with it. He turned to Corrine who had just stepped in the doorway.

"Okay sexy, what's for dinner?" Corrine smiled and answered, "Your favorite, tacos." Not certain why she said that, Michael sat in the kitchen and pulled his napkin across his lap. Corrine worked all day and no longer bothered to cook any fancy meals. She was frequently silent during dinner. Whenever she brought up anything that bothered her, they never agreed. Michael also seemed to be in thought and somewhat quiet during the evening. Corrine became restless and uneasy when Michael looked at his watch and indicated he would leave a bit early. Michael didn't offer to stay the night.

Corrine put the kitchen in order, the dishes in the dishwasher turning it on. Her kitchen was small but efficient. Looking up at the kitchen clock, she wondered if her friend Roz was still up. "I'll wait until nine o'clock to call, she may have a date." Later that evening Corrine called Roz.

"Hi Roz, I hope I didn't wake you."

"No Corrine, what is new with you?"

"Well, remember when you were talking about Michael and his friend Angelo?"

"Yes, what about it?"

"I really think Angelo is more my type."

"What do you mean? Are you kidding?"

"No, I'm fed up with Michael, he isn't interested enough in me to stay over, we don't seem to have much in common anymore… I don't know."

"Why, I thought he was staying over with you at least once in a while."

"Yes, once in a very long while. Wouldn't you think by now he would consider either a long relationship or even marriage? No not him," she started to explain. "His daughter is getting married and I'm not even invited. He said he would be too busy at the wedding to have a date. I just think he doesn't want me to meet his family. And then I overheard Angelo make a comment about some woman Michael used to date." She started choking up.

"You should have seen his face light up. Then he looked over at me and it just isn't the same. I think it is time to start looking around. I don't think this is going any place."

"Oh, Corrine, I'm sorry."

"And Roz you should have heard his dumb comment the other night. He can't stay over and be with me, but he asked me to go outside to dance in the rain or something. I don't get him at all. It is time to look around, don't you think?"

"That is up to you Corrine."

"Yes, I know. Oh, how are things working out for you? We haven't talked in weeks."

"The hospital? I really like it here, and besides I'm dating one of the doctors now."

"What?? You should have called me! Well, good for you, but don't do what I've done and hang on too long. I really think there is a small window of excitement. If they don't jump to marry you then, forget it. It's over."

"What is your day like? I'm going to the Pompano Salon for a shampoo and set."

"That's funny. Me too, but I have an appointment tomorrow at the Gino Salon, I really like it there."

"Well I have to go now. I have lots to do tomorrow."

"Yes, me too. Well I'll see you soon. Take care."

Chapter 64

"SHERRY, ISN'T THIS GREAT spending our first anniversary here in Dallas?"

"Yes and even better to have grad school behind us. Your mom was a love to give us this trip for graduation and our first anniversary."

Jim bent over the bed and kissed his wife. A sweet kiss and she smiled and invited him back into bed. "Honey it is close to noon and we had better be at the travel agent's on time!"

Sherry smiled, grabbed a towel, and walked towards the hotel shower. He looked at her lovely bare figure, but decided not to follow her. He glanced at his Rolex, his father's Rolex. He very much wanted to resemble his father and he even dressed as he remembered him. Standing six foot two with well shaped arms and shoulders, he wore sporty style shirts and designer jeans. A slim black leather belt showed his slim build. Since he would be walking a lot today, he had designer sneakers on.

Jim was fully dressed by 6:00 and had already begun looking at the morning paper with his coffee. Sherry towel dried her hair, leaving it natural and applied body lotion. The fragrance was light and sweet. She quickly slid into a summer outfit, a cotton navy and white stripped shirt over a white panel skirt, comfortable slip on shoes, matching canvas tote bag purse and a darling hat.

Soon they both were ready and gathered the needs for the day, Sherry, her purse, Jim, the tour tickets. They could hear the ding of the elevator as they closed the door to their room. The other couples on the elevator seemed to want the street floor too. Soon they were walking through the lobby to the garage.

"What a beautiful day," Sherry exclaimed as Jim drove the car to the main street. Jim realized the travel agent was across town. He looked at his watch. Jim was very conscious of schedules and was seldom late. Sherry was looking over the tour brochure, pushing her sun glasses up and then down as they caught the sun. The traffic was congested and Jim was all of a sudden sorry he had not pushed for an earlier start.

Jim looked up and noticed the attractive woman coming out of the store. She was laughing into her cell phone as she stepped off the curb on to the street directly in front of the car ahead of Jim.

Tires screeched and squealed, but it too late. The car struck her with a thud and she rolled from the top of the car and flew on to the pavement. Sherry quickly reached for her cell phone, flipped it open, and called 911 giving the information as Jim jumped out of his car to help. Several individuals came rushing over to help; one announcing she was a nurse. The police arrived and soon the street was cleared by a police officer as the ambulance arrived. The Emergency Medical Team (EMT) efficiently and most professionally assisted and soon the lady was taken away. As the ambulance pulled out, Sherry noticed the lady's cell phone. She picked it up and threw it in her bag. Back in their car, a bit shaken up from the experience, Sherry opened the cell phone, but easily found the identification on a clear sticker on the back of the phone, Return to: Corrine Casey, 1818 Sawyer Street, Dallas, Texas. Sherry called the number listed and the woman's housekeeper answered her home phone. Sherry gave the person the information about the accident. Upon hearing the information, the woman replied, "Oh, no, then they would have taken her to Dallas Medical Center, that is the nearest hospital in that area. Thank you for calling." The party hung up before Sherry could make plans to return the phone. She turned to Jim.

Jim said, "Sherry, don't worry, after our tour we can go visit the lady, what's her name...Corrine.... in the hospital."

The young Austins were refreshed from their tour around Dallas and the air had become comfortably warm once the evening hours set in.

"It was interesting to see and hear about the early years and how the city became a city" said Jim.

"Yes and the ice cream was good too" Sherry laughed.

"I know it's late, but before we go for dinner, let's return Corrine's cell phone and find out how she is doing."

Parking the car was easy and entering the hospital reception area wasn't as quiet as one might think. "We are here to see

Corrine Casey," Jim said with a pause, unsure if visitors would be allowed. "She was brought in this morning."

"Room 2803 in the West Wing, take the elevator to the second floor and go right, you'll see the nurses station, they'll point you in the right direction." the receptionist said.

"Thank you." Jim wavered for a moment, "Want to use the stairs, Sherry?"

"No, I'm feeling a bit tired now, let's just go and stay just a minute or two and then eat. I'm famished, too."

They arrived at the nurses' station and asked for Corrine Casey's room number. The nurses glanced back and forth at each other before answering. Finally one said, "I think you can go in, but just for a few minutes."

Upon entering the room, they could see it was a private room and the patient was bandaged from her shoulders to the top of her head and had a sling. A nurse appeared, smiled and said "thank God it was only a broken shoulder and a concussion. We thought at first she had fractured her skull, but thank God she hadn't, just a lot of bleeding."

"We aren't going to stay; we just want to return her cell phone. It was lying in the street. We called the number and found out where she might have been taken. We are just visiting Dallas, so it was a mystery to us."

"That is very nice of you. I'm sure Corrine will appreciate that."

Jim and Sherry paused for a moment then decided to go to dinner.

"We'll leave now and wish her well."

The young couple left the room and got back on the elevator. The sun was still out and it was warm and dry. They were looking forward to a leisurely evening dinner in one of the restaurants that had been recommended to them.

Michael drove in to the hospital parking garage. He was on his cell phone talking to Rosie. He had dated Corrine almost exclusively for two years and yet he knew he would not marry her. Michael had tried to balance their relationship and keep it light. He had gotten sick of her pushing to move in, talking about a future, but he knew she was not the one. He had actually planned to tell her this tonight, but now this happened and again it was not the right time. He couldn't get away from the fact that he still loved Lily.

Chapter 65

"Michael my son, the years will fly past and I've said before--- that life is simply what you make of it. You are so stubborn, more and more like your brother Eddie. You make a good amount of money and have faithfully saved. Your bank account must be very healthy by now."

"Dad, what are we talking about here?"

"Your life, that is what we are talking about."

"My life? Things are okay, Dad."

"Okay is not enough, Michael. When you first came home, you were very upset about Lily. You were concerned that you could not afford a life with her for two reasons. First, you said that you didn't have a job that would continue to pay you enough money to afford her."

"Dad I told you about Lily, she came from a very different life than we had."

"Well, Michael the way you described her over and over was that she didn't care."

"You are right Dad, but I wanted to be able to afford anything she wanted. She would never even think about the difference in our stations in life. You are right Dad. That was Lily."

"And Michael you are not one hundred per cent committed to this other lady, Corrine. Am I right?"

Yes, you are right, but what is your point? What do you want me to do?"

"You could easily support Lily now in the style to which she was accustomed. And you say she never cared that your backgrounds were so different. So… son, if you still care for Lily, then why don't you try to contact her?"

His father was right. What was stopping him now? When he got home, he Michael wrote Lily a brief email about his departure, perhaps too much stress with the relocation and new position etc. He used the email he found on her company's webpage and kept it brief. He quickly pushed the send button before he lost his nerve.

Lily was very surprised to receive the message, and delighted. In her personal, yet non personal way, she wrote back: "You went through Hades at the office. I'm sure I don't even know the half of it. It was probably a wise decision to leave that position. As you know, stress usually is worrying about the unknown future. And Michael you have a beautiful future. I am in the business of looking down the road, and believe me, there is no one I know has a better prognosis than you. You are a great man, one I believe in fully…

Michael could almost hear Lily's voice through that email. He secretly wished she would have signed it 'love', but that was more than he could have hoped for. He was just grateful that she returned his note and didn't chide him about leaving in that way. He could tell that she still cared for him and yet wouldn't say. She was always pretty reserved. That is, except in the proper place and then her love flowed forth. He wanted to see her and be with her, but there was a logistic issue. She was in New England and he was in Texas.

He knew it was possible, but how? He knew he wanted Lily to be herself, but with him. He had only wished they had continued some type of relationship. It would have helped so much, he thought. He felt she must have been hurt and felt abandoned. He knew he had nothing to offer her at the time and was too hurt and concerned for her to say goodbye. Michael hadn't wanted her to talk him into staying, it wouldn't have worked. He knew that.

Perhaps he should have told her. If she only knew how often he reached out for her, picked up the telephone and put it back. His tears and longing for her. Oh, how he needed her. Now he was in the position to care for her, but maybe it was too late. What he really needed was a second chance.

Lily didn't know what to think. When she first opened the email, she was elated. Then she felt let down. It had been too long and too much had transpired. She answered it most professionally, stunned at his brusqueness and lack of emotion.

"What impression had I given him that it was okay to simply reappear without care or concern? How had I misled him? What have I done?"

Chapter 66

THAT EVENING RON CALLED and later came over to Lily's house. He pulled her to him, placing his powerful arms around her shoulders. Her blonde hair fell next to his cheek. His smooth face felt so good. Sitting next to her on the beige sofa, with few sofa pillows next to them, he held her for a long time. He knew a little bit about the case and understood it was a draining experience. Lily felt like he was a true friend. She began to feel secure thinking she knew him. Cary must not really know him, she thought. Either that or he really had changed.

The very warm air made the change of seasons most noticeable. In New England the rainy season is usually April, this year it came in late June. For nearly a week it had been raining.

Ron was dressed for the event in a navy blue Hickey Freeman suit, white shirt and flowered tie. He was about to go to the dance to meet Lily. She was also dressed most carefully in a paisley printed designer dress with a soft lustrous swing skirt and had her hair styled in a new look with curls in back. Her new leather wedge sandal made her ankles look especially trim as she made her way to her Lexus. Feeling the warm rain on her face she returned to her house and called Ron, reaching him before he left his house. "Please come to my house before the dance," she said.

Ron got in his car, flipping on the windshield wipers. The blades moved to the rhythm of the rain, rhythm, the soft gentle summer rain.

"I wonder why Lily changed her mind about meeting me at the dance. I hope there isn't anything wrong, yet, she sounded so good, and perhaps she has some news from her son..."

He drove by the back of the house, but couldn't see anything, not that he expected to. Her backyard was very secluded. "The only light on is upstairs...hmm..."

He turned into her driveway and shut off the car lights. He could hear just the faint sound of music coming from the house. He strained to hear the familiar song, trying to place the tune, "Ahh, The Commodores, that's right, yes, Lionel Richie singing...." The street light shone onto the glass door on the porch. Ron opened the car door and started walking toward the house. The music was clearer now, "Once, twice, three times a lady." No truer words were ever said.

Ron hurried toward the door and noticed a note taped on it. He laughed seeing her words. "She is such an amazing woman!" He read, "Come dance with me...leave your clothes on the porch... let's not waste such a warm soft rain."

He stepped inside, removed his jacket, listening to the words. "And I love you, I love you." So appropriate he thought. First the striped tie came off, then the white shirt. He struggled for the collar button.

"Yes, Once, twice, three times…" The music was getting more mellow. He removed his leather belt, suit trousers and finally his leather loafer shoes, socks and last his brief shorts.

Through the moonlight he could see Lily's beautiful naked body swaying to the music. Her lightly tanned skin was golden and her hair moved with her body, gently covering her shoulders. She turned at the waist momentarily, her hips gently rounded and her eyes were beckoning him. Ron in his full nakedness stepped off the porch onto the soft wet grass as if it were a mat beneath his feet. He walked around back of the house and over to Lily.

Not a word was spoken, she extended her hand, he took her hand, it was warm and covered with rain drops, then the rain fell from a ringlet on her hair onto her forehead, she smiled. First he kissed her wet lips, and in dance position he felt her hand on his shoulder, his left arm around her back, and with his right hand holding hers they began to dance to the music as the rain dropped on their bare bodies, first the right foot moved to the right, then the left foot followed. Ron repeated the movement, then took a double step to the right. They danced within a four foot square, almost dancing in place, a slight amount of movement and just perfect for the dance.

He sang the words, at first in his head and then, softly into her ear, "When we are together the moments I cherish with every beat of my heart, to touch you, to hold you, to feel you. There's nothing to keep us apart, once, twice, three times a lady and I love you."

Ron could feel her wet body next to his, wrapped together in a blanket of rain. As the music ended, he felt a firmness in his body, as Lily's body felt so much a part of his.

"Dancing in the rain is the best part of summer," she said as she looked up at him. The grass was soft and wet beneath their feet. And together they danced the evening away as the rain dropped on their bare bodies.

He knew he would succumb to the warm and moist body and fill it to overflowing with his love.

That night as was every night together, it was sex with a passion of kissing, handling, licking, sucking and loving, never on the level of street talk only lovemaking. It was true lovemaking. "My life will never be the same again, thought Ron. Lily is the best thing that ever happened to me."

Chapter 67

IN THE LAW OFFICE there was talk of promotions. Cary had brought this to Lily's attention and even Jamie made some comments regarding advancements. Lily was happy with her position and having been there only three years, she didn't concern herself about raises and titles. Not yet.

Jamie left her reception desk and walked over to Lily's office doorway. Having Lily's attention she smiled and said, "Mr. Kincade wants to see you in his office."

"About what? Do you know Jamie?"

"Well, Lily, what do you think?"

"Gosh, this is unexpected. I hope I didn't somehow foul up any paperwork. I have been so out straight lately. Did he mention what it was about?"

"No, Lily, he just asked for you."

Lily quickly looked in the mirror on the wall near the coat rack. She looked fine and hurried off to 'The Great Mr. Kincade's Office'. Forty minutes later, Lily wearing a great big smile as she made her way to the coffee room. If she had it timed right, her friend Cary would be there. Whoa…when she stepped into the room a round of applause was followed by congratulations from everyone.

"Now Lily, you are really one of us and you got a raise to boot! Hope you're ready to go to the Catwalk later for drinks," said Cary.

Lily was ecstatic and in a hurry to call her parents and let Dad know. He will be so proud, she thought.

The following week when Lily walked from the elevator she noticed the mail man arrived simultaneously with his usual handful of mail. She paused at Jamie's desk. Jamie looked up at her, "Oh, Lily, some flowers just came for you, I put them on your desk, a new beau?"

"Don't be silly, Jamie, I hardly have time for the dances I go to, never mind another beau," she said laughing at the thought. As she entered her office the flowers made a statement, a beautiful assortment of carnations, roses and lilies, in various shades of pink and white and all exquisitely arranged. An unusually large note was attached to the bouquet. It read, "Dear Lily, Lily-Anne was born yesterday. I hope you don't mind us naming her after you. She is beautiful. Mom and I and Lily-Anne are moving to Vermont soon. We want you to be the godmother when the time comes. Thank you for my second chance in life. Love, Donna."

Lily being Lily, simply cried and thanked God it all came out right.

"Gosh I'll have to share this one with Ron. Maybe I'll call him."

Chapter 68

EARLIER THAT DAY, IN the bright sunlight, two men were standing near a large building talking intently as people walked around them. They moved further up the sidewalk to avoid the crowd.

"Yes, I can give you a pretty good discount. You are Al's friend. Do you know exactly what style a ring you want?"

"A nice size diamond, a filigree setting, something in white gold. Only a few thousand dollars, I'm not spending every dime I have on this. Do you understand?"

"Yes, of course. And how soon do you want the ring?"

"A month or so is okay. Take your time."

"Okay, we have a deal."

The men shook hands and parted.

Chapter 69

THE NEXT DAY IN the construction office, Al and Ron were busy kibitzing and laughing about old times when the subject of legal action came up. "Did you get the lease you wanted?"

"Yep and it certainly is iron clad. I won't have any problems this time. Lily knows her law, that's for sure. "

"Ron is everything okay?"

"Ya, sure,why?"

"I just wondered."

"By the way, there is a new girl in my office. My wife and I are going

out to dinner tonight, do you want to bring her?" Ron hesitated and asked,

"What is she like?"

"What do you think?"

"I don't know, I'll have to think it over."

"No, probably not."

"What's the matter, afraid Lily will find out?"

"No, I think she is playing bridge with the girls tonight."

Well, come along then, who would be the wiser?"

"I guess it is okay."

That same evening, Cary was talking with her baby-sitter. She and Craig had made reservations for dinner to celebrate his sister's birthday. The weather was warm and Cary had found a replacement for her bridge game so the celebration was on. Craig and Cary heard the music and were joining Craig's sister Nancy and her husband Paul at the Candleworks.

It was Nancy's 30th birthday. The music was good, the drinks just right and the food was the absolute best. Nancy most innocently called Cary's attention to the handsome couple dancing. Cary could hardly believe her eyes. At the same time Ron Hollander's eyes caught Cary's. They seemed sad. Craig noticed the expression on Cary's face. Craig asked Cary what was wrong. Cary said, "Oh, nothing, I just thought I saw someone I knew." Nothing more was said.

At the office the following day, Lily came into Cary's office all smiles and cheerfully talking about the bridge game and how she and Pat had won.

"Can you believe that Pat made a small slam the first time and a grand slam the second?"

Cary smiled and congratulated Lily on the game. "That's great Lily. I'm glad you and Pat hit it off easily." Somehow Cary's voice sounded flat. Lily had been so excited about the game, it took her a minute to realize Cary's demeanor.

"Cary, what is wrong? Are you ok? How did your evening go?

Cary had talked it over with Craig and decided not to mention the incident. "No, nothing's wrong. I must just have a touch of the flu or something," she said quickly. "No, it went well. Nancy was happy with the celebration and Paul had given her the bracelet she wanted, you know the tennis bracelet."

Later that day, Lily was thinking about the emotional rollercoaster she was on with Ron. One minute he was so attentive and loving, the next he could be as cool as he was in the beginning. She never knew which Ron was going to show up. Lily thought about Cary's original comments about Ron being needy and needing to have many girl friends. He was afraid to know what true happiness was, she said. He had shown some disinterest, and was often rather cool. Perhaps he was deeper into this relationship than he wanted.

It was so difficult for Lily to understand his real feelings. He seemed to vacillate from day to day. She doubted if he knew what he wanted either. He didn't seem to be able to commit to one person, but led her to believe he could and would. Cary thought Ron was one of those who would keep women at arms length, away from getting to really know him. Lily realized that is probably what Cary meant when she said, "I know what it is to wake up next to a man who makes me truly happy."

She acted like it didn't matter, but deep down, she knew it really did matter. The worst part was that it made Lily realize how much she missed Michael. With Michael, she was always special. He had always made her feel he wanted her and only her.

Ron's thoughts ran again in his head and heart. As his breathing slowed down and his body was satisfied, he thought "Perhaps now is the time." He was a bit uncertain about telling her about the ring, then he thought, "What the hell. This will seal it for real and we can always have these great times." Ron took her hand and drew her face toward his.

"Darling, I'm having a ring made for you. I'm ready to make a commitment to you, just you." He felt great getting the words out.

Lily looked confused and then haltingly began to speak, "As much as I enjoy you, as much as we have together, I can't make that kind of commitment."

"Wh..what are you saying?"

"I can't make that kind of promise to you or anyone else. It's not fair to you or me. I still believe Michael will appear again in my life. You need to know I still miss and love him," said Lily. "I thought I could get over him, I really did, but I just can't. I feel that he is my destiny. I don't know how, or when, but…." her voice trailed off as she noticed his face.

His heart sank and he felt like he had been punched in the stomach. He never felt so hurt, like a knife going through me. His head felt light and he suddenly felt dizzy. It was as if cold water splashed in my face. He realized he looked out of control and quickly tried to regain his composure.

"I'm sorry, I understand." But he didn't. "How could I have been so blind," he thought. "She is just like the others. I can stop the ring thing. Thank God I just put in the order. I'll call tomorrow. And Al didn't even know when he arranged for me to date his secretary. Like I thought, great friend!"

My brain was numb repeating over and over those cold words. I needed to leave. I pretended there was nothing wrong as I joined her in the shower. Slowly I towel dried her body, her back, her legs, and as I dried her shoulders I couldn't help it. I kissed her neck. She reached for her clothing as I turned my back so she couldn't see how upset I was. We finished dressing and she followed me down the stairs to the kitchen.

"Just a cup of coffee in the travel mug."

It was ironic that she asked for a travel mug. It would be the last time. In the garage, he bid her farewell, kissing her delicate fingers. She placed them on my lips and said 'goodbye'. She looked particularly lovely as she started her Lexus. Yes, she might have been the best thing that ever happened to me, but the door was closed on that chapter. After her words, there would never be anything between us.

Ron went back in the house and poured himself some coffee. He knew it could have been different. He wanted her, really wanted her and probably could have had her. "I always had to act so damn smug," he thought. "I would pull her to me, then push her away. What was I protecting myself from, he wondered. And all the time I thought no one could get to me again, she worked her way into my heart."

That evening alone in bed Ron pondered his recent meeting with Al's new secretary, Crystal Cormier. She was funny and could be an easy mark. One you would not have to worry about wanting a life-long commitment. "Not bad for a one night stand," he said aloud. Well, I keep telling myself to stop living in the past. It's time to listen to my own words of advice. Living in the present makes for a much happier man. Well, thank goodness for Al, what a buddy...another gal so soon! A new conquest! Just my type - not too smart and plenty good looking. At this rate, it won't take any time at all to get over Lily...

Chapter 70

No alarm this morning, just the California sun shining through the window. Jim just loved to sleep with the window open and the gentle breeze blowing the sheer curtains. Sleeping in made for an even more wonderful Saturday morning. Sherry had been up many times during the night. At seven months pregnant with their first child, it was to be expected. The doctor had said each month's growth would make her body ache a bit more. These nightly trips to the bathroom were all part of the great joy of becoming a mother.

She pushed her pillow flat and carefully touched Jim's face near his ear. He smiled and rolled over to kiss her cheek. Good morning Mommy, he teased. They were so delighted to be having a baby and Jim was more than delighted to learn it might be a boy.

They had discussed names, deciding on Jim's father's name if it was indeed a boy. Jim had been very excited and supportive throughout the pregnancy and felt a deeper closeness to Sherry and to this new addition to their lives.

"Honey how do you feel this morning?"

"Like a woman seven months pregnant."

"I bet you can hardly wait for the next two months to be over with."

"You've got that right. Not just because of the baby, but to get my figure back, too."

"Sweetheart you look great pregnant."

"Thank you darling. Now can we get up so you can make coffee?"

"Me, oh yeah, it is Saturday, okay."

Jim started for the shower and turned on the warm water. Sherry carefully got on her feet, looking in the mirror at her full tummy and arrived at the shower just in time for Jim to help her in. Stepping over the threshold Jim steadied her and stepped back, placing her in front of him directly under the water. Carefully washing her soft ivory skin all over, her tummy, swollen breasts, her arms, legs and all the while kissed her back. He helped her out to towel dry and carefully unfolded a soft fluffy towel. She wrapped the towel around her and sat on the small chair waiting for Jim.

Jim began singing as if it were opera, hoping she would laugh. Sherry laughs and called out to him to "get with it." Jim turned off the shower and reached for his towel. Sherry carefully and playfully put it away, waiting for him to beg. "Okay mother, my towel please?" Jim grabbed for it and dried them both thoroughly. He reached for the lotion to softly rub it all over Sherry.

Soon both are robed, with coffee in hand, starting their day. The quiet was interrupted by the phone.

"I'll get it honey," says Jim, reaching for the kitchen extension phone.

Sherry could hear the conversation.

"I don't know how Sherry is feeling today, so I'll have to call you back about tennis."

Sherry called out, "Jim go ahead and play, I'm fine."

Jim looked at her and smiles. "Thanks honey." He quickly tells Kenny, "I'll meet you at the tennis court in an hour, okay? Thanks."

"Is that the mailman? Isn't he kind of early today"

"No Jim, it's Saturday, and it always comes early on Saturday."

"Oh, yeah," Jim said as he gathered up the mail and began to look through the envelopes.

"Oh Sherry, here is one from Rosie. You remember Rosie, don't you?"

"Oh, yes, your dear friend from Yale."

"Yes, without her I would have never passed Spanish!" he said laughing at the thought of how badly he was failing before she became his tutor. She had become his best friend on campus and they still kept in touch.

"I know. What is it?"

"Wow," he said as he opened the off white square. "It is an

invitation to her wedding, with a little personal note requesting our presence. She wants me to usher as well."

"Jim, when is it? You know I can't travel right now, I simply cannot do it. It is hard enough for me to walk with all this weight, never mind being on an extended flight."

"I know Sweetie, but I would really like to go. It's only in Dallas."

"Look, Jim why don't you go anyway? My mother would love to come and stay with me. It would be an excuse for her and a little vacation time for you before the baby comes."

"Sherry, I really don't want to go alone. Thanks anyway."

"Hey, Jim, it has been some time since you've been with your mom, why not ask her. A trip would do her good. Don't you think?"

"Now that's an idea, are you sure you don't want to go?"

"Sweetheart it isn't that I don't want to go, it is simply that I'm seven months pregnant."

"Are you sure?"

"Yes, I'm sure. I'm sure I'm pregnant," she laughed.

"No I mean that you think I should ask my mother?"

"Yes, when you get back from tennis, call her."

"Oh, yes, tennis, okay I'll call her then."

Chapter 71

LATER IN THE DAY Lily's telephone rang. It was Jim on the line.

"Mom, do you remember my friend Rosie, you know, the girl that helped me through my Spanish classes?"

"Yes, Rosie.....Rosie Lopez"

"Well, Mom, she and Freddie are getting married. I knew it would only be a matter of time. Well, anyway, I received an invitation to her wedding. She wants me to be an usher. It isn't until next month."

"Jim that will be fun and what a nice honor, too."

"Yes, but Mom, the reason I'm calling is that I want you to go with me. It has been ages since you've really taken a vacation, a real one, not just those conventions. Sherry really doesn't think it's wise for her to travel. She's getting very uncomfortable now."

"Oh, Jim I don't know, perhaps you should go by yourself."

"Come on Mom, Your volunteering work will always be here. The biggest thing you do is that Sunday tea for the ladies in the nursing home. Honestly Mom!"

"Son, what kind of a function is it?"

"I don't know, what do you mean what kind of function?"

"What does the invitation say, read it to me. I just want to know how formal this wedding will be. If I don't know that – how can I pack?"

"Oh Mom, thank you so much! Then you'll go?"

"Yes, I'll go. How could I toss over my son for some old lady's tea?" Lily laughed. "Now read me the invitation, please!"

"Ok, let's see, 'The daughter of Michael Lopez, Jr. ....'"

Lily stopped breathing for a moment, not hearing anything after those words. "Where did you say this wedding was?"

"Dallas, Mom. Remember I told you that was where Rosie's family came from."

She couldn't believe the words. Finally she caught her breath "Read that again Jim."

"Mom what is the matter? They are nice people. I met her father years ago at college when he came to see Rosie.

"Yes, Jim, I know" Lily began to sob quietly. She tried to cover the phone so he wouldn't hear her.

"Are you crying Mom? What are you crying for? I'm not getting married, I'm already married. Are you ok?"

"Yes, Jim. I'll call you when I've made my flight arrangements." Was this the way God wanted us to meet again?

In the morning, Lily decided that she was curious to see Michael after these years. Had he married, had he forgotten her except for that little email he sent her? Oh, well the trip would be a good change of scenery. What was it Cary said? Oh, yes, according to Cary, her kick-ass therapist said, "It is results not regrets." Well, we'll see. At the very least, her head would know whether her heart was right or not.

Lily called Jim and left the message since Jim and Sherry were out.

"Yes, Jim, just to confirm, I'll join you. Just note that two will be attending the wedding, no other comment please."

The plane arrived near three in the afternoon. Jim knew he had time to check in at the Marriot and shower and change for the evening. A dinner was scheduled for the bridal party and that included Jim and his guest. He and Lily took a taxi to the hotel. Jim asked for rooms on the fourth floor.

"I'm sorry sir, that floor has been reserved for the guests of the Lopez wedding party."

"Well, that we are. Are there rooms available next to each other?"

"No sir, however if you need two rooms…"

At that moment, Lily said, "Jim excuse me, I would rather have my room on the fifth floor."

"Oh, okay Mom."

Soon both parties were checked in. Lily chose to rest and have dinner in her room, while Jim dressed and went to the dinner party. Lily was feeling anxious, but tried to keep herself calm. Although she seemed calm, her thoughts raced out of control. She wondered what Michael would think when he saw her. Then, could he have remarried? Does he have more children? The invitation had listed Rosie's mother's name, too. What if he is not pleased I came, too, oh dear Lord, maybe I shouldn't have tagged along. But I had to see him, if only just once more.

It was like torture to be so close and yet, it has been so long ago that we were one with each other. He probably isn't even the same person he used to be. Well, I am here now and need to make the most of it. I'll stay out of sight until the actual wedding tomorrow. With so many people here, perhaps he won't notice me. I wonder how he looks...

Lily was tired from the trip and she welcomed the nightfall. The next day would be everything or nothing, Jim met his Mother for breakfast and then they went to their rooms to dress for the wedding. Jim called her as soon as he was dressed. "How handsome you look," Lily said proudly with a mother's smile. Soon they were off to the church.

It was a beautiful sunny day. The church was packed. Jim looked so handsome in his tuxedo, walking the guests to their seats. The prelude music was very traditional, Pachelbel's "Canon in D Major." The bridesmaids were so pretty in lovely shades of blue and carrying pink flowers. Right on cue, the moment arrived and the organist began Wagner's famous bridal chorus, "Here Comes the Bride". The audience all stood as the bride was announced by the change in music. Father and daughter hesitated and then began the walk down the aisle.

Chapter 72

LILY QUIETLY GASPED. TIME had been very kind to Michael thought Lily, sitting down as he presented the bride to the groom. The priest's words made an impression on Lily. The Gospel according to Luke and St. Francis prayer both brought a rush of thoughts each in its own way to both Lily and Michael. There were memories of their own marriages, times of joy and times of sadness. Moments later, the ceremony was over and the celebration was about to start. Lily had remained quietly tucked inside the large group of guests. Michael only had eyes for his radiant daughter anyway and didn't seem to notice anyone else.

By the time Lily went through the receiving line, Michael had excused himself to go make some arrangements for the reception. Lily was introduced to Rosie, and Rosie hugged her and thanked her for coming with Jim.

The reception was held at a private club. It was fabulously decorated and elegantly appointed. As the guests arrived, they marveled at the surroundings. Each table had a fresh flower arrangement, matching the bride's theme. The wine was poured and the guests were mingling when a host began introducing the various members of the bridal party. Everyone was in high spirits.

The music began and Michael and Rosie stepped on the floor for the father/daughter dance.

All eyes were following the couple around the floor; beautiful music and a beautiful couple executed the dance steps. Lily couldn't help but admire the dancers. She strained see if Michael was wearing a wedding ring or not. Then some men don't wear them, so it wasn't a sure sign. The toast was made by the best man.

"May faith, hope, and love become the mainstream of their lives together, our wish as we toast our friends Freddie and Rosie." Freddie and Rosie beamed at their good wishes and blessings. Michael sat at the table with his own parents. Pleased that his part was over, he took a deep breath, and began to look over the guests. Just then, Michael saw Lily for the first time. At first Michael questioned in his mind whether or not it was really Lily. He looked closely to make sure it was really her! There was no mistaking that face. It was Lily.

She was talking to the person sitting next to her. She looked up, almost as if she felt his eyes on her. Her eyes connected with Michael. Wait, how did she happen to be at the wedding? His eyes darted around the room, then from Jim back to Lily. Then it all came together, Jim Austin was the son of Lily Arnold Austin. And there she was right here in Dallas at his club enjoying the wedding of his daughter Rosie. God had been good to him.

He felt he must be dreaming. He had tried so hard these years not to care about her, and now at this moment he felt the rush of excitement throughout his body. He knew he could never let her go, no matter what. Then another thought entered his mind, he hoped she was not with someone, a husband or fiancé.

Lily had been watching him; she couldn't take her eyes off of him. Since her husband had died, she dated, but there had been no one else she really loved, just Michael, and she had longed for him these many years.

Just then, the dance floor was opened up to everyone. Quickly, Michael stood up and walked directly to Lily, he extended his hand. She smiled, "Hello Michael." He said very softly, "Hello Lily." Michael took her by the hand to the dance floor, not another word was spoken. The music was a waltz and they danced in silence. At first they danced very formally, as they had many years ago, then cheek to cheek, not saying a word to each other. The way they glided on the floor, it was as though they had never been apart.

Soon people around the room began to take notice of their dancing. They fit in each other's arms so perfectly and they didn't take their eyes from each other's faces. Michael Sr. and Maria gave each other that knowing look. He said very softly to Maria, "If I didn't know any better, I'd think that was his Lily." Maria said "You know, Michael, it has to be her. I don't know how or why, but, I've never seen our son look so complete with another woman."

And at another table sat Eddie and Roseanne, never married,

but holding hands. Eddie nodded towards Michael as Roseanne gave that agreeing smile. They best understood the body language of the dancers. According to Lily, nothing ever needed to be said. And Michael so wanted to say what was in his heart so many years. They spent most of the time dancing and not talking. Finally, Michael took Lily to his parents and introduced her. Maria nudged Michael Sr. under the table as they tried not to stare at Lily.

When the reception was over and the many guests had left, Michael took Lily's hand in his and kissed her fingertips. As the late afternoon sun glinted through the windows, Michael took Lily back to her hotel. They sat in the lounge and spoke in soft voices, unfolding the lonely years and answering each other's questions. As the hour passed, Michael realized Lily was single and available. His fate was sealed. They got on the elevator and pressed the button for the fifth floor. Michael moved toward her and pressed her gently against the elevator wall and kissed her so fully that it took her breath away. They walked in silence to room 510.

"Lily I am so sorry for leaving without telling you, and you will never know how many times I started to write you and stopped. I am so sorry for the pain I may have caused you. Only God know why our lives went this way."

"Yes, Michael you're right, only God knows why our lives unfold as they do. But now we have a second chance." She handed him the key, they both entered the room.

It was late morning, the sun was up and room service brought their breakfast.

"Michael my love, do you remember that our grandchildren are coming next weekend?"

"My darling Lily, of course I remember. We promised to take them to Nantucket Island this summer and to Texas' South Padre Island next winter. Now that we are both retired we can enjoy Rosie and Fred's two boys, Robert and Richard, and Jimmy and Sherry's son Richard and their three girls Rhonda, Tanya and Kennedy. What a blessing that Rosie with her family and your son Jim with his family simply love being together. A real family, the way it was meant to be all along.

"And sweetheart, we'll teach them to dance in the rain."

"Lily my wife, how about a second cup of coffee?"